Juggle
WITHOUT
Struggle

**Five Secrets,
Four Weeks,
Nine Minutes
to Inner Peace**

Peggie O'Neill

CRADLE CONCEPTS

Published by Cradle Concepts

ISBN: 978-1-4675-4552-5 (paperback)

ISBN: 978-1-4675-4553-2 (hardcover)

Printed in the United States of America

Dedication

To Our Lady of Good Remedy,
who guides and protects me always.

To my husband, Frank, who makes me laugh when I want to cry:

To Frank, Judi, Laurie Beth, Kyle, Michelle, and Keith; Brian,
Miriam, Little B, Allegra, Shannon,
Julian, and Lawrencia;
Joe, Ione, Joey, Chloe, and Inez;
Mike and Jeannie, young Jeannie, Jacqueline, Michael,
Lauren, and Ryan;
Bill;
Vince, Alice, Vincey, Owen, and Maggie.

You are my inspiration and guiding light; I love you.

Contents

Foreword

I received a phone call a few months back from the sisters of Peggie O'Neill. They were dear friends of a writer that I had worked with in the past. They were familiar with a book project that was brought to market by my partner, Megan, and me. They were calling about a very important book project.

The story that followed about Peggie O'Neill and her family was filled with so much love and passion that they, indeed, had me from "hello." What followed was nothing short of inspirational.

I learned about Peggie O'Neill and her "Courage of One" outreach that she had championed before her death. Peg had written a novel, *Juggle Without Struggle*, which Peg's niece (Mary DeCarlo) and Peg's daughter-in-law (Alice O'Neill) were determined to get published. I was truly blessed to assist in this "labor of love" so passionately brought to the finish line by these lovely ladies and their family. The outpouring of their love for Peg (and one another) in this quest to honor Peg's last wish was inspiring. I quickly bonded and connected with these women who were driven to get this done.

The rest is history.

Juggle Without Struggle speaks to the heart of every woman. There are five secrets that are revealed through the story of four women from various walks of life: two wealthy, a single mom, and a struggling young wife and mother in marriage. Problems include bankruptcy, divorce, marital problems, single parenthood, family issues, additions, and other struggles that many of us have to deal with. In Peggie O'Neill's own words: "Each woman ultimately discovers the five secrets that help her find the courage, wisdom, strength, and inner peace to meet and rise above the overwhelming challenges that confront her."

After visiting Peg's family and hearing so much about her it is clear that Peg touched so many souls and emulated St. Francis of Assisi, who said, "Preach the Gospel at all times and when necessary use words." *Juggle Without Struggle* is an extension of Peg's constant works of charity in helping others.

Peg inspired others by her daily example. True to her Catholic Faith and deeply rooted in the love of the Eucharist, she rallied thousands to pray every week for priestly vocations. Yet she clearly reached beyond her Catholic circles. When it came to someone in need, Peg was there. She founded pregnancy help centers for women in crisis and she listened on her own time for countless hours to the heartaches of those whom she trained in corporate America over the years. She also prayed and consoled many chemotherapy and radiation treatment patients who walked the journey alongside her in her own battle with cancer.

Juggle Without Struggle is the work of this compassionate heart who knew that the greatest help and gift that a person could be given is a way to achieve inner peace. Peg understood that problems in life cut across all barriers of faith, race, and socioeconomic status. She understood God's love for every single soul regardless of where they are standing at any given moment. She knew that the only way from fear, anger, busy-ness, desolation, sarcasm, despair, and bitterness was by way of daily prayer and blind faith that God has a special plan for all of us as individuals to fulfill in our lives.

Peggie O'Neill has left behind a beautiful book which reminds us that "earth has no sorrow that heaven can't heal." In all the juggling that life demands of all of us, this book is a great reminder that although we all have suffering at one time or another, we can accomplish our purpose in life without the struggle. It all begins with a daily discipline of giving yourself the gift of time alone everyday with God.

I am told that Peg was gifted at connecting those who needed to know each other. Apparently, she is still doing so! *Juggle Without Struggle* can transform your life from chaos to peace. It is up to you to begin your walk down the path toward inner peace, with 5 secrets, 4 weeks, and 9 minutes.

Jenn Giroux
Wife and mother of nine
Registered Nurse, speaker, writer
Vice President, Public Relations, Cradle Concepts

My mother, Peggie O'Neill

My mother, Peggie O'Neill, was an extraordinary mother, businesswoman, leader, friend, and wife. She was the most positive and enthusiastic person I ever met. My brothers and I always called her "Muz". It was our affectionate title for our amazing Mother. When we were young teenagers, she routinely woke us up at 4:00 in the morning, made us read self-help books such as *Think and Grow Rich*, had us run around the block five times, and then allowed us to go back to bed. Of course, after doing that, it was impossible to go back to bed. When summer started, we were thrown out of the house and told not to return without a job. Needless to say, we always got a job on the first day of summer and had more cash in our pockets than anyone in the neighborhood. She did not tolerate inactivity. Muz constantly read biographies of great leaders to us and encouraged us to do the same. She insisted on a spiritual household and any friends who were around the house prior to dinner were forced to kneel in front of the Blessed Mother and say a rosary. Muz had great courage and was fearless. She worked with unwed mothers at Birthright and routinely visited inner city families to counsel against abortion. Peg started many organizations including Prayer Power, which had over 5,000 women praying every day for their assigned priest that "he would be on fire with the Holy Spirit" and for a general intention that families would be strong and holy.

Aside from being my mother, Peg O'Neill was also my best friend. She had a passion for life. I remember the time she rented a camper and went on a driving tour of the United States and Canada with six boys, a babysitter and a dog in tow. After the fifth day camping out, she said she had had enough and we began checking into hotels. We giggled and laughed and explored together. My brother Frank was the oldest and he was only 12 years old. Mom approached each day with an extraordinarily positive attitude and an unrivaled spirituality. Her charisma was a beacon of light that extended to everyone she met, from the cashier at Genuardi's Food Store to the Dalai Lama. Everyone wanted to be around Muz. Despite her popularity, however, she always exercised a high degree of humility.

Muz had great business savvy and spent a lot of her time studying the human psyche and matching people with roles that best suited their talents. She was a great teacher and mastered the art of teaching people to use their God-given talents to be the best at whatever they did. She was a great motivator with a strong hand. She taught us to pray to be good husbands and fathers and to be successful in our personal and business lives. I spoke to Muz every day, often two or three times a day. We laughed together, prayed together, compared business notes, and shared our struggles. Peg O'Neill was the ultimate entrepreneur, philanthropist, friend, partner and cheerleader. I spent a lot of time with her during the 20 years that she battled cancer. I watched her endure excruciatingly painful chemotherapy treatments and numerous elongated stays at various hospitals, but never once did I hear her complain. On our 6:00 a.m. trips to the University of Pennsylvania Hospital for her treatments, she always bought a box of chocolates for the nurses and receptionists. It was no wonder that she always got the first appointment. I recall her telling me what a great tribute people paid when her father passed away at an early age. That was only surpassed by the thousands of people who waited in line for hours to pay their respects to our "Muz" when she died. She was a remarkable human being. She devoted herself to substituting stress and heartache for prayer and God.

I miss her greatly and talk to her every day, with never ending love.

Brian O'Neill
Son, Husband, Father of 5

Introduction

In today's fast-paced world, the minute a woman opens her eyes in the morning and her feet touch the floor, she is off and running until she collapses into bed at night. Most women usually do everything for everyone else, with little or no time for themselves.

In *Juggle Without Struggle,* I share with you five simple secrets for inner peace. They transformed me from an overwhelmed supermom to a peaceful and more joyful woman. I used to struggle to juggle family, friends, children, work, doctor and dentist appointments, games, cooking, shopping, cleaning, laundry, church, school, and community involvement. Let's face it, women's work is overwhelming. These five secrets for inner peace have helped me struggle less and love more.

The five secrets are revealed through the story of four women who struggled with problems such as bankruptcy, divorce, marital problems, single parenthood, family issues, and addictions. Each woman ultimately discovered five secrets that helped her find the courage, wisdom, strength, and inner peace to meet and rise above the overwhelming challenges that confronted her.

Although the heroine Kitty Bradshaw Murphy is a fictitious character, she could be you or me. She could be the woman down the street, or the woman sitting next to you in church. We all have a little bit of Kitty in us. The stories of Kitty, Jenny, Maria, and Caroline are inspired by anecdotes I've heard over the years from friends, family, clients, and students in my seminar classes.

My first encounter with the concept of inner peace came in 1965, when I had two stillborn baby girls within 14 months of each other. In those days, if you had a miscarriage or a stillborn baby, it was treated as if you had had a tooth pulled. Get on with your life, be thankful for the four healthy boys you do have. These well-meaning comments only made me feel more guilty and depressed.

I tried to get over my depressed, empty feelings, but I couldn't shake them. As usual, when my feet touched the ground in the morning I was off and running to take care of our four boys and do the things I was supposed to do. But my heart wasn't in it. I existed. I was irritable. My husband didn't understand, and I was lonely.

I visited a nun friend of mine, who suggested I try to find time just for me. I needed time to pray and reflect on who I am, why I am here, and what's important in life. She suggested I get up a half hour earlier so I could get this time to myself. I thought she was crazy. What would a nun know? I was already getting up at 6 a.m.

I resisted her stupid idea. She urged me to try it for 30 days. If it didn't work after that time I could look for something else. I figured I could do anything for 30 days. I agreed to try it, and those 30 days turned into 43 years. It was during those morning hours that I discovered the five secrets to inner peace that transformed my life. My hour to myself in the morning is the most wonderful time of my day.

The five secrets that I share with you in *Juggle Without Struggle* helped me find motherly insights and wisdom to raise six adventuresome sons whose mission was to test our fortitude. Most families have one black sheep. Our family was reversed: We had five black and one white. As teenagers, our sons were blessed with the great gift of leadership. They were leaders in drinking, smoking, and partying. Because of this wonderful talent a few of our sons were invited to leave several different high schools.

Thanks to my husband's guidance and example, prayer, and the five secrets (which are really peace principles), our sons have grown up to be wonderful, responsible, caring men. They are good husbands, fathers, and businessmen. They generously contribute their time, energy, and money to community service.

People are always saying to my husband and me, "You must be so proud." We *are* proud of our sons. More than proud, however, I really feel blessed, so blessed. We have five wonderful daughters-in-law and 16 grandchildren. Most important of all, they all love and enjoy each other.

The five secrets also helped me navigate through three major financial crises and several recurring bouts with cancer.

I pray that the peace principles you discover in *Juggle Without Struggle* will bring you and your family the peace and joy that they have brought my family and me.

— **Peggie O'Neill**

Chapter 1

FEAR

"You can tell the size of your God by
looking at the size of your worry list;
the longer your list, the smaller your God."

– Author Unknown

Born into the privileged class, Kitty Bradshaw Murphy lived a fairy tale life as the only child of Douglas and Katharine Bradshaw. Her father, a renowned Philadelphia lawyer, indulged Kitty's every whim.

She married the handsome University of Pennsylvania quarterback Matt Murphy, who adored her. Matt, a successful stockbroker, specialized in technology stocks. They had three children and lived on a beautiful three-acre estate.

Kitty lived in a bubble. She didn't know that bubble was about to burst and her life would change forever.

**

Kitty Bradshaw Murphy woke with a start; soft rays of sunlight beamed in through her bedroom windows. She sat up, blinked, and looked at the clock; it was 7:05 a.m.

Kitty used to love waking up in the bright beauty of the spacious bedroom, but lately she woke up tense, wondering what unexpected crisis was awaiting her. She sat on the side of her bed collecting her thoughts. *Realtors at 11, lunch at noon with her bridge group.*

I can't do lunch. I can't sit around making small talk, pretending ev-

*erything is wonderful when my whole world is crumbling around me. I just
can't do it.*

Kitty eased back under the covers, pulled them up to her neck,
and clung to them. *I don't want to lose our house.* Tears rolled down her
cheeks.

When they were first married, Kitty and Matt loved driving around
the Main Line, an area of wealthy suburban neighborhoods just outside
Philadelphia, looking at the beautiful estates. Then one day they peeked
through a set of iron gates and gazed up the long driveway to an elegant
brick Georgian mansion. From that moment on, they agreed this was
going to be their home. When they passed it, as they often did, they
would laugh and kid about their future house.

Kitty clipped articles on kitchens, bathrooms, gardens, fabrics, and
design from *House and Garden*, *Architectural Digest*, and various home
décor magazines. They planned and saved. Matt's stockbroker business
grew, and finally a miracle happened – the house came up for sale. They
settled on the house on their fifth wedding anniversary.

Although architecturally beautiful, the house was built in 1929 and
needed a complete renovation. Kitty and Matt spent hours, months,
and even years planning, re-planning, renovating and decorating. They
talked and laughed and argued about design, furniture, and paint colors until they had their home exactly the way they wanted it to be,
blending modern luxuries with Old World charm.

This is the house where they laughed and cried, discussed their
dreams, talked over their hurts, taught their children to play ball, swim,
and ride bikes. For 20 years, this was the home, the house where their
children, Ken, Doug, and Susan had grown up.

Unfortunately, Kitty and Matt were heavily invested in technology
stocks. The technologies crash in 2001 drained their resources. They
were struggling. Although neither one of them wanted to sell their
home, they didn't have a choice after the past few years of their finances
steadily plummeting.

Kitty sighed, threw the covers back, and slid her long, slender legs
out of bed. Wrapping herself in a short silk robe, she glided over to the
opened French doors, stepped out onto her veranda, and inhaled the
scent of freshly turned soil and newly cut grass. June was Kitty's favorite

month, but today the gorgeous weather only made her sad. She mindlessly gazed at her rose garden below. Her award-winning roses needed trimming, but she hardly noticed; she was too preoccupied with the events of the day. She walked back into her bedroom. *I'll think better after I have my coffee.*

Anticipating the comfort of a freshly brewed cup of coffee, she hurried down the spiral stairs, crossed the grand white marble hall, and headed for the kitchen. She glanced at the clock on the kitchen wall: 7:15 a.m. She pushed the button to start the coffee maker, but it didn't go on. She shook the machine and scolded, "Come on, you stupid pot, start!" Nothing happened.

Kitty flicked the light switch; no light. She opened the refrigerator. The light was off, of course. She groaned. Of all mornings for the power to be out, why today?

A second glance at the clock revealed it was stuck at 7:15.

She looked at her wristwatch; it was 8:30. "It can't be 8:30," she cried. "The realtors will be here in two hours!" A group of realtors was coming to the house to take a tour and determine how much the Murphys could get for the property.

She tried to call the electric company, but the phone was dead. Using her cell phone, she navigated the power company's phone directory and endured what seemed like hours of recorded music. Finally, she reached a human. He checked her records and informed her that the power company had turned off the electricity because of an unpaid balance.

"That can't be," Kitty uttered in disbelief.

She had to pay at least part of it immediately if she wanted it restored. She promised to deliver a check within the hour, and looked at her watch again: 8:50. She panicked.

"Damn you, Matt! I hate you for this," she said as she dialed her husband's office.

"May I please speak to Matt?" she asked politely, trying to control her anger.

It seemed like hours before Matt picked up the phone. "What's up, Kitty?" he asked.

"The electricity's off! What will I do?"

"Check the fuse box."

"You didn't pay the electric bill. They turned it off."

Matt didn't speak.

"Matt, are you there? They won't turn it on until we pay the bill."

"Kit, I can't talk. I'm in a meeting."

"You have to talk to me."

With resignation, Matt told Kitty he needed to switch phones. After a quick hold, he returned to the line. "Okay, what's the problem?"

"We have no electricity, and the realtors will be here in two hours."

"Write the check, and I'll cover you tonight," he answered abruptly. "I can't discuss this right now."

"What do you mean? What's more important, our home or your precious meeting?"

"The precious meeting is with our bankers," Matt responded. "If they don't extend our credit, we won't have a home."

Kitty couldn't believe her ears. "And you want me to write a check with no money in my account? What would your precious bankers say about that?"

"Calm down, Kitty. I told you I can't talk now. Grow up and write the damn check. I'll deposit cash in your account today." He slammed the phone down.

Matt never talked to her like that. She gazed at the dead phone. "You bastard," she said and slammed her phone down.

She struggled to write the check. *What am I doing? I can't do this but I must.* Kitty knew her bank balance to the penny. She had watched it shrink from $10,000 to $5,000 to $2,000. Every day she woke up expecting money to come from somewhere as it always had. But no funds came, and her balance continued shrinking from $2,000 to $500 to $235.

How did we get into this mess? I've never worried about money before. Kitty was, after all, born a Bradshaw. The Bradshaws were a respected Philadelphia family who had built up a prestigious law firm over five generations. Her father, Douglas, had been tall and thin, a well-regarded lawyer at a powerful firm, and had a twinkle in his blue eyes. Kitty had grown up in a beautiful house similar to the one she now lived in. *The one that currently was dark and had no power.* That would never have happened to the Bradshaws. *My father must be turning over in his grave watching me deliberately write a bad check.*

She slowly wrote out a check for $2,000, tears rolling down her cheeks. *What is going to happen to us?* She felt lost as she headed upstairs.

Kitty turned on the shower and stood motionlessly in front of the three body sprays. *Daddy, you always took care of Mummy and me. We never had to wait in line in restaurants or theaters. Everyone knew and respected us. We attended charity balls. You donated hundreds of hours in free legal advice and assistance to the low income families of Philadelphia. You encouraged us to give back to the community and never said no when asked to host a fundraising party. Our home was filled with beautiful antiques and artwork. We had conversations about politics, theater, flowers, music: the topics were endless! I never worried about money. How could Matt let this happen? Doesn't he have any pride? Letting the electricity be turned off.* She sighed. *What are we going to do? Daddy, I wish you were here.*

She stepped out of the shower, wrapped herself in a large Egyptian towel and methodically dried herself off. Why hadn't Matt sold their technology stocks when the market started to spiral downward? Kitty Kittcarefully put on her makeup, accentuating her high cheekbones and piercing blue eyes, and mechanically brushed her glossy dark hair. She dressed, picked up the check from her desk, and was heading for the garage when she remembered the realtors. She'd have to cancel, but she dreaded calling Sophia, her nosy realtor, on Sophia's ever-present cell phone. Instead, she left a message in Sophia's office voice mail, hoping Sophia would get it in time to call off the house tour.

Frustrated and tired, Kitty got into her Jaguar XJ8 to go to the electric company. Suddenly she realized that the garage door was closed and the power was off. Matt had shown her how to manually open the garage door if they ever lost power. Kitty was grateful she remembered how to open the door. It was not that heavy; she was somewhat relieved. As Kitty reached the end of her driveway she was wondering how to open the black wrought iron gates. Luckily, the gardeners had opened them earlier when they came to cut the lawn.

On the way to the electric company she again thought about her late father. "Oh, Daddy," she sighed out loud. "I wish you were here." Her cell phone rang, interrupting her thoughts.

"I'm glad I reached you," chirped her friend, Caroline Evans. Caroline, a successful marketing executive whom Kitty had known for more than 20 years, spoke in her usual confident tones. "The others can't go to lunch."

Kitty had been so absorbed in her problems that she'd completely forgotten she had lunch planned with friends. "So lunch is off?" she clarified, sighing with relief. "Good, I have a lot to do anyway."

"Oh," Caroline said. "I thought you and I could have lunch like we used to. What do you say, Kit? We never spend time together anymore."

The last time Kitty had gone to lunch with her, Caroline sent her food back three times and called the waitress stupid. Kitty wasn't up for another embarrassing scene.

"I'm really busy today."

"Don't say no," Caroline pleaded. "Come on. Let's have a few laughs, for old time's sake."

Kitty couldn't help but wonder why Caroline was being so insistent. *We're not close like we used to be. Does Caroline know about our situation? Is she going to pump me about what's going on?*

She thought about Caroline's son, Chuck; maybe he was the reason Caroline was so eager to get together. Although Caroline never mentioned it, Kitty had heard rumors that Chuck, a junior in high school, was doing drugs.

Worn down by the morning's events, Kitty wearily agreed to meet Caroline at the Four Seasons, Philadelphia's most elegant hotel, at 12:30.

Kitty's hands trembled as she pulled into the electric company's parking lot. She looked around to make sure she didn't see anyone she knew. No one must ever know their electricity had been turned off. She was a Bradshaw, and she wasn't going to let her family name be disgraced. As she reached for the door handle, her phone rang. Matt's name appeared on the screen.

"What do you want, Matt?"

"I made payment arrangements with the electric bill."

"Really?" Kitty shot back.

"I made a partial payment with a credit card."

"When were you going to tell me, after I humiliated myself and gave them a bad check? I'm in the parking lot right now."

"I didn't think of it until I got out of my meeting. I wanted to save you the embarrassment."

"It's a little late for that, don't you think?" Kitty snarled.

"Kit," Matt snapped, "we're going through some hard times right now, like a lot of other families. We'll get through it, and you'll live." He hung up.

Kitty banged her hand on the steering wheel and again swore: "Damn you, Matt!" She pulled the check out of her handbag and tore it up. Somehow, though, she felt even worse after the empty gesture.

Chapter 2

Remember When

"We do not remember days; we remember moments."

–Cesare Pavase

Kitty opened her sunroof and steered her burgundy Jaguar toward Kelly Drive. She cruised along the river thinking about the night she and Matt were having dinner at the General Wayne Inn and Matt's best friend, Nick Evans, introduced them to his girlfriend, Caroline, a blond beauty.

Caroline was different. She had attended public school and worked after class; Kitty went to a private academy and played sports after school. Caroline took the bus to school; Kitty drove her Mustang convertible. When they'd met, Kitty was a senior in college, while Caroline was already a single parent with a young child she'd had in her teens, before meeting Nick. Ironically, Caroline wanted a career, while Kitty wanted a family.

In spite of their differences, they became close friends. They talked on the phone every day after each had married; however, their relationship changed when Caroline started working at a marketing firm and her career took off. Although their husbands remained close friends, Caroline and Kitty drifted apart. Caroline threw herself into her career, and Kitty immersed herself in her family and charity work.

Caroline made all the right moves for success. She got her MBA, mastered the art of networking, and climbed the corporate ladder, becoming vice president of a niche marketing company.

And over the last few years Kitty had begun avoiding Caroline; Kitty thought her friend had become self-centered, rude, and arrogant.

She regretted accepting her lunch invitation. But on the other hand, she thought as she pulled up to the Four Seasons, anything was better than being home without electricity.

Vincent, the doorman greeted her. "Good afternoon, Mrs. Murphy! Nice to see you again." She was pleased that he remembered her.

Caroline was already seated at a table, watching as tall, elegant Kitty walked toward her in a Chanel pastel linen suit, carrying a Hermes Birkin bag. Most of the men in the dining room stopped talking long enough to glance at tall, brunette Kitty, as they always did. Kitty had olive skin. Her long dark hair glistened in the sunlight. She was 5'8" with long, slender legs and walked with poise and confidence. Her attention to every detail of her appearance, her skin, makeup, clothes and hair, gave her a regal look that was "undeniably Kitty."

When Kitty sat down, Caroline was relaxed and chatty, almost giddy. Kitty tried to listen but found Caroline's joyful mood annoying.

"What's with you, Caroline? You're so happy you almost glow," Kitty told her.

Caroline's hazel eyes lit up. Her blond hair was pushed back behind her ears, which accentuated her oval face and delicate features. Caroline was 5'4" and had a petite frame. Caroline had pearly white skin with slightly pink colored cheeks. Her lips were full and usually painted with a mauve colored lipstick. She usually wore her hair back in a barrette and had a warm, friendly smile.

Kitty could see that she wanted to tell her something, but instead she complimented Kitty's handbag. Kitty squirmed in her chair, adjusting her skirt.

"I've heard that bag is selling for thousands of dollars on eBay," Caroline said.

Kitty pulled her handbag closer to her side while eyeing Caroline suspiciously. *Why is she talking about selling my bag? Could she possibly know about our financial situation?*

Kitty decided to cut right to the point. "I can tell by your smile you're dying to tell me something. You're giggling like you did when we first met. Are you having an affair or something?"

Caroline laughed. "An affair? Well, I am in love," she teased.

Kitty leaned over the table. "Tell me about him."

Caroline just laughed again, and changed the subject. "How does Susan like Boston University?"

Kitty stiffened. Her daughter, Susan, had just finished her freshman year at B.U. She didn't want Caroline to know that Susan wasn't going back because they couldn't pay her tuition. "She likes it, but I don't think she's going back." Before Caroline could ask another question, Kitty interjected, "You're holding back on me. Tell me about your affair."

Caroline smiled nervously. She ran her fingers up and down her water goblet. "It isn't what you're thinking. I'm having a love affair with life," she said, which only confused Kitty more. She began to dread the possibility of a long and tedious lunch and suggested they order wine.

Caroline agreed and beckoned the waiter. Kitty watched anxiously: She didn't want one of Caroline's embarrassing scenes. But her friend smiled at the waiter and thanked him politely.

She is different; something has definitely changed her. Kitty pushed Caroline to elaborate on her love affair with life.

"I don't want to bore you," Caroline told her.

"Try me."

Caroline's face lit up. "Every now and then something extraordinary touches your spirit and teaches you the joy of living. It sets you free to be who you were meant to be."

The joy of living. There's no joy in our life. Susan's angry, we've lost our money, our electricity is turned off.

"Joy of living?" Kitty repeated.

"Yes," Caroline said. "The joy to be free to recognize and appreciate the people, the beauty, and the love all around you. To live in the moment."

Kitty gazed at Caroline. Just then the waiter brought the bottle of wine to the table. He held it at an angle to show Caroline and Kitty the label. He poured a small amount into Caroline's glass. She sipped it. "Lovely," she said, complimenting the waiter.

"How do you get this joy of living?" Kitty persisted.

Caroline smiled. "I began by re-evaluating my life and what's really important. I started making some changes, beginning with my job. I resigned."

"You did what?" Kitty gasped. "Why?"

Caroline's face was pensive. "Have you ever felt like you were trapped in a situation and you couldn't get out?"

Kitty panicked. *She knows something, she knows we're trapped in a financial disaster.* Kitty sighed. "You feel like your life is out of control. Is that what you mean?"

Caroline nodded in agreement. "I struggled to be the super mom, super career woman, and super athlete. I drove and pushed everyone to live up to my expectations."

"Don't you think all moms try to be super moms?" Kitty asked reassuringly.

"But they don't claw their way to the top, stepping on anyone who gets in their way. I was uptight and miserable and I made everyone around me uptight and miserable. I didn't like the person I was becoming."

This doesn't sound like Caroline. Something has happened to her.

"I think we all have times when we don't like ourselves," Kitty reassured her. "I don't like myself sometimes either."

Caroline seemed surprised. "But you never show it."

"Neither did you," Kitty commented.

"Speaking of liking yourself," Caroline asked, "How much money did you raise from the breast cancer ball?"

The question took Kitty by surprise. It had been a long time since Caroline had actually showed any interest in what Kitty was doing. "It was our best year. We netted $600,000," Kitty said proudly.

"Wow, $600,000!"

Kitty told her they raised most of the money from corporations. When Kitty's mother, Katharine Bradshaw, was diagnosed with breast cancer, the Bradshaw-Murphy family turned all their energies to raising money for breast cancer research. "I had a lot of help," Kitty added modestly.

"You're too modest," Caroline replied. "It's more than the people you know. It's your passion for a cure that inspires people to give."

Kitty's face flushed. "Well, that's over. I'm taking a sabbatical from all charities."

"You're kidding! You're so good at it."

Kitty felt emptiness in the pit of her stomach. She didn't want to talk about what had been. It was too painful. She was glad the waiter interrupted them, and she and Caroline both ordered a shrimp salad.

Kitty sat back and looked at Caroline. "Tell me about this extraordinary thing that happened to you that helped you change your attitude."

"It was a series of things. I guess it started when I decided I was going to take Valerie Morrel's job."

"Wasn't she your boss?"

"Yes, she was in line to be the next president. I tried to show her up every chance I got. To my surprise, she let me grab the limelight and take all the credit for our success. She encouraged me and gave me recognition in front of the president and the clients. At first, I thought she was stupid."

"It sounds like she *was* stupid."

"Stupid like a fox," Caroline said, adding that their department won sales awards for the last four years. "It was Valerie's leadership. She was tough, but fair," Caroline continued. "She didn't miss a beat, yet she was calm and relaxed. No matter how stressful things were, she was always smiling and at peace."

Kitty took a sip of wine and kept listening.

"I envied her joy. She had that extraordinary balance of being peaceful and productive. I wanted to find peace and joy in my life. I wanted her secret."

While Caroline was talking, Kitty's mind wandered to her conversation with Matt earlier. *You can't have peace without money or electricity or a home. The heart and soul of our family is hidden in the walls of our home. How can we possibly have peace without a home?*

Caroline gave her a funny look. "You seem distracted."

"I was thinking about peace," Kitty admitted, picking up her wine glass. "Did Valerie tell you her secret?" she persisted.

"On my last day at work she told me she struggled to be a super career woman, super mom, and super wife, but the harder she pushed, the more miserable she became. Then, pointing to her heart, she said 'When I discovered that happiness comes from the inside out, not the outside in, I began struggling less and enjoying life more.' "

"What made her realize this?"

Caroline leaned forward conspiratorially as the waiter delivered their salads. "A friend, a book, and five secrets."

"Is that it?" Kitty's disappointment was obvious. "Did she give you the book?"

"The day I left she gave me the book, and we've been practicing the secrets together."

Kitty took a sip of wine and sighed. "So your love affair with life isn't with a person, it's with a book?"

"You're really curious about this, aren't you?" Caroline seemed pleased.

"It's hard to believe you are so lighthearted because of a book and a few secrets," Kitty admitted. "It just sounds too simple."

"It's more than a book." Caroline's hazel eyes glistened. "It's a way of life that brings peace and joy."

Kitty was getting irritated by Caroline's pie in the sky attitude. She arched her eyebrows, took a bite of her salad, and asked, "Are you trying to tell me that when you follow these secrets, your alcoholic husband and drug-addicted son become peaceful, and all is well?"

The minute the words were out, she regretted saying them. A hurt look swept across Caroline's face. She had occasionally alluded to her son, Chuck, having some problems, but had never elaborated. And whenever people even intimated Nick had a drinking problem, Caroline immediately defended him. Kitty expected her to retort with her usual sarcasm, but Caroline didn't dispute the remark.

"I'm sorry, Caroline," Kitty apologized immediately. "I don't know why I just said that. I'm really sorry." Her mind scrambled. *I can't believe I did that. Is it the wine or is it because I'm uptight and irritable about selling our house?*

Caroline didn't say anything. Kitty nervously sipped wine.

"It's okay," Caroline finally responded. "You've always said what's on your mind. That's an admirable quality." She hesitated before continuing. "But it hurts, especially coming from you."

"I don't know why I said that," Kitty responded. The next words out of Caroline's mouth surprised Kitty further.

"Kit, practicing the peace secrets has helped me realize that finding peace is not about changing others; it's about changing *me* and my attitude. I either choose to be angry and sad, or happy and peaceful. For example, it isn't the things people say or do that make me angry or happy. It's my perception of what they say or do. I can take your comment as a personal affront, or I can accept it as a direct question from a good friend. I know you didn't mean to hurt me."

"Thank you," Kitty responded. She watched Caroline's long, tapered hand gracefully fork up a bite of salad. "I didn't mean to be so harsh."

Caroline looked directly at Kitty. "You asked a good question."

Caroline continued talking. "For years I blamed my unhappiness on Nick, the schools, the coaches, the business, our house. At the same time, I always felt guilty for working and being away from home. I constantly second-guessed myself. Remorse and regret were my daily companions."

Kitty looked up at her with surprise. "Why should you feel remorse or regret?

Caroline hesitated. "I had remorse for not spending more time with my family, and regret at missing events that were important to Nick and my children. I lost my sense of fun and family."

It was like Kitty was talking to herself. "Did the book you mentioned help you let go of your remorse and regret?" she asked.

Caroline smiled and nodded. "When I follow the peace secrets, I'm able to let go. But when I ignore them and try to control the outcome of everything myself, I go back to my usual irritable self."

"I can't take the credit," Caroline admitted. Then she said something that stunned Kitty.

"The credit belongs to God. Every day I'm more confident that God loves me and is watching over me. He loves and watches over you, too, Kit."

A sudden wave of sadness swept through Kitty. No one loved or watched over her anymore. She choked up, feeling like she was about to cry, and glanced at her watch.

"I have to go." She leaped up, waved goodbye to Caroline, and said, "I'll call you" as she rushed out of the dining room.

"Kit, where are you going?" Caroline called after her. But Kit disappeared.

Kitty cried all the way home.

Chapter 3

Grief

"There is no pain so great as the memory of joy in a present grief."

—Aeschylus

When Kitty turned into her driveway, the tall, black wrought iron gates were closed. She held her breath when she pushed the button to open them; they slowly opened. She exhaled and relaxed.

The electricity was on, but the house was empty. Susan, her youngest child, was up in Boston at school, and Matt worked late. Their sons, Ken and Doug, had moved out. Ken was living in Los Angeles now, near Kitty's favorite uncle, Chip.

Kitty felt restless, and wandered through the house picking things up, putting them down, and fluffing up pillows in an attempt to keep her mind off her problems. She thought again about Caroline's joyful attitude at lunch, and wondered if she would ever be happy again.

Kitty picked up an old picture of her and Matt taken after a Penn University football game. She'd met Matt while she was still in high school at a fraternity party at the University of Pennsylvania. She remembered giggling when the friend she'd come to the party with suggested they go over and talk to Matt Murphy, the star quarterback.

Matt greeted them like he already knew them. Everything about him surprised Kitty. He was about six feet tall, but didn't seem as tall once she was standing next to him. He had broad shoulders, yet he wasn't bulky. He had the warmest brown eyes and a wide smile. When they shook hands, their eyes met, and Kitty tingled all over. She didn't want to let go, and she felt he didn't want to either. She loved the way he unconsciously pushed back the black curls from his forehead, and the way he shyly offered to get her a drink.

After their first meeting, Kitty constantly thought about Matt. She casually asked people about him, dreaming about him inviting her out, even though she knew he wouldn't. She was only a senior in high school, and he was a junior at Penn.

She learned from her friends that his father died when he was 15, he was a city boy, and he had graduated from public high school. Their backgrounds were quite different. She came from a wealthy family; he came from a middle-class Irish clan. She was raised on a 40-acre horse farm, while he grew up in the city. She was an only child, and he was the eldest of four. Kitty spent July traveling in Europe with her parents, and August at their summer home in Spring Lake, New Jersey. Matt's family took an annual one-week vacation in Ocean City – that was the highlight of their summer. Although Kitty knew her parents weren't snobs, she didn't think they would approve of her dating Matt Murphy.

She learned every little detail about him. Each new piece of information fueled her desire to date him, although she heard that he rarely asked girls out. Everyone liked and admired him. He waited on tables every weekend, except during football season, to help out his mother financially. He didn't have much time for partying.

That was so long ago. Kitty ran her fingers across the photo, and the old tingling stirred when she looked at Matt's chiseled features and square jaw. She touched the scar over his right eye, and ran her finger over the dimple on his cheek. She gazed at the picture for a long time, tears rolling down her cheeks. *How did we get into this mess? What went wrong?*

Kitty thought about taking a swim, but couldn't muster up the energy. She meandered through the gardens; she tried watching TV, but nothing interested her. She picked up a book, but couldn't concentrate. The night dragged until it was time to go to bed, and then she couldn't sleep.

She heard Matt come in, and listened to his familiar footsteps traversing the hall. Matt hesitated in front of their bedroom door, and then turned back toward the guest room where he'd been sleeping for the past month. Kitty lay there listening, wondering if she should jump out of bed, scream at him, and shake him for losing all their money, but that wasn't her style. After much turning and twisting, she finally drifted off to sleep.

The telephone jarred her awake early the next morning.

"Hello," she answered, trying to disguise the hoarseness in her voice.

"Kitty, dahling! Is that you? This is Sophia. I didn't wake you, did I?"

Kitty rolled her eyes. Sophia, their real estate agent, consistently annoyed her. She was furious at Matt for listing their house with her.

"No, you didn't wake me," she said curtly, glancing at her clock. Almost 9:00 a.m. She never slept this late!

"My office was very unhappy about your last-minute cancellation yesterday," Sophia told her. "We scheduled our morning around you, and you didn't give us enough notice to make other appointments."

Kitty apologized.

"Well, I'd appreciate it if you give us more time when canceling an appointment."

Kitty felt she was being reprimanded and her blood boiled. "Pardon me. Who do you think you're talking to, Sophia? I am the client, remember?" Kitty didn't even try to hide her anger.

There was silence on the other end of the phone.

"Is there anything else?" Kitty asked.

Sophia hesitated. "I have a family interested in seeing your house. They're from out of town, and can see it only today. But I'd like to bring my appraisers over beforehand. Can I bring them around in an hour? Say about ten, so I can bring my clients at one o'clock?"

"I thought the open house wasn't until Sunday!" Kitty was annoyed with Sophia, and with herself for sleeping in. She usually never slept past 7:00.

"The open house *isn't* till Sunday," Sophia said. "But my appraisers have to price the house before we show it, and if these people buy, we won't have to have an open house. I drove them by last night. They want to see it. Is ten o'clock okay?"

"No, ten is not okay!" Kitty responded angrily.

Sophia persisted, "If you want to sell the house, we need to show it!"

Kitty tried to calm down, and said into the phone, "You understand what I mean, Sophia. I raised my family here. It's just painful closing a chapter in your life." Kitty was getting in much deeper than she wanted to.

"I do understand," said Sophia, softening a little.

"Look, Sophia, we're wasting time. Come at 11 o'clock. Goodbye." She slammed the phone down harder than she intended.

A half hour later, Kitty gulped her last sip of coffee and ran from room to room straightening up. She raced back upstairs, made the beds, took her shower, and dressed.

A final inspection of the house included walking from the hall to the living room, the dining room, and the library. The house was so beautiful with its sunny yellow walls and bright touches of blue and green everywhere. Kitty stopped at a library table and absentmindedly straightened a family picture. She paused and took another look. It was a picture of her mother and dad, with her and Matt, Ken, Doug, and Susan. Kitty gazed at the picture, gently touching each smiling face. It had been taken 11 years ago, on her 35th birthday, during a cookout they'd had with all their friends. *Mummy and Daddy look so healthy, the children so young, and Matt and I so in love. Wish I could go back for just a day.* She was still holding the picture when the doorbell rang.

Kitty took a last look at the photo and carefully replaced it. She smoothed her skirt and moved toward the front door. Sophia and five of her colleagues entered the house.

It's an army. She invited them to take their time looking through the house. She headed to the garage with newspaper in hand and decided to go hide out in Starbucks.

Chapter 4

Sorrows Turned to Joy

*"Every woman has her secret sorrows
which the world knows not.
Often times we call a woman cold
when she is only sad."*

–Henry Wadsworth Longfellow

Entering Starbucks, Kitty was surprised to see Caroline sitting at a corner table by the window, reading a book. She immediately turned to leave, but Caroline spied her.

"Kitty! Join me," Caroline beckoned. Kitty was always running into people when she least wanted to.

Kitty sighed. She'd wanted to be alone, but maybe Caroline was just what she needed right now. She bought a grande cappuccino and headed toward Caroline.

"I just escaped a bunch of realtors," Kitty found herself telling Caroline. "Including Sophia Sardon – dahling," she added with a laugh, using Sophia's favorite word.

"Are you selling your house?" Caroline looked surprised.

Kitty nodded. "We're thinking about it."

"You're talking to Sophia Sardon?" Caroline asked. "Well, she's the best. She won't let up until she sells your house." Kitty's eyes grew misty at this.

"Kit, what's the matter?" Caroline asked, alarmed.

"I just get a little emotional when I think about selling our home. Let's not talk about the house." Kitty tried to change the topic. "Yesterday you said you had discovered the secrets to peace. Tell me more about that."

Caroline smiled. "This is the book I was telling you about." She held up the slim volume bound in purple; on its cover were the words *The Peace Way.*

"We're so busy we don't have time to notice the precious moments in our life, but the secrets in this book will help you do so," Caroline said earnestly, her skin taking on a golden glow from the sun coming in the window.

"That's what makes the secrets so magical," Caroline explained. "They help us see miracles all around us."

"Magical secrets? Miracles? Caroline, do you really believe this?"

Caroline smiled. "Let me give you the book and see for yourself."

"That's very kind of you," Kitty acknowledged. "But I don't have time to read a book right now. Why don't you just tell me the secrets?" She longed to feel what Caroline felt, but her stomach was tied up in knots.

Caroline ran her fingers across the book. "I can tell you the secrets, but it would be like trying to tell you about a garden, rather than taking you there to experience the lushness of the colors, scent, and beauty of the flowers for yourself."

Kitty saw the intensity in Caroline's hazel eyes.

"The secrets are revealed in the lives and challenges of the women in this book." Caroline held up the book.

Kitty took a sip of her cappuccino and slowly put her wide-rimmed cup on the small table. "I'm not sure I can buy into the secrets," she confessed, "but tell me the most important secret, and I'll try it." She raised her eyebrows and smiled. "If it works for me like it has for you, I'll read the book. That's a promise."

Caroline repositioned herself in the big leather armchair, and adjusted her green-and-white golf skirt. "All the secrets are important," Caroline said. "But one secret is the foundation for the other four."

"What is it?" Kitty asked, leaning toward Caroline.

Caroline took a deep breath. "The first secret to finding joy is praising and thanking God in all things."

Kitty stared at Caroline. "What do you mean?"

Caroline laughed. "You praise and thank God for everything in your life, both the good and the bad."

Kitty wrinkled her forehead. "Can you give me an example?"

Caroline put her cup down. "Well, I thank God for this coffee, and for your company. I also praise and thank God when things go wrong, and when I feel my life is out of control."

"Caroline, praising and thanking God for coffee and even for my problems just doesn't make sense," Kitty said, feeling frustrated.

"You're right. It sounds crazy, but when you read the book and learn how the secrets evolve, you'll realize that praising God in all things makes a lot of sense."

Kitty started to laugh. "If it was anyone else other than you saying this, I'd swear they weren't all there."

Caroline laughed. "If you told me six months ago I'd be talking like this, I'd think you weren't all there."

"Well, we agree on that," Kitty said, laughing. "Can you give me an example of a problem that you praise and thank God for?" Kitty examined Caroline's face. She'd always had beautiful skin, but today it glowed. She looked absolutely regal.

"Well, when I'm trapped in a situation where I have no control, like when I'm stuck in a traffic jam, I praise and thank God for the traffic jam and ask his blessings for all the other people stuck along with me. I begin to relax and actually enjoy the quiet time."

"You praise and thank God for being stuck in a *traffic jam?*"

Caroline giggled. "That's the miracle. God's peace and love is everywhere. He wants to free us from our self-imposed traps." She looked into Kitty's crystal blue eyes. "He loves you, Kitty. He wants to fill you with His joy."

Kitty suddenly felt trapped. An overwhelming feeling of loneliness swept through her. She wanted to get up and run.

"Look, Caroline," she said weakly, trying to fight off the sadness. "I'm glad you're so happy, but this isn't for me. Besides, you know me. I'm not afraid of anything." Kitty felt a lump swelling in her throat, and whispered, "I have to go." But before she could get out of the chair, tears erupted and cascaded down her cheeks uncontrollably. She tried to hide her face.

"Kit, what's the matter?" Caroline asked, visibly upset. "Did I say something to upset you?"

Kitty tried to speak but the words wouldn't come. Finally she was able to choke out, "No, no, it was nothing you said. I don't know." Kitty sobbed. Trying to control her crying, she blurted out, "Everything is wrong!"

Chapter 5

Cleansing the Heart

*"A true friend is someone who reaches for your hand
and touches your heart."*

—Anonymous

Rubbing her fingers around her coffee cup, Kitty got control of herself, and slowly spoke. "Susan barely talks to me. Matt and I sleep in separate bedrooms," she whispered. She couldn't believe she was telling Caroline all of this but she couldn't stop herself. "We've lost everything. We have to sell both houses." Kitty and Matt had owned a house at the Jersey Shore for more than a decade. She wiped her eyes and hesitated. "We're broke, Caroline. One day we were millionaires, today we're destitute."

Caroline looked shocked. "What about your dad's money?"

"Gone. It's all gone," Kitty whispered.

"Your trust fund is all gone?" Caroline cupped her hand around her mouth so no one could hear what she was saying.

Kitty looked around the coffee shop. She was relieved that there was no one sitting near them.

"Matt invested it in the market, and there's nothing left. I'm so ashamed. I ask myself over and over again, 'Why did I give all that money to Matt?' All our family memories are wrapped up in our home and we have to sell it." Her stomach began trembling as she tried to hold back the sobs coming from deep within her. She turned her body toward the window so no one could see her.

"Kitty, I'm so sorry. I've been rattling on about myself. I had no idea."

"I'm sorry for what I said yesterday about Nick and Chuck," Kitty told her, pulling herself together.

"That's okay," Caroline told her. "We've been friends a long time, Kitty, and although we've had our differences, I love you. I wish I could take away your pain."

Kitty could feel the tears starting again. She put her hands up. "Let's talk about something else, anything," she said, dabbing her eyes.

Caroline looked at her. "I don't know if this is the right time, but I would like to talk to you about Chuck."

"Sure," Kitty said, feeling herself squirm a little.

"Kit, I never told anyone about Chuck. I was amazed when you mentioned his drug problem yesterday. Does everyone know about it?" she asked, looking Kitty straight in the eye.

Trying to hide her embarrassment, Kitty looked into her coffee cup. "I'm sorry I said that, I really am. Susan told me. You know kids know everything."

"It's fine, Kit," Caroline said. "I'm actually glad you mentioned it. Now I can talk to you about it without feeling disloyal to Chuck." She looked at Kitty and smiled. "If I can't talk to you, who can I talk to?" She hesitated. "They tell you in rehab that the first step to recovery from addiction is honesty. Don't hide it."

"How is he doing?"

Caroline glanced out the window for a minute. "He's doing great. He's off drugs, and very involved in Narcotics Anonymous. It follows the same program as Alcoholics Anonymous." Caroline leaned over the table. "You know, Kit, before I started practicing the peace secrets, I nagged him. I worried about him. I got in the way of his recovery. I didn't realize it but I was so scared for him that I never let up on him. I thought I could control his addiction."

Kitty felt an overwhelming desire to protect Caroline. "Don't you think you're a little hard on yourself?" she asked. "After all, what mother wouldn't try to get her child off drugs?"

Caroline smiled and pushed her hair back behind her ears. "You're so right. We want the best for our kids. But trying to control them often gets us the opposite results from what we want."

Kitty thought about the fights she had with her daughter, Susan, and how distant Susan had become. "I don't understand what you mean," she said.

Caroline leaned over and rested her elbows on her knees. "Nagging someone aggravates the situation and makes things worse. I knew nagging wasn't working but I didn't know what else to do until I learned the peace secrets."

Kitty thought of a conversation she had with her son, Doug, when he wanted to quit college and sell Jaguars. *That's what Doug kept saying to me.* She could hear his words replaying in her head. *Stop nagging me. I know what I'm doing. I love you, Mom, but your nagging is just making everything more difficult.* She stared at Caroline. "You don't praise and thank God for Chuck's problems, do you?"

Caroline laughed and told Kitty that praising and thanking God for Chuck helped her change her attitude about him. She said it was hard at first, but the more she praised and thanked God for Chuck, the better she felt about him. She said she began realizing God loved him and was taking care of him, although she couldn't see it.

"Don't you think God expects us to be responsible for our own problems?"

"I thought it was my responsibility to change Chuck's behavior. I was trying to change him from the outside in. It wasn't working. "

"You're his mother. A responsible mother will do anything she can to change her children when their behaviors are self-destructive," Kitty argued.

"That's true. But we want to be successful at it, don't we?"

"Naturally," Kitty affirmed.

"I'm slowly realizing I can't change Chuck or anyone else. I can only change me."

"I don't agree with you," Kitty insisted. "I think we can change people."

"I used to think I could change people," Caroline confessed. "But I'm learning that happiness comes from the inside. No one else can make me happy. It's my choice. And Chuck's happiness has to come from inside him. No one can make him happy. He has to want to change his behavior and choose to be happy." Caroline tilted her head to the side. "I guess we have to ask ourselves, 'Are we effective when we try to change our children?' "

Kitty couldn't believe her ears. "Caroline, are you suggesting that when our children's behavior is self-destructive, we shouldn't try to change it?"

Caroline shook her head. "I'm saying we have to help our children think things out for themselves. They have to *want* to change."

Kitty thought about that for a moment. "How do you make a person want to change?'

Caroline looked at Kitty. "I can only tell you what works for me. When I began praying and thanking God for Chuck exactly as he was, my attitude toward Chuck began to change. I became more patient with him. I'm not afraid to hear him out and explore his thinking with him. I'm often surprised by his wisdom." Caroline looked down at her hands.

"Don't you advise him on what he should and shouldn't do?" Kitty asked.

"The one big 'aha' I've gotten from all of this is showing my children respect. When I listen to them verbalize their thoughts and I explore the principles behind them, I'm showing them respect. When they feel respected, they're more open to suggestions."

Kitty didn't speak. She wished she could have Caroline's joy and faith. She and Matt had an unspoken agreement about religion. They thought most people used God as a crutch, one that they didn't need.

Caroline looked at her watch. "Oh Kit, I'm sorry, but I have to run. I have to pick Sammy up at the club, and take her to her softball game." Sammy was Caroline's 12-year-old daughter. She picked up her coffee cup and put it on the tray in the corner.

The two women hugged each other.

"Kit, try praising and thanking God for finding you the perfect home. It will be difficult at first. But you'll be amazed at the peace you'll experience."

"Caroline, thanks for the suggestion, but I don't think so," Kitty told her. "Thanks, anyway. See you soon."

"Here," Caroline said, handing her the slim purple volume. "Take a few minutes and just look at the book while I make a quick phone call." Caroline walked outside to make her call, and Kitty gathered her handbag and keys to leave. The book was open on the table before her, and she couldn't help but pause to read part of the opening pages.

> Thank you for joining me while I share with you my journey from fear to faith, from hate to love, and from panic to peace.
>
> As we journey through my story together, I invite you to stop and think about the peace secrets that have transformed me from a helpless victim to a hopeful victor.
>
> You will discover the secrets to juggling your daily life with a peaceful and calm heart. When you uncover a secret, stop and reflect on how you can weave it into your life. I also encourage you to try the prayers that Maria taught me. These seemingly simple prayers can be as powerful and rewarding for you as they are for me.

Feeling confused, Kitty waited until Caroline was finished with her call. Then she handed Caroline the book, thanked her, and drove home.

Chapter 6

Loneliness

"The surest cure for vanity is loneliness."

–Thomas Wolfe

On the ride home, Kitty's thoughts were preoccupied with Caroline. As close as they had been, Caroline never told Kitty about her life before she married Nick. Matt, Nick, and Caroline's brother, Tom, grew up together. Caroline left for college in New York and came home three years later a single parent with an 18-month-old baby, Malcolm. Malcolm was four when she married Nick. When or where Caroline had Malcolm was never discussed. Matt thought Malcolm was born in New York, but no one knew who his father was.

Kitty was always curious about Malcolm. Caroline talked about regrets. *I wonder if she regrets the deep, dark secret about her life with Malcolm's father.* Kitty shook her head, trying to drive thoughts about Caroline out of her head. *Malcolm is a wonderful young man. Nick obviously enjoys having him in the company. I wonder if Caroline sees Malcolm's father or even knows who he is? Why am I wasting my time thinking about Caroline's past? I have problems of my own.*

She thought about her own children. *If Matt and I get separated, I have to find a place for Susan and me to live when she's home from college. What's Susan going to do? She'll have to get a job.* It had not occurred to Kitty that she, too, would have to find employment.

She was anxious to get home and see how the realtors had left her house. Strolling through the living room, Kitty ran her fingers gently over the furniture. Memories flooded her mind. She thought about the weeks she'd spent walking until her legs were sore, picking out materials and planning this room. She thought about the nights she and Matt stayed up late discussing how much they could spend furnishing the house.

And now it was over. Although the room was filled with furniture and beautiful art, it felt gloomy and empty. The emptiness screamed at her. *This is a bad dream.* A wave of loneliness swept through her whole body. Caroline's words ran through Kitty's mind. "I can't begin to tell you how many wonderful things have happened in my life since I started praising and thanking God, and sending love out to all the painful situations in my life."

She picked up a pillow from the couch and hurled it across the room. "Oh!" she cried, sobbing. "I can't stand this empty house." Kitty grabbed her keys and headed toward the garage. It was then she noticed a beautiful flower arrangement on the hall table. The card read:

"Dear Kitty and Matt,
Your home radiates love and care.
My clients loved it. I'll call you. S. S."

Kitty turned the card over in her hand. *Well, that was nice of Sophia. I should call her.*

She phoned Sophia from the car and left a message thanking her for the flowers. She then dialed her daughter's cell: no answer. Next she rang her son's office. He wasn't in. *Just as well. I'm too out of control to talk to them right now.* She started to cry again.

Doug, their 22-year-old second son, had left Harvard after his sophomore year because he knew his father was having financial hardships. Kitty was furious with him. She thought he was being melodramatic, making a big issue out of nothing. Worse yet, he started selling cars and he seemed to have no interest in going back to college.

Kitty drove around killing time and going nowhere. She drove to the King of Prussia Mall, a luxury shopping center near her house, and wandered aimlessly for an hour or so, her mind a blank. Loneliness consumed her. She bought a large soft pretzel, slathered it with mustard, took two bites, and threw it into a trashcan.

I hate this feeling. She attempted once again to pull herself together. She tried standing up straight, but she couldn't shake the loneliness.

When she got back into her car, she sat in the parking lot for a long while. She thought about Matt, her children, and her parents. She considered how much Susan, her only daughter, had changed.

Susan had been the ideal daughter. She and Susan had spent considerable time together laughing, sharing stories, and being friends, until the middle of Susan's junior year in high school. Susan had planned to go to Kitty's alma mater, Vassar, before Matt began pressuring her to look at Harvard.

Out of nowhere, Susan decided she was going to Boston University. *What got into that girl?* Kitty shook her head. Although everything Kitty read or heard about Boston University gave it rave reviews, she simply didn't want Susan going there instead of Vassar. Kitty had tried to change Susan's mind by highlighting all the reasons Boston University wasn't the right school, but Susan resented her mother's negative remarks.

It was the beginning of a love-hate relationship. They became vicious enemies. Kitty was condescending toward Susan, constantly criticizing everything she did. Susan changed from a sweet, gregarious daughter who shared everything with her mother, into a guarded, irritated young woman. They couldn't be in the same room together without fighting.

Kitty put her head down on the steering wheel and cried softly. Suddenly, she sat up straight. *I could drive into the median and end it all.* She started the car and headed toward Route 76. She imagined what it would be like to drive into the median. She thought about all the nice things her family and friends would say about her at her funeral. She thought about how sorry Susan would be.

She paused and shook her head. *"Kitty, stop. This is insane thinking. Go home. Susan will be there soon."*

One of Susan's close friends from Boston University lived in New York, and Susan had spent the last few days visiting her. She planned to be home for dinner.

Thinking about the breast cancer marathons she and Susan had run together, Kitty smiled remembering the fun they had. She resolved to change her attitude toward her daughter. *Tonight, I'm going to listen to her ideas with true interest.. I'm not going to fight with her. I'm going to enjoy the time with her. That's what I'm going to do.* She sat up straight. *I'm going to enjoy the moment.*

Chapter 7

Control

*"Speak when you are angry and you will make
the best speech you will ever regret."*

–Ambrose Bierce

When Kitty returned home, Susan's car was in the driveway. As Kitty opened the door, she felt a nervous twinge, almost fright. She called up the steps, "Susan?"

Susan looked over the banister. "Hi, Mom, what's up?" she asked.

Susan was in a good mood. Kitty was relieved. "I'm glad you're home. How was New York?"

"It was great," Susan answered.

"Do you want to go out to dinner?"

"Gee, Mom, I'd like to but I have a lot to do tonight. Why don't I run out and pick something up, and we'll eat here?"

While Susan picked up dinner, Kitty turned on the music and set the table out by the pool. She set out two large candles. She was feeling much better and was looking forward to spending time with her daughter. Kitty stepped back and admired the beautiful setting.

She had covered the wrought iron table with a crisp white tablecloth. Midnight blue goblets complemented midnight blue napkins, and candles flickered in the summer breeze. It was a perfect setting for a perfect June evening.

The dinner started out well. Susan was enthusiastic about her recent visit with Sally. Kitty didn't like Sally but she kept her thoughts to herself. She didn't want to start another argument. Finally she changed the subject and told Susan about the realtor bringing someone through the house.

Susan was empathetic and told her mom how sorry she was about all their problems.

Kitty pushed back tears. She held her head up and said firmly, "We'll get through it. We always do." *Why don't I show Susan how I really feel? She's being so sweet. Let your guard down, Kitty.* But she couldn't. She had never allowed her children – or anyone else – to see her vulnerable side.

She glanced at her daughter. *She's beautiful. She has Matt's deep brown eyes and my mother's oval face. What a gorgeous combination.*

She curiously asked, "What are you doing tonight that you couldn't go out to dinner?"

"Oh, just unpacking and straightening up a few things," Susan said as she reached for her second roll.

"That's your second roll. You'll never lose weight."

Susan dutifully pushed the roll aside. "What did the realtors say about the house?"

Kitty tried to control the irritation she was feeling about Susan's weight. She abruptly answered, "I'm not sure yet. Susan, look at me when you talk to me. What is it that you're doing tonight?"

Susan looked at her mother. "Mom, why do you talk to me like I'm five? You know I hate it when you treat me like a child." She pushed her plate away, threw her napkin on the table, and got up, shoving her chair aside.

"Don't be so moody," Kitty rebuked. "I'm asking you a simple question. I'm your mother, and I expect an answer. I have a right to know what you're doing."

"I'm a woman, not a child," Susan fired back. "You may be my mother but you don't have any rights over me. I want to tell you what I'm doing but you're so critical about everything I do. It's easier to avoid having a conversation with you. 'Susan, don't eat this, don't do that.' "

"Don't you talk to me like that, young lady." Kitty's voice rose and she pointed her finger toward Susan. "You're spending too much time with that Sally. She's a bad influence on you."

Susan stepped farther away from the table. "You don't like Sally because she's not from the Main Line! Oh, and her mother's a sales-woman. You don't want your daughter associating with those types of people. What would your friends say? You only like thin, beautiful people." Susan's fury mounted. "Funny thing is, Mother, if you ever gave Sally a chance, you, of all people, would love her," Susan told her while walking into the house.

"Where do you think you're going?" Kitty yelled.

Susan came back to the sliding glass doorway. "I'm going to pack," she answered. "I'm moving into an apartment tonight. I was hoping that if I waited a couple of days, we'd have some quality time together. But you're so full of yourself and what you want. You have to be in charge of everything and everyone. Well, mommy dearest, I'm out of here!" She turned and stormed into the house.

Kitty was frozen in her chair. Susan returned to the terrace. Kitty was staring at the flame of one of the candles she had lit to set a serene mood for dinner.

Susan held the back of the chair she'd been sitting in and continued her rant. "You know, Mom, you don't have a clue about the real world. There are families right in this city who don't have a place to live. They have to scrounge just to survive. Stop feeling sorry for yourself. This is the first time in your life when you can't have everything your way, ex-actly like you want, when you want it. And guess what? You'll survive."

"Who do you think you're talking to?" Kitty shot back. "I'm your mother."

Susan continued talking as if she hadn't spoken. "You don't seem to get it. My college ended abruptly this spring. Dad says there's no more money for tuition. So now I have a job and I'm enrolled in Temple for the fall. I was hoping that for once in your life you'd maybe even say, 'Susan, I'm proud of you. It takes a lot of courage to strike out on your own.' But no, not you. You can't give anyone credit for anything you don't control."

With that, Susan slammed the chair against the table. But she wasn't finished. Heated words continued to spew from her mouth. Thoughts that apparently had been building up for months poured out. "You're going to end up a lonely old woman, Mother, if you don't take a good, hard look at yourself. This may come as a big shock to you, but you're not the only one hurting. We're all hurting.

"Your friends think you're wonderful because you listen to their problems. You're always the strong one – the composed one with all the answers. You have it all together. Well, guess what? You don't! You're afraid to be anything but Mrs. Perfect. I feel sorry for you."

Finally, she ran up the steps and slammed her bedroom door.

Kitty couldn't move. Susan's words were devastating. Too weary to move, she stared at the candles for almost 20 minutes.

She finally focused her thoughts on the events that just transpired. *How dare that spoiled little snip talk to me like that?* Abruptly she pushed back her chair and headed for the steps. She was determined to win this battle and put Susan in her place but the phone interrupted her.

"Hello?" Kitty answered, trying to control her shaking voice.

"Mom, how are you? It's Doug."

"Douglas, where have you been? I've been trying to get you," Kitty said coolly.

"I'm sorry, Mom. I've been really busy. This is the first chance I've had to call. What's up?"

"The realtor, Sophia, came through the house today. She really annoys me," Kitty complained.

Doug laughed. "She can come on a little strong. Remember, I went to school with her son, Ted. But Sophia is a good woman. She's a single mom and she works her tail off. She gets results. How much did she say the house was worth?" asked Doug.

"Sophia thinks we can get about $2.8 million. But thinking and doing are two different things," Kitty replied sarcastically.

"That's great. That'll really help," Doug responded cheerfully.

"Honey, that won't even scratch the surface," Kitty assured him. She could feel tears welling up inside her. *Oh God, I can't let Doug hear me cry.* She stood up, threw her shoulders back, and put on her game face. As a little girl she'd learned she could stop tears by changing her posture and facial expression. She was a master at hiding her feelings.

"Mom, are you okay?" Doug asked.

"Of course. What makes you think I'm not?"

"You sound a little uptight. I wish there was something I could do to help you and Dad."

"You're sweet, Doug. But there's nothing you can do. Your dad's the one who needs to do something." Kitty's voice quivered slightly.

"He's doing the best he can," said Doug. He quickly changed the subject. "What's up with Susan?"

"Susan? She's a whole other issue," Kitty said bitterly.

"What's the problem?"

"She wants to move into her own apartment in town. Sally put ideas into her head. I knew Sally was a bad influence."

"Mom, you did a great job with Susan. She's like you – competent, smart, and independent. You should be proud of her."

Not saying a word, Kitty rolled her eyes. A sense of isolation welled up inside her again. It was paralyzing. She felt too weak to comment. Caroline's smiling face flashed across her mind. She could hear her say, "I can't begin to tell you all the wonderful things that have happened in my life since I started praising and thanking God and sending love out to all the painful situations in my life."

"Mom? Are you there?"

"Yes, I'm here."

"Do you want me to come over?"

"No, not tonight, dear," she said. "You're sweet, but I'm fine, honey. I'm just a little tired. And you're right about Susan. I should probably thank God she wants to be out on her own."

"Well, you do have a lot to be thankful for," Doug said, surprising her. He hesitated and then said something that took Kitty aback. "You know, Mom, if you thank God for your blessings, you'll be surprised at how much easier life will be for you. And everything will work out."

Kitty stiffened. "Not you, too!"

"Huh?" Doug asked.

"Oh, nothing. Just something Aunt Caroline is into." The Murphy children referred to Caroline and Nick Evans as Aunt Caroline and Uncle Nick.

"Look, honey, why don't we have dinner together tomorrow night?" Kitty suggested.

"I wish I could but I'm working," Doug apologized, but quickly added, "How about the next night?"

Kitty hated being turned down. "I think I'm busy, too. We'll make it another time. Good night, Douglas."

She climbed the stairs and was relieved to see Susan's bedroom door closed. She stopped in front of it and was ready to knock, but changed her mind. *I'm too exhausted to get into another fight with Susan. I'll talk to her tomorrow.*

Chapter 8

Susan Reflects

*"It's not only the most difficult to know oneself,
but the most inconvenient."*

–Josh Billings

Susan made plans to leave early in the morning, before her mother
got up. Accordingly, she threw herself across the bed and fell into a
deep sleep. She woke around 2:00 a.m., finished packing, then sat in
her rocking chair and wrote in her journal. "I can't believe that this is
the last night I'll ever spend in this room," she penned as she rocked
and cried. She then turned her journal back six weeks – to the day she'd
received a letter from her father telling her he couldn't pay her tuition
for next year. She read what she had written earlier that morning, May
6th. "Today is going to be a wonderful day. Sally, Josh, and I had coffee
at the coffeehouse. We had so much fun planning for next year."

Later that day she wrote: "Today is the worst day of my life. I received a letter from Dad. I was excited to open it but I was completely
unprepared for its contents. It was a short, cold, factual letter explaining
that he couldn't afford to send me back to B. U. for sophomore year. I
tried to call Doug but I can't get him on the phone. I tried calling Dad
but I can't reach him either. He's doing this because I defied him and
didn't go to Harvard. He's angry I went to B.U. I won't be able to see
my friends. He's ruined my life. I hate my dad for doing this to me."

She sighed. *That was only six weeks ago, yet it feels like six* years. She
looked back at her journal entry where she had written about Doug's
phone call. "Doug finally called me around dinner time. I screamed at
him. He was disgustingly patient and listened while I ranted."

Susan was embarrassed, thinking about how nasty she had been on the phone to her brother that night. She looked back at her journal to see what else she had written about Doug's call: "He empathized with my pain. He said Dad's having serious financial troubles, and he hated writing that letter to me. Doug said Dad had no choice but I don't believe that. If Dad were in this much financial trouble, I would have known it before now. I told Doug that I'm having trouble believing Dad's story. Besides, Mother has money. Why doesn't she pay my tuition?"

Susan couldn't read anymore; it was too painful. She set her journal down, packed her makeup, and tried to forget that day. She sighed. It was useless; she just couldn't drive the events of that day from her mind.

"In six short weeks, my whole life turned upside down. I was acting like a spoiled brat," she conceded. She shuddered when she thought about how she'd kept screaming at Doug on the phone, "Mom has a trust fund. Why can't they pay my tuition out of that?" She was irritated with Doug.

Doug had simply taken a deep breath and a long pause before he spoke again. He told her he would rather talk to her face-to-face.

"Since when have you become so wimpy, Doug?" she yelled into the phone. "I want to talk about it now. It's fine for you to say, 'Wait till I come home.' You're not the one whose college dream was just shattered because Mom refuses to dig into her trust fund, and all because she hates B.U."

She knew by the sound of Doug's voice that she had pushed him too far.

"I'm sorry for your problem, Susan. I'm also disappointed by your selfish behavior. Until now, I've tried to protect you from the problems Mom and Dad are having. It's time you grow up and learn the facts of life," he admonished.

She knew Doug well enough to know he was trying to control his anger. She could visualize his muscular jaw twitching sporadically. She remembered him saying, "I can give you the gruesome facts now or wait until we're face-to-face. You decide."

Susan smiled wryly to herself, remembering how she backed down when Doug gave her the ultimatum. She wanted to know what was going on but she was also afraid to know the truth.

"Can we meet for breakfast on Friday morning?" she asked. "I want to know what's going on before I see Mom and Dad."

She thought about Sally and how disappointed she had been when Susan told her she wasn't coming back to Boston.

Back in the bedroom where she grew up, Susan continued to rock in her favorite chair. *It's like some kind of nightmare. I'm going to wake up and find out that's all it ever was – a bad dream.*

She vividly remembered her breakfast with Doug that Friday in May. She'd left Boston around 11:00 at night and arrived at Pete's Diner in Philadelphia just after 6:30 a.m. Doug was waiting for her. He was somber – not at all his usual self. Like their father, he was over six feet tall, but not as lean. He looked like a football player: broad shoulders, solid, muscular arms and legs. Susan couldn't help noticing how much he looked like their mother's Uncle Chip – their mother's only living relative. Everyone loved Uncle Chip. Doug was exactly like him. He was fun, kind, considerate, strong, and always dependable. And like Uncle Chip, everyone loved Doug.

As Doug explained to Susan that he'd left Harvard because of their parents' financial situation, Susan cried. "Doug, I'm so sorry for the way I spoke to you on the phone. Why didn't you tell me? I feel so foolish. Poor Dad." She noticed her brother's eyes looked glum when she mentioned their father.

"You asked about Mom's money." Doug went on to explain that several years ago their brother, Ken, had been selling stocks in their dad's firm. Like most first-time investors who start out in the beginning of a bull market, Ken thought he had the secret to lifetime wealth. He tried to get his mother to change her portfolio from mutual funds to tech stocks, but their mother resisted Ken's suggestion. She didn't think dabbling in stocks was the proper thing to do. After all, she was a Bradshaw, and Bradshaw women never discussed money. But she changed her mind when some of her bridge partners from the country club started an investment club and invited Kitty to join. Women investing in the market became the "in" thing to do.

At first their mother invested small amounts of her monthly income in the market. When she saw her investments double in value, she began selling some of her conservative mutual funds and investing the money in technology stocks. Her stock returns were much better than her conservative mutual fund yields. She became more and more interested in the market, and eventually transferred all her money into the technology industry. It was the sophisticated thing to do. It was a thrilling time in the market, and their mother got caught up in the excitement.

Doug further explained, "Dad begged Mom not to invest all her money in tech stocks. He kept insisting that her money was a safety net, but she ignored him. Dad was considered a technology stock expert. He helped a lot of people make a lot of money, and Mom thought she should be making the same kind of money that Dad's clients were making. Unfortunately, like most amateurs, Mom thought she had the perfect formula. She margined herself – as did Dad. Then the market tanked. They both lost everything."

Susan remembered that Doug's voice had gotten very soft. He almost sounded like he was going to cry. But he didn't.

Doug said, "Now, Mom's angry with Dad for not stopping her. The sad thing is that Grandfather originally had Mom's inheritance invested safely. She had no control over the way it was invested. But when Grandfather saw what an investment genius Dad was, he gave her more power, assuming Dad would control their investments."

Doug told Susan their parents were selling the house, and worse, they were going to separate. "They both have to find a place to live," he said. "If you're living on your own, you won't have to take sides."

Susan was stunned but she knew Doug was right. She definitely didn't want to take sides. Doug knew their parents would not approve of Susan moving into an apartment, and he suggested she move in with him, so she gratefully accepted.

When they parted that day, Doug gave her a big hug. He assured her everything would work out and tried to convince her that she was a lot stronger than she realized.

Susan was disappointed with herself. *I can't believe I had such awful thoughts about Dad and Doug. Boy, was I clueless. I have to make it up to both of them by making them proud of me.*

It was 3:30 a.m., still too early to leave for Doug's. Susan lined her things up by the door, turned out the light, looked out the window, went back to her rocker, and dozed off.

She woke with a jolt at 4:10 and took a quick shower, the last one in her own bathroom.

Tiptoeing down the stairs, she carried load after load of her things to her car. Each time she returned to her room, she stopped in the hall and listened to make sure that her parents were still asleep. On her third trip, she thought she heard her mother moving around. She stopped and listened. All was quiet, and she was silently thankful that her room was at the top of the stairs.

As she picked up the last of her things, she took one final look around her bright, cheerful room. She loved the soft green, floral wallpaper and her white organdy spreads. *I love this room. It's been my sanctuary for as long as I can remember. I can't imagine living anywhere else. But it's time to go.*

She was determined to take care of herself. Susan closed the bedroom door so her mother wouldn't miss her until after she had her breakfast. Kitty was always in a better mood after breakfast.

The sun was peeping up over the pool. Susan wiped her eyes as she got into her car, determined not to cry. She was halfway down the expressway before her pent-up tears broke loose. "Oh, God, please help me get to Doug's," she prayed. She regretted leaving without saying good-bye to her mother. She'd tried to talk to her mother about their situation but Kitty always cut her off.

"Oh, Mom, you should be so proud I want to be independent," she said out loud, as if her mother were sitting right next to her. "You should be proud of the way we're handling this crisis. Rather than whining, we've taken it on the chin. We're doing something for ourselves." Susan's anger toward her mother resurfaced. "But if you weren't so stubborn, Mom, if only you'd listened to Dad when he tried to advise you on how to invest your money, we wouldn't be in this position. It's your fault."

Susan tightened her grip on the steering wheel. She rationalized with herself that she shouldn't feel badly about her mother. Kitty had brought these problems upon herself, and everyone in the family was suffering because of it.

**

Kitty had another restless night. At one point she thought she heard Susan wandering around. A look at the clock revealed it was 4:30 a.m. She started to get up but her weary body wouldn't cooperate. She finally fell into a deep sleep.

The sound of Matt's car pulling out of the driveway woke her. *Oh gosh, it's 7:30. I can't be sleeping like this.* She jumped out of bed, stopped in front of Susan's door, and went downstairs, thinking she'd wake her daughter after having coffee.

At 8:15, Kitty called up to Susan. No answer. She called again. "Susan, it's time for you to get up."

Kitty decided to let her daughter sleep for 15 more minutes, but when she took the trash out and saw that Susan's car was gone, she realized why no one had answered her. Panic gripped her. She ran inside, flew up the stairs, and opened Susan's bedroom door. Susan was gone. She walked around the room, gazing at the marks on the wall where pictures once hung. She lingered by the closet and then slowly opened the door. A few empty hangers dangled from the closet bar.

Defeated, Kitty sat on Susan's bed and wept. "Susan, Susan," she sobbed out loud. "How could you leave without saying good-bye?"

Chapter 9

Matt's Anxiety

"Many of us crucify ourselves between two thieves —
regret for the past and fear for the future."

–Fulton Ousler

Matt was driving down the parkway, lost in his thoughts, when his cell phone rang.

"Hello, Matthew, this is Sophia."

Matt rolled his eyes. Sophia could rattle off every sale she'd made in the past 20 years, and Matt wasn't in the mood to listen.

"Hello, Sophia. Do we have an offer?"

"Dahling, you know me. Of course we have an offer," she shot back.

"Give me the numbers."

"It's a good one: $2.7 million, 30-day settlement, no contingencies."

Matt was praying the house would sell quickly but not this quickly. *Kitty will have a fit. But we have to take the offer. It's coming just in time.*

"Matthew," Sophia continued, "my buyer just purchased a big company in this area, and he wants to settle as quickly as possible. When can you let me know? They don't have time to fool around. If you don't take their offer, they have a second choice."

"Sophia, why don't you call Kitty? I'll be in meetings all day, and I won't get a chance to talk to her until late."

"You want me to call Kitty?" Sophia asked, sounding alarmed.

He smiled to himself. *Well, I'll be darned. Kitty's even intimidated*

Sophia. It was the first time he'd ever heard Sophia not in complete control. He decided to have some fun with the situation.

"Don't you think that would speed things up?" he asked her.

"No, I don't," she answered emphatically. "You two have to discuss it. You talk to Kitty, and let me know."

"I'll tell you what. Tell them it's a deal for $2.8 million and settlement in six weeks."

Sophia agreed to go back to the buyer with this deal, and hung up.

Matt sighed. He was on his way to his lawyer's office to discuss the possibility of declaring bankruptcy. He had tried everything he could to avoid it, but it was looking more and more grim.

"How did we ever get in this mess?" he asked himself over and over again. He thought back to the night he'd met Kit. She was so young. He remembered the sparks he felt the first time he shook her hand. Even now, with all their problems, she still excited him.

He laughed to himself, recalling the shocked look on her face when she saw him on Christmas day at Mr. and Mrs. Charles Frenche's annual open house. He'd asked her for a date. The Bradshaws were very protective of their one and only child – their precious Kitty – but he'd quickly won them over.

He loved both her parents but he had a special bond with Kitty's mother, Katharine. They hit it off the first time they met. She laughed at his jokes. She used to say, "Oh, Matthew, I love your boyish ways and your Irish wit. But I love you most for the way you love my daughter." He wondered what Katharine Bradshaw would say if she were here now.

He smiled, thinking about the elegant, fun-loving Katharine Woodward Bradshaw. Tall, chic, warm, and friendly, she loved life, and she loved people. She was always on the go, either planning events for the Junior League or cooking at St. Julian's Home for Abused Women. She was well known for her generosity and compassion for the poor and underprivileged. Every Tuesday she volunteered at St. Julian's, working side by side with the other volunteers, scrubbing the bathrooms, cooking, washing dishes, and teaching the women how to read and sew. The other volunteers knew her as Katharine. They assumed she was a housewife whose children were grown. No one at St. Julian's knew who she was until she died.

In fact, Katharine was one of the Grande Dames of Philadelphia. She had a chauffeur and maids. She could snap her fingers and people would jump. She never did, though; she was too gracious to be haughty. *She had it all together.* Matt thought of her fondly. *She was a great woman; Kit has a lot of her mother's traits.*

For the thousandth time, he started beating himself up for his financial losses. *I thought I was invincible. I thought I had a foolproof investment system. How could I be so stupid? I did all the stupid things I warned everyone else not to do. When Kit invested her money in technology, I should have cushioned our risk by investing in a Vanguard fund.* He gave a deep sigh. *I'll get out of this somehow. I have to think positive.*

There wasn't any equity in the house, but somehow he'd get enough money to help Kit get settled. Not in the style she was used to, but it would be better than nothing. She certainly was used to the finer things. *What a shock this must be for her. She's never had to worry about money. She was raised with the proverbial silver spoon in her mouth. She's never wanted for anything. No wonder she's so unbearable. She must be petrified.*

His mind continued to wander. *What happened to our marriage? We had everything going for us. When did it begin deteriorating?* He smiled as he thought about the good times at the beach, the trips with the kids, and the weekends when he and Kitty sneaked away alone. *We were so in love. Those were precious weekends.* He couldn't help but think about how happy they were before he made all his money.

Loneliness and gloom overwhelmed him. He felt a sharp pain in his stomach – again. "Ahh!" he yelped out loud. *I have to do something about this pain.* It slowly subsided, and Matt continued to wrestle with his thoughts. *I was too anxious to prove to Kitty that I was as smart as her dad. She always said she loved me for me.* He recalled the way she used to stroke his hand and tell him he had more character in his little finger than most people had in their entire bodies. *Obviously she doesn't think that now.*

The stomach pain hit him again. It always came when he was stressed, and he certainly was at the moment. *How am I going to tell Kit about the house anyway? I'll make her feel that the price we accept is her idea, not mine.* Matt parked his car in his reserved space. He was early, so he decided to call Kitty from the car.

His wife wasn't enthusiastic about Sophia's offer. "You're going to counter, of course?"

Matt always included Kitty in the decision-making process on family matters. "What do you suggest?"

"At least $2.8 million," she answered without hesitation. But she sounded really down, almost depressed.

"Are you all right, Kit? You sound upset."

"Of course I'm upset. This whole mess is tearing our family apart. What do you expect me to be? Did you know that Susan moved out last night? She moved into her own apartment. Did you know that?"

"Susan moved out? I talked to her right before I went to bed. What makes you think that?"

"Because she told me she was moving out, and everything's gone from her room, including Susan." Kitty's voice rose. "She left a few empty hangers in the closet." Then she started to cry.

"Kit, I'll find her and bring her back home. Don't worry."

"Don't you understand, Matt?" Kitty replied, "She doesn't want to come back home. She thinks she has to work and pay her way through college. She wants to be as far away from our problems as she can get. It's this horrible mess we're in." She started sniffling again.

"It will all work out. I'll find her," Matt repeated. "She'll come around. She's a smart young woman. Maybe she just needs a little breathing room. She's had a lot of upsets in the past six weeks."

"And I haven't?" snapped Kitty. "We're all upset, not just Susan. This is so selfish of her. She's acting like a spoiled brat. Let's not talk about it anymore, Matthew. Tell Sophia we want $2.8 million, nothing less. Let me know what happens."

"I'll present it and get back to you," Matt said as he hung up. He put his head down in his hands. *What else can possibly go wrong? Susan sure picked a lousy time to play Miss Independent. I'll check with Doug. If he knows where she is and thinks she's okay, I won't interfere with her plans. How can I, after the way I let her down?*

Doug told Matt that Susan was living with him and he was watching out for her. "Dad, you and Mom have a lot to handle right now.

Don't worry about Susan. Just do what you have to do, and I'll take care of Susan." Just as Matt was ready to hang up, Doug said, "Hey, Dad, I love you, man. You're a great dad. Don't ever forget it. We all love you."

Matt couldn't respond. He choked up. He knew Doug understood. "See you, Dad," said Doug, hanging up. Matt stared out the car window. *Matt Murphy, you're one lucky guy. So get on the ball and do what you have to do.*

Chapter 10

Frustration

"Anger is just a cowardly extension of sadness. It is easier to be angry at someone than to tell them you are hurt."

–Tom Gates

Kitty knew the offer on the house was a blessing, but it was a blessing she didn't want. She walked around the pool to the rose garden where even the roses looked lonely. She held a yellow rose between her fingers and spoke to it. That was a habit she learned from her mother, who'd said, "Whenever you feel blue, go find a flower and talk to it. It will listen, and it will answer you with its fragrance and beauty."

Kitty missed her mother. She looked at the rose again. "Speak to me; I'm lonely," she said to the rose. "Are you as lonely as I am? You dear rose, you should be enjoyed and appreciated. I'm sorry." She sighed. "There's no one here to enjoy you. You're so beautiful. Will you miss me as much as I'll miss you?"

She took a handkerchief out of her pocket and wiped her eyes. *What's happening to me? I must get hold of myself.* She threw her shoulders back and headed to the house to call Sadie.

Sadie began working for Kitty's parents when Kitty was a little girl. After Ken was born, Kitty's mother suggested that Sadie go to work for Kitty and Matt. She'd worked for the Murphys until six months ago, when they'd had to let her go. Sadie had helped raise the three Murphy children; she was part of the family.

Years ago Matt had set up an annuity for Sadie, so when they had to let her go, Kitty felt good knowing that at least Sadie was taken care of.

At the last minute, Kitty decided not to call Sadie. She didn't want to tell her they were selling the house until they actually sold it. Instead, she started cleaning closets on her own. Kitty usually avoided unpleasant feelings by jumping into activities that distracted her. She hated clutter, and she became immersed in her chore. The time passed quickly. She finished three closets before lunch, and Susan called just as Kitty was finishing her last closet.

"Where are you, Susan?" Kitty asked immediately.

"Mom, I wanted to say good-bye but you were asleep."

"Most normal people are asleep at four in the morning."

"Mom, I can't wait for you to see the apartment," Susan said, trying to sound enthusiastic. "I want to make it more attractive. I was hoping you'd help me."

"You mean you were hoping I'd pay for it," Kitty shot back.

There was silence on the other end of the phone. "It probably wasn't such a good idea," Susan responded, rather hurt. "I really thought we could have some fun like we used to, and I wasn't going to ask you for a dime. I was hoping you would help me find what we need at the thrift shop. I'm sorry I bothered you, Mom." There was a click on the other end of the line.

"Susan?" Kitty asked, holding the phone out in front of her. She immediately began to question her actions. *Why was I so sarcastic? What's wrong with me?* Kitty wanted to spend time with her daughter, but Susan agitated her. She tried going back to cleaning closets but she couldn't focus, so she wandered around the house, rearranging items, and then replacing them as they were. Finally she grabbed her car keys and headed out for a drive.

Chapter 11

Focus on the Goal

"Good planning shapes good decisions. That is why good planning helps to make elusive dreams come true."

–Lester Robert Bittel

On the way home that evening, Matt prayed for guidance, then rehearsed what he would say to Kitty about the house. He'd already told her the offer over the phone, but he hadn't told her the potential buyers wanted to settle in 30 days. When he walked in the house, Kitty was standing in the kitchen.

"Oh, I didn't expect to see you," she said, in a surprised but pleasant voice. "I'm glad you're home. The house seems so empty when no one's here."

Matt noticed his wife straightening up and throwing her shoulders back. He knew that meant she was determined to accomplish something. It could be a good sign or it could be a bad sign.

"Did you have dinner?" she asked.

He relaxed., *Maybe she's determined to be nice. I hope so. I'm too tired to fight.*

"I had a late lunch," he answered. "Did you eat?"

"I was going to grill fish and broccoli," Kitty replied. "Would you like some?"

He wasn't sure how to answer her invitation. He *was* hungry, and it would be nice to eat together, but he was apprehensive. Lately when they were together, they ended up fighting; that was the last thing he wanted. But memories of wonderful summer nights with dinners they'd shared on the terrace flashed across his mind. "I'd love it," he said. "Here, let me help you."

He set the table out by the pool. It was a beautiful, bug-free, June evening, perfect for outdoor dining. He turned on the music and lit the candles. At first their conversation was strained but then they started reminiscing about the children and all the fun they had in the house.

"More wine?" Kitty asked, as she filled Matt's glass.

"What happened to us, Matt?" she asked, gazing into his eyes. "Was it me, was it you, was it the money? When did we start drifting apart?"

"I don't know, Kit," Matt answered truthfully. "I've asked myself that question many times." He hesitated. "I know one thing. No one will ever make me feel the way you used to make me feel." He paused again. "I want you to know I'm sorry for the way everything turned out, Kit. Someday I'll get it all back for you. I promise."

Kitty instinctively leaned over and stroked his little finger. "You have a lot of character, Matt. You'll get it back." She watched him slowly relax.

"All I Ask of You" from *Phantom of the Opera* was playing in the background.

"Let's dance," he suggested. Just then the phone rang. "Don't answer it," he pleaded as Kitty leaned over to pick it up.

"I'd better. It might be one of the kids."

Unfortunately it was Sophia. "Hello, Kitty. Is Matt there?"

Kitty handed the phone to Matt. "It's Sophia, *dahling*."

"Hello, Sophia." He listened for a moment. "So he's offering $2.7 million?" Matt asked.

Sophia shot back, "What are you talking about, Matt? We agreed today to $2.8 million, and a six-week settlement. The answer to both is yes. Is it a deal?"

"He wants a decision now, and he wants to be in the house in four weeks?" Matt repeated into the phone. "I have to talk to Kit about that. I don't think we can do that."

"Matthew, are you drunk or something?" Sophia asked with irritation. "You told me six weeks and he's agreed to that. Do we have a deal?"

"I'll call you back. I want to discuss it with Kit."

"Matt Murphy, are you playing some kind of game with me?"

Matt hated playing this game but the house had to be sold, and he knew Kitty would never accept the first offer. If things were different, they would talk about it and make a mutual decision. He sighed because he knew the situation, and he knew what he had to do.

"What's happening, Matt?" asked Kitty.

"Their final offer is $2.7 million with a 30-day settlement."

"Thirty day settlement?" Kitty cried incredulously. "That's impossible. We have no place to live. We can't possibly get out of this house in 30 days. Are you crazy?" Kitty calmed down, straightened up, and held her head high. In a controlled voice, she bitterly lashed out at Matt. "You got us into this mess. I told you on the phone today, we won't take that offer."

She took a moment to think. "We'll take nothing less than $2.8 million and we'll need at least three months to pack and move out. No sooner."

"Kit, if they go up to $2.8 million, will you agree to a six-week settlement?"

"Six weeks! I don't think I could get the job done in six weeks."

"I don't think we can afford to let this one go."

She took a sip of her wine.

Finally she said, "See if we can get $2.8 million. If they agree, I'll agree to six weeks."

"I'll call Sophia back."

He dialed her number.

"Hello, Matthew. I hope this isn't going to be another nonsensical conversation."

He appreciated his realtor's persistence; that's why she was so successful. She made deals happen, and he needed to have the house sold and settled at least 90 days before he declared bankruptcy. He felt obligated to give Kit back some of her money and to pay off the mortgage on the house. If they were divorced, she wouldn't be liable. He wanted her to have some financial security. He owed her that much.

"Tell your client $2.8 million and 45 days to settle, and we have a deal."

They cleared the table, cleaned up the kitchen in silence, and then went upstairs, still not saying a word. Matt went into the guest room and was emptying his pockets, placing everything on the bureau, when Kitty came in.

"How do you think I'm going to get out of this house with no help?" she demanded.

"We'll work it out. We can get Sadie to help you."

"Sadie isn't as young as she used to be."

Matt looked at his wife. "We're both tired. Can't we talk about this tomorrow?" he asked, as he gently led her out of his room. "I have a big day tomorrow. I'm going to bed." He closed the door behind her.

"Don't close the door on me! Who do you think you are?"

Kitty was trembling as she returned to her room. Her rage had turned to tears. She threw herself face down on the bed and pummeled the pillow again and again before crying herself to sleep.

Chapter 12

Move Forward

"Today is the tomorrow we worried about yesterday."

–Author Unknown

Kitty woke the next morning in a cold sweat. *Oh my God, where am I going to live? Matt and I can't live together. What am I going to do?* For the first time in her life, she avoided getting out of bed. She pulled the sheets up over her shoulders, turned on her side, and tried to go back to sleep, but her mind wouldn't rest. *I've got to get up and get moving.* Kitty dragged herself out of bed, showered, and dressed. She grabbed her Blackberry and headed for Starbucks.

Kitty called Sadie from the car. Without going into detail, she told Sadie they were selling the house. Sadie knew they had problems but she didn't know how serious they were. She agreed to help Kitty pack and move.

Sadie's granddaughter was graduating in Atlanta, so she couldn't help Kitty until the following week. "After next week, I can help you all summer if you want me to, honey," Sadie promised.

Panic gripped Kitty but her voice remained calm. "Not until next week?" she responded, as she straightened up and poised her head high. "Okay, next week will work. Oh, Sadie, what would I do without you? Have a good time in Atlanta. Tell Michelle I said 'Hi.' And one more thing. Do you mind calling me at home and leaving Michelle's address on my machine? I want to send her a gift."

"Kitty, honey, that's too much, with all that's on your mind," Sadie replied.

"Please, Sadie, I want to. Will you do that for me?"

"Okay, honey, but don't you be putting yourself out for Michelle."

For the next three days, Kitty stayed busy. She hardly noticed the void in the house. The movers dropped off packing boxes while she sorted and separated things into piles of things to keep and things to give away. She called the Salvation Army to pick up the clothes and other items she was donating.

On the fourth day, Caroline called. "Can you meet me at Starbucks for coffee at about 10:00?" she asked.

"I'd love to," Kitty replied, relieved. "I'm ready for a break."

Chapter 13

Seeking Advice

"Seek and you shall find."

(Luke 11:9)

With cappuccinos in hand, Kitty and Caroline headed for the corner lounge chairs. Kitty filled Caroline in about selling the house, and Caroline listened intently. "Let me help you," she offered.

Kitty thanked her but declined the offer. "Sadie is going to help me next week," she told her friend.

Kitty was feeling better until Caroline asked, "Do you know where you're going to live yet?"

Kitty's face changed. "I don't know. I thought I'd start looking today." She sat up straight. "Forget about me. Tell me about you. Are things still going well for you?" Kitty asked. For the first time in her life, she envied Caroline.

Caroline laughed. "You know, Kit, things are still pretty much the same. God bless Nick. He's struggling with his business and he still comes home angry and drunk. But I'm different. I used to confront him, but now, when I find myself getting angry, I remind myself that there's peace in this moment, and I disappear. That's something the kids learned a long time ago. I wasn't as smart as them." She laughed.

"I don't think I could do that," Kitty commented. "I'd probably kill him if he were my husband."

"But I don't just disappear out of fear or anger," Caroline explained. "I disappear so I can praise and thank God for working in Nick's life. After five or ten minutes, I start feeling good about me. I feel safe. I feel God's protective love around the children, and Nick, and me. Well,

enough of that," Caroline said, changing the subject. "Why don't we go
out together and look for a place for you?"

"I don't even know where to begin. I don't know how much I have
to spend." Kitty hesitated as she looked down at her coffee and tried
to sink the froth with a spoon. "But I think you might be able to help
me solve another problem." She looked up at Caroline. "Believe it or
not, I keep thinking about what you said about the wonderful things
that have been happening in your life since you started praising and
thanking God and sending love to all the painful situations in life. The
change in your attitude is miraculous. I need to make some changes in
my relationships, and I thought you might have some ideas."

"You want to change your relationship with Matt?" Caroline asked.

"No. Not Matt. I need to change my relationship with Susan."

Caroline looked surprised. "I thought you and Susan had a wonderful relationship."

"We used to, but not anymore. She resents everything I say."

"Like what?"

"You know I didn't want her to go to Boston University. She was
going to Vassar but Matt started pressuring her to go to Harvard. She
did a complete reversal, and out of nowhere she chose Boston U., very
much against our wishes. That's when our relationship deteriorated."

"I'm sure she'll come around. She adores you," Caroline reassured
Kitty.

Kitty shook her head. "Not anymore. She has this friend, Sally,
who's a big influence on her. I don't like Sally. Boston U. was wrong for
Susan, and Sally is the wrong friend for her. She refuses to listen to me
when I try to talk to her about it."

Caroline paused for a few moments, framing her words. Finally, she
asked, "Why is it so important for you to tell Susan she's wrong? How
do you know she's wrong? Maybe Boston U. *was* the best place for her."

Kitty, a bit dejected, looked at Caroline. "That's easy for you to say.
You don't know anything about B.U., and you've never met Sally."

Caroline made eye contact with Kitty. "Kit, you're right! I don't
know Sally, and I don't know much about B.U., although I know several people who went there and loved it. But that's beside the point.
You know I tend to be very courageous when it comes to pointing out

people's faults, but I don't like it when they give me feedback about my negative behavior. Do you?"

Kitty thought for a minute. "Well, no, I don't like it. And Susan has been doing a lot of that lately. The only conversations we have are when she tells me all the things I do wrong."

"Why do you think Sally is a bad influence on her?"

"Sally's an independent woman. Her parents are divorced. Her mother's a saleswoman; Sally is on her own most of the time. I can't explain it, but she's giving Susan ideas about being an independent woman. Susan's moved into an apartment downtown."

"Did she move in with Sally?"

"No, I don't think so. Sally lives in New York."

"I'm sure you tried to discuss it with her."

"Not exactly. I forbade her to get an apartment. She left in the middle of the night."

"Kit, I'm sure she'll come around," Caroline said sympathetically. "Susan's always had a mind of her own, like you. Maybe she's teaching *Sally* how to be independent. You never know."

Kit half smiled. "Everyone says she's like me. However, I never left home, and I never talked to my mother the way Susan talks to me."

"You said you thought maybe I could help you. What did you have in mind?"

"I keep thinking about what you said about sending love into painful situations. I was wondering if there is a way I could send love into this situation. It seems rather hopeless, but maybe, just maybe..." Kitty hesitated. "It's probably a stupid idea."

Caroline took a sip of her coffee. She didn't say anything.

Kitty spoke up again. "I can't praise God, but do you think there is any way I could make your secrets work for me?"

"I don't know if this will help," Caroline said, "but Valerie gave me good advice about interacting with my children when I disagree with them. She said, 'Rule number one: No one is ever all wrong. We just have differences of opinion.' "

"That's a cop-out," said Kitty brusquely.

"Wait, hear me out. This really helps me with my children."

"Okay, go on," Kitty agreed reluctantly.

"Rule number two: Try to understand the feelings behind what the other person is saying." Caroline ticked off the rules on her fingers, one by one.

"Rule number three: Acknowledge that the other person is making some good points.

"Rule number four: Make your point by asking the other person what they think about it. Carry on a dialogue. Acknowledge what the other person is saying, and explore the reasoning and thinking behind what is being said."

Kitty thought for a moment. "Your rules are good in theory, but putting them into action is a different story. I'm constantly promising myself I'm going to be nice to Susan, but the minute we're together, we're at each other's throats."

"You're so right," Caroline admitted. "It *is* hard. I could never follow these rules if I didn't first praise and thank God for the situation. Prayer helps me slow down, think about these rules, and follow them."

"You don't think I can improve my situation without prayer, do you?" Kitty asked in defeat.

Caroline considered this. "You can try, but I haven't been able to improve my relationships without prayer. Lately, when I think someone's wrong, I try to praise and thank God for them and their behavior exactly as it is before I get too annoyed. Then I ask myself, 'What can I learn from their behavior?' "

Caroline looked at Kitty and continued, "Maybe you can stop and ask yourself what you can learn from Susan's behavior. Susan may feel you're criticizing her good judgment. For example, how do you know Sally isn't good for Susan?"

She's right. Susan was doing her own thing long before she met Sally. She probably does think I'm insulting her judgment when I criticize Sally. Kitty's eyes got teary as she realized it was no wonder Susan was always so angry. A wave of sadness engulfed her. She hadn't heard from Susan since the day she'd called to go shopping. *I can't believe I was so mean to her.*

"I'd like to find some magic formula like your praise and thanks, but I don't think I really believe in God. I don't have time to experiment," Kitty said.

Caroline nodded. "If you don't believe in God, Narcotics Anonymous suggests you acknowledge a higher power, a power greater than you. Why don't you try praising and thanking universal love for Susan exactly as she is, and for your relationship exactly as it is?"

Kitty fidgeted with her coffee. "How will that help? I hate our relationship the way it is."

"Praising and sending universal love into this situation will slow you down," Caroline said with a gentle smile. "It will help you obtain insights and it will help you change whatever you need to change. It's simple."

"I'll think about it," Kitty promised.

The two women went their separate ways, Kitty pondering Caroline's words. Later that evening, she called Caroline.

"I've been thinking about our talk today and about the way I've been treating Susan," Kitty told Caroline. "I'm going to praise and thank universal love for Susan just as she is and for our relationship just as it is. Is that right?"

"You got it," concurred Caroline. "Good luck. And be patient."

"How long do I have to be patient?"

"I don't know. It's not easy, but it is simple."

"What do you mean it's not easy? I thought you said it *was* easy!"

Caroline laughed. "It's very simple. Just praise and thank God for your life and the situation exactly as it is. It's challenging; we want to control things and people. But whenever we persist in praising and thanking God, we feel better. Prayer gives us confidence that an infinite love is taking care of us. The more we let go, the better and easier life becomes."

"I thought you said I could praise universal love," Kitty said skeptically.

"You can."

"You keep talking about God."

"Kit, I believe in a higher power whom I chose to call God. When I speak about praying and praising, I can only talk about praising God. You chose to call your higher power universal love."

Kitty laughed. "Okay. Got it."

She carried her dinner out to the pool, closed her eyes, and began praising and thanking universal love for Susan. "If you're all love, and you love Susan and me, then I thank you for working our relationship out. I thank you for our relationship exactly the way it is."

Caroline was right; it was hard to say this prayer at first. But Kitty discovered the more she said it, the easier it became, and the better she felt.

On Sunday morning, Kitty was about to take her latte out by the pool when she saw Matt doing laps. She retreated to her bedroom to praise and thank universal love for her and Matt exactly the way they were. She couldn't say it at first. But she stuck with it, and to her surprise, she slowly began feeling better.

"Look, universal power, I'm tired of being miserable. If thanking you for my misery will make me feel better, I'll do it. I genuinely want to feel better," she prayed aloud.

She called Caroline again. "I'm glad I caught you. Do I have to praise and thank for my misery? It's ridiculous. Who in their right mind praises and thanks for their misery?"

The two of them laughed together.

"You praise for what you want as if you already have it," responded Caroline. "Praise and thank for your joy, for God placing joy in your life right now."

"But I thought you praised and thanked God that Nick is an alcoholic."

"I praise and thank God for Nick being exactly as he is, because I know God is working in Nick's life in ways I can't see or understand."

"Oh." This was different, Kitty realized. "So you're not praising and thanking God that Nick's an alcoholic."

"I'm praising and thanking God for Nick exactly as he is. God knows what Nick needs in order to experience his abundant love. I don't. I just let go and turn him over to God."

"That sounds better. Okay, thanks. I'm practicing. See you later."

Caroline laughed.

"Oh, by the way," Kitty added, "I can hear you saying to yourself, 'This is typical of Kitty. She has to get everything perfect.' You always say that, and you're right," she joked.

"Now you're a mind reader?" Caroline chuckled. "That's exactly what I was thinking."

Kitty realized she was looking forward to seeing Matt, but when she finally went downstairs he was gone.

Suddenly she felt sick, alone, and lonely. *Should I praise and thank universal love for this terrible feeling? Universal love, take this feeling away. I hate it. Please remove it.* The more she begged to be rid of the feeling, the worse she felt. *Damn it. If you're universal love, fill me with peace. Take this damn feeling away, right now.* She pleaded but loneliness overwhelmed her. She gave up. *This doesn't work.*

Kitty began to clean. She started with the refrigerator. *It's just as well Matt isn't here.* But she couldn't shake the loneliness. The house haunted her. Finally, she called Caroline back.

"Hello, Evans family."

Kitty recognized Chuck's voice. She sank back, smiled, and sweetly raised her voice in pitch. "Hello, Chuck. This is Aunt Kit."

"Hi, Aunt Kit. How's Susan? I haven't seen her in a while."

"She's great. How're you doing?"

"Fantastic! I got honors this last semester."

"I'm proud of you, Chuck. Keep up the good work. I'm sure Susan will be delighted to hear how well you're doing. You two used to be such good friends."

"Tell her I said 'Hi.' Mom ran out for a minute. I'll tell her you called."

Kitty was surprised at how disappointed she was that she'd missed Caroline. She went back to cleaning. She tackled the cupboards but she couldn't focus.

Caroline finally called back.

"I'm sorry if I'm being a pest, but this isn't working," confessed Kitty. "I feel rotten and I can't shake it."

Caroline empathized as Kitty told her how she had demanded that universal love take away her lonely feelings.

Caroline listened and suggested. "Let me pray with you now. I'm going to pray to our Lord. Is that okay?"

Kitty didn't object.

Caroline began her prayer. "We praise and thank you, Lord, for surrounding Kitty with your peace. Thank you, Lord, for loving her and caring for her. We praise you for showing her your love in this moment. We thank you for the healing that is taking place in her heart right now."

Caroline continued, "Lord, we ask you now to still Kitty, calm her heart so she can focus on your love for her. Fill her with your praise and silence. Help her enter into your peace."

Caroline finished and remained silent.

Kitty wiped a tear from her cheek. "Thanks, Caroline, I feel better already. I was demanding that universal love take my pain away. When you're used to controlling, it's hard to let go. You're right. That doesn't work," she confessed.

Kitty went back to her prayers. *I'm doing it wrong. I don't like the term "universal love." God, if you exist, I praise and thank you for this feeling.* The more she praised, the better she felt.

Although the loneliness was still there, she began to feel peace. *This does work. I'd better praise and thank God for Susan. I want to mend our differences.*

Kitty sat at the kitchen table thinking about her daughter. She praised and thanked God for her. The more she did, the more blessed she felt having Susan as her child.

Chapter 14

DISCOVER What Is Really Important

"Truth hurts – not the searching after; the running from!"

–John Eyberg

Kitty didn't know how much time had passed when she heard Susan calling from the front door.

"Mom, are you home?"

"I'm in the kitchen."

"Hello," responded Susan as she stood awkwardly in the doorway. "You look radiant this morning."

What do you expect me to look like? Kitty kept that thought to herself and graciously said, "Thanks, honey, I appreciate that."

"I just heard about the house. I'll be glad to help you pack, or do whatever I can to help." Susan looked at her mother. "Maybe you, well … I didn't know if you wanted to do anything today. I have some time," Susan added.

Kitty felt tears welling up again. She sat up, arched her shoulders back, smiled, and said, "Honey, do you know why I look so good this morning?"

"No," Susan answered nervously.

"I think you'll be surprised. I've spent the past half hour thanking God for you. You're a blessing to Dad and me, and I just didn't appreciate how blessed I am that you're my daughter."

"Mom …." Susan couldn't say anything else. She looked at her mom as her eyes started to blur with tears.

The two women gazed at each other.

"Mom," Susan blurted out, "I feel the same way about you. I was always proud you were my mom. My friends envied me because I could tell you anything. Then, well, I don't know what happened. I've asked myself a hundred times, what did I do? Why are you so angry with me, what changed between us?"

Kitty was about to say, "Me? Angry at you?" But she caught herself. She remained silent for a moment and then admitted, "I've asked myself the same question. I thought you were angry with me." Kitty tried to hold back the tears but couldn't. "I'm sorry. I can't seem to stop crying," she confessed. "I hate being such a baby."

Susan reached out to hug her mother. "Mom, I love you." They held each other in silence. Finally, Kitty pulled herself together and moved away. Susan tried to speak but couldn't stop crying. Finally she managed to say, "Don't you see, Mom, it's okay to cry. I always felt ashamed of my feelings. You're so stoic and disciplined. I felt inadequate around you."

Kitty was shocked. "I never wanted you to feel inadequate."

"I always felt like a sissy around you. Seeing you cry helps me know I'm not a sissy. This isn't like you. I don't want to see you hurt, but it helps me to know it's okay to cry," Susan added.

"I don't know what's gotten into me. All I do is cry," Kitty admitted as she wiped her eyes.

They looked at each other without speaking. Then Susan spoke up.

"Mom, thanks for your honesty. You know I used to tell everyone you were my best friend."

"Used to? What happened?"

"I guess I grew up. I'm not a little girl. I'm a woman. I still need your advice and I need your wisdom." She hesitated, "But Mom, I want you to respect me as a woman. I don't want you to treat me like your little girl. I want you to be my friend, my mentor, not some domineering authority figure."

Kitty didn't know what to say. She looked at Susan and had an idea. "Let's forget the house today. Sadie is coming next week to help. We can do it then. Can you come back next week?"

Susan looked at her mother. Asking people for help was not Kitty's style. Susan started laughing. "I can help you for a few days, sure."

Kitty said cheerfully, "Let's you and I take the day off. We'll have lunch and visit your apartment. Then we'll shop for whatever you need."

"Oh, that'll be fun," said Susan. Kitty, remembering she was short on cash and unsure of her credit card status, suggested, "Let's just eat in the food court at the mall."

"That'll be fun. And my treat," Susan insisted.

They chatted all through lunch, just like old times. Just as they were finishing lunch, Susan took a deep breath and said, "Mom, there's something I have to tell you. I hope you won't be upset."

Kitty stopped eating, said a silent prayer that her daughter wasn't pregnant, and looked at Susan. "What is it?" Kitty asked, trying to hide the panic in her voice.

"Mom, the apartment I'm living in – it's Doug's."

"*That's* what you wanted to tell me?" Kitty asked, praising God under her breath. "Why didn't you just tell me?"

"I wanted to," Susan explained. "But you were so upset about me moving into an apartment, I couldn't tell you anything."

Kitty stared at Susan. "Why didn't Doug tell me?" she asked with disbelief. "Why would I be upset that you're living with Doug?"

Susan hesitated. "You were so convinced that Sally was a bad influence on me and that she'd convinced me to get my own place. I thought you'd be angry with Doug and blame him for my moving out."

Kitty gazed at Susan and softened her voice. "Susan, Sally's influence and Doug's influence on you are two different matters. Doug's your brother and he loves you." Kitty caught herself just as she was ready to say something negative about Sally. *I can't thank God for Sally. That's ludicrous. But thank you, God. Thank you that Susan's living with Doug. Thank you.*

That was the only glitch in the day. The rest of the day was precious for both of them.

Chapter 15

Brace for Change

*"If you realize that all things change, there is
nothing that you will try to hold on to."*

–Byron Katie

There was more work involved in moving than Kitty anticipated. Sadie was a big help, but she was older now. She wasn't as fast-thinking and quick-moving as she used to be.

Susan helped pack the china, crystal, and other breakables. Kitty occasionally caressed a piece of china while telling Susan the story behind it. Most of her china and antiques came from her parents. Each piece had a story about a country, a trip, or family members that gave meaning to it.

One afternoon Kitty gently touched the Danish silver centerpiece that had been displayed on the dining room table for as long as Susan could remember. Kitty sighed as she held it up for Susan to see, and together they admired it.

"This is my favorite piece," Susan said. "I love the cherubs around the base, and the three groups of cherubs on the center bowl. The top angel is so graceful. I used to love to watch them when I was little. I imagined they were my friends."

"My mother and I found this in a tiny shop in Paris when I was pregnant with you," Kitty explained. "I fell in love with it. Mother really bought it for you. When you're ready for it, it's yours."

Susan wiped her eyes and forced a smile on her face. "Mom, I love hearing your stories." She hesitated and dabbed at her eyes again with the back of her hand. "You know this is the only house I've ever lived in

– I can't imagine what life will be like with you and Dad living some-where else. Every time I think about it my stomach hurts."

Kitty returned the centerpiece to the table and hugged her daughter. "I know, honey. It hurts. But we'll get through it and everything will be all right. I just know it."

Susan let her mother hug her for a long time before she gently pushed away. "We better hurry up and finish what we're doing," she said, wiping her eyes.

As Susan spoke, Kitty kept praising and thanking God under her breath.

**

Although Kitty had been too busy to talk to Caroline, she was faithful to her thanking-and-praising regimen for the first two weeks. But by the third week she didn't have time for it. She and Matt were having major blowups. On top of that, Kitty knew how she wanted things done but everyone helping her pack was sloppy, even Sadie. Kitty never remembered Sadie being so careless. Kitty fought with everyone.

During the first two weeks of emptying the house, making deci-sions was relatively simple for her. Sadie and Kitty worked late most nights. Susan came by every day but left by 3 p.m. By Thursday of the third week, all the crucial items were packed in boxes and labeled. The boxes were lined up neatly in the living and dining rooms.

In spite of all their work, there was still more to pack and more to give away. On that Thursday night, Susan took Sadie home early. Alone, Kitty wandered around the house trying to gather her thoughts. *What am I going to do with all this stuff? In three weeks we have to be out of here and I have no place to live.* She sat down on the living room floor amidst the boxes, hugged her knees, and rocked back and forth.

She was in such a state of anxiety that she couldn't get up. She was glued to the floor. Then the phone rang. She couldn't answer it. Her mind was spinning. It rang again. She pulled herself up and slowly moved toward the kitchen to answer it. *What will I do? What will I do? Where will I go? I wonder if Matt already has a place. He doesn't seem to care.*

She answered the phone.

"Kit, is that you? It's me, Caroline." Caroline's cheerful voice blared across the phone. "Are you okay? You sound down."

"Wouldn't you be down if you were losing your house and your husband and you had absolutely no place to go?" Kitty responded bitterly. "We have to be out of here in three weeks and I have no place to go. I don't want to hear any more about praising and thanking God, or universal love, or whatever it is. God helps those who help themselves."

Caroline was silent. Kitty continued tensely, "No one is going to help me. I have to help myself. I'm sorry, Caroline. I'm in a lousy mood and I'm very scared."

"I would be, too," Caroline empathized. "You're in a scary position."

Kitty's anger softened. "I didn't mean to insult you, Caroline. You're a good friend and I appreciate your friendship. It's just that all that praise and thanks stuff works for you but it's not really helping me. It did work with Susan, but that was easy. We just had to talk things out."

"Kit, I understand. You have a lot on your plate. You're a very courageous woman. I just called to say hello and see if I can do anything for you."

Kitty didn't say anything.

"Kit, you don't have a place to live right now, do you?" Caroline asked.

"I just told you I didn't."

"What do you have to lose by praising and thanking God for your new home? You agreed to experiment. Suppose it does work? What alternatives do you have?"

"Caroline, you don't get it! I don't have five cents. Even if I did find a place, how would I pay for it? When I try to talk to Matt, he cuts me off."

"That's just it, Kit. You have nothing. What alternative do you have? You have nothing to lose and everything to gain." Caroline hesitated before continuing, "I don't know how you're holding up so well. I'd be a basket case. Just try it for a week."

Kitty remained silent.

"Kit, it's hard when we're upset. I could do it for you," Caroline suggested.

"No, no, I don't want you to do that. If I believed in it, I'd do it myself. Look, Caroline, I know you want to help, but no one can help me right now." Kitty stiffened and locked her face in a determined pose. "See you later. Bye." Kitty hung up.

She wandered around the house on autopilot, fraught with anxiety and helplessness.

She picked up a picture of her parents with Matt. "Mom, Dad, I'm glad you're not here to see this," she said out loud. She picked up the phone to call Doug and then put it down. She tried dialing her oldest son, Ken, in California. He didn't answer. Ken was never good with stress and managed to disappear when problems arose. It was probably just as well he didn't answer.

Kitty had always been faithful to her three-times-a-week workout, but lately she had let that slip. She hadn't exercised at all in the past few weeks. She knew she'd feel better after working out, so she went down to the exercise room and looked around their in-home gym. She thought how much she would miss her private exercise room with the mirrored walls. She'd miss her rowing machine, the treadmill, and the weights. She sighed. *I'm going to miss the freedom of exercising when I feel like it.* She picked up two five-pound weights and commenced with arm curls, but couldn't get into it. Finally she put the weights back and tried the treadmill.

Kitty managed the treadmill for 15 minutes, half her usual 30. *Boy, I am really out of shape.* Next, she decided to swim. The night was dragging. It was 7:30 when she jumped into the pool. The cool water felt good. She forced herself to do ten laps, though she wanted to quit after each one.

She was just finishing her eighth lap when Matt appeared at the end of the pool. "How's it going?" he asked, already knowing the answer.

At first she ignored him and kept swimming. He stood silently watching her. When she got to the end of the pool, he again asked, "How are you doing?"

"How do you think I'm doing?" she snapped. "How does someone do who's moving out of her house in three weeks and has no place to go?"

"Kit, we'll find a place to live."

"What do you mean we'll find a place to live? I thought you decided it was better if we lived apart. What's this 'we'?"

Matt sighed. "We'll find a place for you and a place for me. We don't need a lot. You'll be living alone and I'll be living alone. It'll work out; trust me." He walked back inside, feeling weary. He had just sold his Porsche, and spent most of the day hassling with lawyers, creditors, and accountants. At night, he tossed and turned, mulling over things he could do to assure Kitty would have some income. He was too tired to deal with her anger. He climbed into his used car and took off.

Chapter 16

Broken Illusions

"A people that values its privilege above its principles soon loses both."

–Dwight D. Eisenhower

"Matt!" Kitty called after her husband's car. *Damn.* She saw his car turn the corner and disappear. Matt never could handle confrontation. *Damn it, I need to talk to him.*

Kitty got out of the pool, toweled off, and went inside to rummage through the leftovers in the refrigerator. *This refrigerator is a disgrace. I can't believe I let it get like this.* Forgetting that Sadie no longer worked for them, she began blaming Sadie. *Why didn't she clean it out? She's slipping.* Kitty got a trash bag and began dumping leftover shrimp, a week-old bunch of broccoli, and a mixture of half-empty takeout cartons into it. She poured various half-filled bottles of soda, water, milk, and juice into the sink. She'd just finished with the refrigerator when the phone rang.

She washed her hands before picking it up. "I hope it isn't Caroline," she said as she reached for the receiver.

"Hi, Mom," Ken's cheerful voice greeted her.

Kitty forced a false smile as she answered, "Hi, Ken. How are you doing?" An inner voice warned her. *Be nice!*

Ken had been a broker with Matt's firm when the market started sliding. He'd never really liked the business, but he wanted to please Matt. When they started losing money, he quit and headed for California to pursue an acting career, against Kitty's advice. Matt gave him his blessing and some money to get started, and Ken was doing surprisingly well, getting small parts in commercials and in local theater productions.

"I'm auditioning for a great movie part," said Ken. "I know you don't pray, Mom, but will you ask Doug and Susan to say a few for me? It would help."

Kitty stiffened and gritted her teeth. *Who does he think he is?*

Again, an inner voice cautioned her to be kind. Ken had always been the religious one in the family. He loved to go to different church services with his friends, and was a pest about it. Every time he went to a new congregation, he would come home and try to sell Matt and Kitty on going to church.

"That's great! What's the part?" she asked her son, trying to sound excited.

"It's like a documentary," answered Ken. "I'll tell you more about it if I get it. I need prayers, lots of them. The competition is fierce. I tried calling Doug and Susan but couldn't reach them. Do you mind asking them for me?"

"No, I'll talk to them," Kitty assured him. "I'm sure Susan and Doug have nothing better to do than say a prayer for you."

Ken paused. "Mom, you don't have to be so sarcastic."

"Kenneth, if there's a God, He's too busy to worry about your audition. You have all the talent you'll ever need to get the part. Just make up your mind that you're going to get it, and you will. God helps those who help themselves. Just go do it." She could hear him breathing on the other end of the phone, but he didn't say a word. Kitty could picture the disgusted look on his face.

"Are you there? Ken!"

"Yeah, I'm here. I'll talk to you soon. Take care of yourself."

With that, Kitty heard a click. *He's so damn sensitive.* She hung the phone up.

She tried to read but couldn't focus. She tried to watch a movie, but it was impossible to pay attention. Had this been the previous summer, Kitty would have been at the beach. But this year, of course, they'd rented their beach house out, and it would soon be put up for sale.

She went on an internal rant. *Why did I ever invest all my money in tech stocks? I didn't have the slightest interest in the market to begin with.*

Matt was the expert; he should have stopped me. Why did he put all his eggs in one basket?

Kitty had never considered touching her trust account until Ken suggested she change her trust portfolio. He kept asking his mother why she left her money in such poor investments. He'd bring articles home from work about some of the companies his dad invested in. "You're still young, Mom. You should be in growth stocks," he urged. Up until that point, Kitty had only thought of money as something to spend. She came from a wealthy family and she'd always had all the money she needed. She never saw a bill. She never thought about investments. But Ken's persistence intrigued her. He taught her about the market and showed her how she could invest in tech stocks and double her trust fund in just a few short years. Once she got hooked on the market, there was no stopping her. Kitty remembered the rush she felt when she watched her stock portfolio soar.

Her Uncle Chip, who lived in California, urged her not to change her trust fund holdings. Kitty's only living relative, Uncle Chip had taught her how to ride a bike and how to drive. He took her to her first movie. He taught her to ski and to mountain-climb.

When Kitty was a child, everyone loved her Uncle Chip. He made occasions special. All the kids in the neighborhood loved to go to Kitty's house for Halloween. Uncle Chip made elaborate graveyards and fabricated ghosts that made spooky noises when trick-or-treaters walked up the Bradshaw driveway. The kids squealed and screamed with delight. Chip was the biggest kid of them all.

Because Kitty's father was 15 years older than his brother, Chip was only nine years older than Kitty. It was a big difference when she was a child, but the gap closed considerably as they aged.

Kitty usually spoke to Chip once or twice a month but hadn't called him in recent weeks. She was ashamed of her financial problems. She often thought about his words of caution. "Kit, honey, Matt is doing very well in the market. It's always good to have a cushion. Don't touch your trust fund. Your dad left you that money in case something ever happened. Please, honey, don't touch it."

Although she appreciated his concern, Kitty hadn't considered Chip a good financial adviser. Her inner voice taunted her. *I guess he was smarter than I thought.* She sighed, turned out the lights, and went to bed.

Chapter 17

Heartbroken

*"Your sadness will be turned into joy...
The kind of joy no one can take away from you."*

(John 16:20, 22)

Except for four place settings of dinnerware, four place settings of silverware, a few glasses, one frying pan, and one saucepan, the kitchen was all in boxes. Susan and Sadie were gone by 3:00 p.m. on Friday.

Kitty was tired. *I wonder what Matt's doing for dinner?* She called his office and his secretary promised he'd call back.

When he did, Matt and Kitty agreed to go to the country club for dinner. It was the first time they had gone to the club in nearly a year. Kitty's family had been members for three generations, and although neither Matt nor Kitty had played golf in more than a year, they had hoped to hold on to their membership. They drove Kitty's Jaguar to dinner in silence. Kitty wanted to ask Matt if they would be able to pay their country club dues for the following year, but she decided not to.

They ran into Caroline and Nick sitting with another couple at the bar, and Matt suggested the six of them eat together. At first Kitty didn't feel like joining anyone. She was worried Caroline might say something about their conversations. But Caroline didn't and they had a lot of laughs reminiscing about their summers together at the Jersey shore. For a few brief hours, Kitty was able to forget about her problems.

On the way home, Matt told Kitty they had two offers on their beach house. The people renting it had made an offer to buy, furniture and all.

He explained to Kitty that he was trying to avoid bankruptcy. He told her if they sold and settled on both houses before more liens were put on them, there should be some cash for her to buy a small place, and he could get an apartment. They agreed to settle on the beach house within the next 30 days.

Kitty found herself surprised at how old Matt looked. He was only 50 but the prominent black circles under his eyes and the taut, drawn skin across his face aged him. A surge of panic ran through her. "Are you feeling all right?" she asked.

He looked at her and said, "Thanks for asking. I'm tired." He didn't say any more and they drove in silence.

"Where's your Porsche?" she asked, afraid to hear the answer.

"I sold it."

"Oh, no," said Kitty. "Matt, what are we going to do? Even if there's enough money to buy a little place, how could we keep it up? It's crazy for us to be considering living apart when we can't even afford one place. Wouldn't it be smarter to live together?"

Matt kept his eyes on the road and said nothing. They were two blocks from their house. Upon their arrival at home, Kit followed her husband to the hall outside the guest room and continued to pepper him with questions.

It was then that he chose to drop the bomb. "Kit, it'll be better for all of us if you and I get a divorce. We can get separate lawyers, or we can get one lawyer and you can have everything."

Kitty was shocked. She couldn't speak. Matt had never mentioned divorce; Kitty was the one who'd kept talking about it. Immediately she wondered if there was someone else. She was almost afraid to ask but did anyway.

"Someone else? You're kidding, aren't you?" he said, looking at her in disbelief.

"No. Why would I kid about that?"

"From the first day I saw you, you were the only woman for me. Good night." He shut his bedroom door.

She moved slowly into her room. She felt pain everywhere and was racked with loneliness. *Oh God, if you exist, help us. Why are you doing this to us?*

Kitty's sleepless night dragged on. She finally got up at 1:00 a.m. and turned on the light. *Will this night ever end?*

She decided that if she couldn't sleep, she might as well do something productive, so she headed downstairs to clean out the den. She opened the patio door for some air. A small gift-wrapped package was leaning on the side of the door. She opened the card:

> "Dear Kit,
> We loved having dinner with you and Matt tonight.
> There is a saying, 'The one who always searches finds.'
> I pray you'll find what you're searching for in this book.
> Love, Caroline."

Kitty carefully unwrapped the present. It was the purple-bound book Caroline had shown her at Starbucks a few weeks ago. Holding the book in her hand, she eased into Matt's large leather chair. She turned on the light and gazed at the cover for a few minutes, repeating very slowly to herself: *The Peace Way: The Five Lost Secrets to Finding Inner Peace.* She glanced through the table of contents and the author's introduction.

> Dear Reader:
> Thank you for joining me while I share with you my journey from fear to faith, from hate to love, and from panic to peace.
> As we journey through my story together, I invite you to stop and think about the peace secrets that have transformed me from a helpless victim to a hopeful victor.
> You will discover the secrets to juggling your daily life with a peaceful and calm heart. When you uncover a secret, stop and reflect on how you can weave it into your life. I also encourage you to try the prayers that Maria taught me. These seemingly simple prayers can be as powerful and rewarding for you as they are for me.
> When we arrive at the final page of our journey, we will go

our separate ways, but our lives will be richer and our hearts will be lighter for having spent this time together. Although our journey together will end, our journey into a deeper experience of God's peace and joy will just begin.

I pray you will share your journey with the special people in your life. And together may you discover God's ever-growing, unconditional love and peace in your heart. And may you have the courage to spread it wherever you go and whatever you do one moment and one heart at a time.

**

Kitty thought about the introduction. *This book* did *change Caroline. She's a much happier person in spite of her problems. I hope it can do the same for me.* She picked up the book and began reading.

Chapter 18

The Peace Way

"Do not be afraid. I am with you."

(Isaiah 43:5)

The book began:
I am Jenny Solomon, a single mother of four. My husband, Jon, deserted us three years ago. For the first two years, I was paralyzed with fear. Oh, I moved about and did everything I had to do, but I was unconscious. His disappearance changed me from a caring, easy going, fun-loving mom to a miserable, uptight insomniac.

Jon left for work one day and never returned. He just vanished, leaving me with four children ranging from age 6 to 12, a mortgage, and two very small savings bonds.

He usually arrived home by 6:30 p.m. That night, the children and I waited and watched for his car. I called him at work; no answer. I called his cell phone. I finally called the police. They said he'd probably come home, not to worry. He never did, and he never called. We sat by the phone 24 hours a day, waiting for a call. Family, police, neighbors, and friends came in and out of our house with food, words of consolation and hope, but no trace of Jon. He had vanished.

I couldn't sleep or eat. Our pain dragged on for six days with no Jon, no clues, just waiting and more waiting. Finally, on the sixth day the police suggested I go through Jon's things to look for some clue that would help us find him. I resisted. I knew something terrible happened to him and I was positive I wouldn't find anything that would give us a clue where he was.

One policeman urged me to just look, and I finally agreed. He waited downstairs while I rummaged through Jon's drawers, and then underneath his shirts I found the note in his handwriting. It was a simple, right to the point note.

Dear Jen,
By the time you find this note I'll be far away.
I can't take it any longer.
I want to live free of you and the kids.
Sorry I'm a louse, but you can keep the savings bonds.
Jon

The room began spinning. Pain shot through me; I opened my mouth to scream but I couldn't. Then I heard what seemed like a far away cry of anguish: "No! No, it can't be."

The policeman came running up the stairs. He gently pried my fingers from the note and read the message. I screamed, "Get everyone out of my house. Get Jon's parents out of here. Get them out!"

From that day on, I refused to talk to my family and friends. I was humiliated. I cried all the tears out of my body. It was like I'd fallen into a deep, dark pit. I functioned physically, but I was dead emotionally. I told the children I'd heard from their father but that he wouldn't be back for a long time.

Then I went from shock to seething rage. How could he desert his children? I wanted to kill him with my bare hands. I was sure I would if I ever saw him again. The children stopped laughing and giggling. They were so young, and I wanted to protect them. But I couldn't. J.J. – a nickname for Jon Jr. – was 12 and Sara, our baby, was 6. Rachael was 8, and Rebecca was 10.

Weeks became months, and the children's questions and accusations irritated and annoyed me. I didn't have the answers. I kept screaming, "I don't know. I don't know. Don't ask me." I hated Jon and I hated the person I had become. The children perceived Jon as the good parent and me as a shrew.

I struggled to hold everything together but my expenses far exceeded my income. I sold the bonds and paid the mortgage. When the bond money was gone, the pile of unpaid bills kept growing and late mortgage notices kept coming. I was too exhausted to discipline the children or prepare a decent meal. At night I slept in spurts or I didn't sleep at all.

I wanted to die. I began saving the sleeping pills my doctor prescribed for me. I was supposed to take one a night, but instead I took one every other night and saved the others. I was planning to amass enough to put myself to sleep forever. Every night after the children were in bed, I'd go to my bathroom and count my sleeping pills. One night I counted 13 pills. I needed to save 17 more.

I was so scared that I didn't know if I could wait 34 days. In desperation I fell on my knees and cried out, "God, if you're here, let me see you, let me hear you. Help me. Please help me." For the first time in two years, I wept uncontrollably, but nothing happened.

**

The next day, I dragged myself out of bed, exhausted and depressed. After the usual nagging, pushing, and screaming I finally got the kids in the car, dropped them at school, and headed to work. A few blocks past the school, I noticed an old brown Honda broken down on the side of the road. A petite, attractive woman in her late 20s was standing beside the car, and I stopped to see if I could help her.

She thanked me, but just then the tow truck she'd called arrived. I started to drive away but something prompted me to wait. I watched the mechanic look under the hood of the car. He yelled out, "Hey lady, I can't fix this junker. I'll have to tow it to the service station."

"Isn't there any way you can fix it now?" the woman pleaded.

"Lady, I told you, I have to tow it."

"It's all I have." Then she stopped herself, took a deep breath, smiled and thanked him. She asked him where he was taking it, how long would it take to fix, and how much.

The serviceman softened. "Gosh, lady," he answered, "I don't know what it will cost." He wrote the service station number on a piece of paper and handed it to her. "Tough break," he added.

The woman walked over to my car. "Thank you for waiting. I'll take you up on that ride, if you don't mind."

I was glad I'd waited.

She introduced herself as Maria Garcia. We shook hands, and she thanked me again and asked me to take her to a nearby bus stop. On the way, I learned that her husband's name was José and she had three small children. I also discovered we worked in the same office complex, so I could take her straight to work.

"God always takes care," she giggled. "Can you believe we work so close to each other, our children go to the same school, and we never met until my car broke down?"

"You think God is taking care of you when your car just broke down and that serviceman was rude to you? I don't know why you didn't tell him off," I commented.

"Oh, you're probably right. But I sent him love instead. And did you see how he softened? I think he's a kind man, a little gruff, but kind."

She was joyful and upbeat, and I felt a strange connection with her. I admitted to her that the tow truck driver did soften his tone of voice and his personality did change for the better. "But he was rude," I protested. "How did you keep your cool?"

"It's a game I play," she told me, pointing to a pin on her collar. "This is my Peace Way pin. One person can spread peace and love one moment, one heart at a time. I love doing it." Her face lit up as she told me this.

"Why would you want to send peace to someone who's nasty to you?" I asked her.

"Well, I guess I know what it's like to be a nasty person. I used to be one."

I told her I couldn't believe she was ever a nasty person. She was too sweet.

Maria laughed. "Trust me, I was nasty. Everything and everyone annoyed me." She laughed again.

"Anyone who can send love to an old grouch isn't nasty," I insisted. I was getting more curious. If she was as nasty as she claimed to be, what had made her change?

She told me she had always been miserable, but she didn't know how truly miserable she was until her co-complainer, Julio, was transformed from a miserable, quarrelsome complainer to a joyful, grateful peacemaker.

"What's a 'co-complainer'?"

Maria laughed again. "A co-complainer is a friend who is as miserable as you are. You're miserable together."

I was puzzled. I asked her how a co-complainer helped her send peace to some old grouch.

"Julio and I met in first grade. From the first time we met, we complained about school, the teachers, the other kids in the class, the mean world, and all the mean people in it. That's how we became co-complainers," she smiled. "We hated everyone and consequently, everyone hated us. That's how it works, you know."

"How what works?" I asked.

"You get back whatever you give out. Send out negative feelings and you get back negative feelings. Hate people and they'll hate you."

"I'm not sure I understand what you mean."

"If we think someone doesn't like us, we don't treat them very nicely; consequently, they don't treat us very nicely."

"Mean-spirited people don't deserve to be treated nicely," I said. "You were lucky to have a friend who empathized with you."

"At the time, it seemed nice," Maria acknowledged, "but complaining is an addictive poison. The more you complain, the unhappier you become. When two people support each other's misery, it becomes like a cancer growing in their hearts. Like cancer, it consumes your every thought."

"Some people are like cancer. They destroy us," I commented bitterly. "They rob us of everything sacred in our life and leave us with nothing to live for except complaining."

Maria gave me a strange look. "Yes, if we had nothing to live for, I guess we would have a right to complain."

I realized I could have turned her off with my remark, but she didn't seem to notice. I was curious to know what changed her. There was something inviting about her and I needed to know what it was. I asked her, "What changed you from a nasty complainer to a smiling peace sender?"

"When Julio found out he had terminal cancer, he changed almost overnight." Maria hesitated. "It was strange. He became grateful for everyone and everything. When I complained about someone he'd say, 'Try to look at their intent, not their action, and send them love.' "

Maria paused and her thoughts seemed to be elsewhere.

"Julio made new friends," she said wistfully. "He began doing kind things for people. He sent birthday cards, get-well cards, and little gifts to people. That was so unlike him."

"He sounds like a nice guy."

"He was a wonderful guy, but he wasn't as much fun. He was positive about his illness. He wasn't facing reality. He made me furious." She looked over at me and asked, "Do you know what I mean? He wasn't willing to complain with me anymore."

"I guess you felt all alone in your misery," I answered.

"Yes, I did. But he was peaceful. The anger was gone. Our conversations were uplifting. He talked about his blessings and encouraged me to talk about mine."

"Is that when you started sending peace thoughts out to other people?"

"Not right away; it evolved. At first he frustrated me. I wanted to chew on my misery. But very slowly, I began feeling better about me and my life when I was with him. I noticed his new way of facing life had a lot more benefits to it than my dark and negative attitude."

"What do you mean?"

"I focused on everything that was wrong. I thought everyone was against me. I was a victim."

I tensed up. She was describing my life. I was the victim and everyone was against me, even my kids. Worse yet, there was nothing I could do about it. I felt trapped. "Life is unfair," I commented. "Some people get all the bad breaks. They are victims."

"I used to think that until I saw the difference in Julio." She gave me a broad smile. "I wanted his joy. He had terminal cancer. He suffered and he didn't deserve it, yet he was joyful throughout his illness."

"Did he die?"

"Yes, almost two years ago."

I felt a weird twinge. Her friend must have died around the same time Jon left me. "How old was he?"

"Twenty-nine."

"Twenty-nine! That is so young. Wasn't he angry about his cancer?"

"At first he was, until he started his radiation treatment."

"How did *that* help him change his attitude?"

Maria laughed. "The treatment didn't change him. It was another cancer patient he met during his treatment who encouraged him to read the Bible. He taught him that the secret to joy is to see the face of Christ in everyone you meet. They did this by living the Peace Prayer of St. Francis. They said the prayer together while they waited for their treatment. Living the Peace Prayer became a way of life for Julio, and he changed. He invited me to practice the prayer with him, but I resisted."

The more she talked, the more I wanted to know about Julio and the prayer of St. Francis. I asked her what she didn't like about the prayer.

"As I told you, I hated the world and everyone in it. There was no way I could get into that prayer."

"What's in the prayer?"

Maria laughed. "It's a prayer that encourages you to be a sap for everyone else."

"Really? Then how did it help your friend?"

Maria shrugged her shoulders. "It's the formula for finding inner peace and he embraced it."

I was baffled. "If you wanted the same peace he had, why couldn't you just suck it up and follow the prayer?"

Maria laughed. "I enjoyed my misery. If I followed this prayer, I would have had to give up my misery."

"But you have changed, haven't you?"

Maria smiled. "Yes, I've changed."

"Was it the prayer?"

"I guess that was part of it."

"Is there some mystical power in the prayer?" I was getting excited. "Do you think it would help me?"

"It will if you want it to."

"I'd love to hear it. Can you say it now?"

"I know it by heart. But I warn you: although it's a simple prayer, it is a very difficult prayer to practice."

"Do you mind saying it?"

Maria closed her eyes, lowered her voice, and reverently said,

"Oh Lord, make me an instrument of your peace.
Where there is hatred,
Let me sow love;
Where there is injury, pardon;
Where there is doubt, faith;
Where there is despair, hope;
Where there is darkness, light;
And where there is sadness, joy.
O Divine Master, grant that I may not so much
seek to be consoled, as to console;
To be understood, as to understand;
To be loved, as to love.
For it is in giving that we receive;
It is in pardoning that we are pardoned;
And it is in dying that we are born to eternal life."

I tried to think about the words as she said them, but the very thought of sowing love where there was hatred, and pardon where there was injury, turned me off. I hated Jon and I would never pardon him.

"What do you think?" Maria asked.

"I can see why you didn't like it. It's all that turn-the-other-cheek stuff, and that doesn't work."

Maria laughed. "I thought the same thing when I first heard it, but Julio did radiate peace and joy and I wanted that peace." She sighed. "Now I love the prayer."

I kept my eyes on the road. I told her I thought it was a nice prayer but that it wasn't reality. I agreed life would be wonderful if everyone practiced the peace principles. "But people aren't like that. If you live this prayer, people will walk all over you."

"That's the whole point," she replied. "When we live this prayer and spread God's love one moment, one heart at a time, we will spread peace wherever we go, and in whatever we do."

"It just won't work." I shook my head.

She spoke gently. "But it *does* work one heart at a time. The great peacemakers of history lived these principles and changed nations."

I glanced at her out of the corner of my eye. "Do you really believe that?"

"Yes, I do."

"It sounds good, but it's pie-in-the-sky nonsense. What made you go for this prayer?"

She laughed. "Julio told me wonderful stories about Jesus' compassion and love for us. He said the Peace Prayer was Jesus' love letter to us, and Julio wanted to deliver Christ's love letter of peace to everyone he met. He wanted me to experience God's peace, so he broke the peace principles down into small, bite-size prayers.

"Bite-size prayers?"

"He wrote small, simple meditations for each peace principle. For example, he wrote a meditation about peace that was easy to understand and follow." She hesitated. "He was so persistent that I agreed to reflect on his meditations every morning for 30 days. It only took a few minutes and I always felt calmer and more relaxed afterward. That was the beginning of a new and wonderful life for me."

I wanted to know more, but we had arrived at our office complex. Maria worked in the first building and I worked across the street. When I left her off at the corner, I offered to drive her home after work – I wanted to hear that magic prayer. I suggested we meet at the same corner at 5:15.

I watched her run up the steps.

"Move along, lady!" a man screamed from the car behind me. I started to give him the finger, but I thought about Maria sending love and peace to the tow truck driver. So instead, I sent love and peace to Mr. Impatient, and giggled to myself as I drove on.

**

Maria was waiting when I pulled up at 5:15. She gave me instructions on how to get to her house.

All day, I'd thought about her mini peace prayers. I was hoping maybe they would help me. I asked her about them.

"Julio wrote eight meditations based on five peace secrets," she told me.

"What are peace secrets?"

She smiled. "When Julio wrote the short meditations on the virtue of peace, he uncovered five simple secrets to attaining it."

I felt a glimmer of hope. I asked her if she thought the meditation would help me.

"If you are faithful to the prayers," she said confidently. "Can you take ten minutes to pray?"

"Ten minutes," I said in a loud voice. "I don't have ten minutes to go to the bathroom." I asked her for a shorter version.

She laughed. It was a warm, caring laugh, not a mocking laugh. "You sound like me: 'Just give me the instant package – peace in a moment.'" She told me there wasn't an instant fix for finding peace. She said inner peace came from finding God's presence within.

I was tempted to tell her I wasn't into talking about God's presence, but I didn't want to hurt her feelings. I simply stated, "I've never been in God's presence."

I kept my eyes on the road but I could feel her large, caring eyes looking at me. "You're always in God's presence. You may leave Him but He never leaves you. He loves you and is always with you."

I shook my head. "How can you say that with such assurance? You don't even know me."

"I don't," she agreed, "but I know God's love, and He loves you. You are His precious child and He is constantly watching over you. Even if you don't feel His presence, He is with you." She took a deep breath. "God promised us:

> "I can never forget you!
> I have written your name on the palm of my hands."
> (Isaiah 49:16)

I felt goose bumps all over. I wanted to believe her. "What do I have to do to experience God's presence?" I asked.

"Just take a few minutes of uninterrupted time out of your day to spend with Him, and He'll open your heart to His love," Maria said.

I felt helpless. "I don't know how to do that."

"It's easy: Set a specific time every day for you and God."

"What would I do?"

"I'll help you get started." She pulled out a notebook, ripped out a clean page, and began writing.

I began to feel uncomfortable. I didn't want to make a commitment. "Are you suggesting I spend ten minutes with God every day? I told you I can't find ten minutes to talk to my kids."

"Well, you said you wanted to find peace, and you didn't want to wait."

"Are you saying if I spend time with God, we'll be friends and I'll have peace, just like that?" I was getting annoyed. I wanted an instant method to help me find some peace that day, but I wasn't into long, drawn-out prayer. We drove a few blocks in silence. I regretted being so sarcastic. Then Maria asked me,

"Do you think you can find *six* minutes?"

She apparently hadn't picked up on my comments and I was glad. I didn't want to end our brief friendship.

"God invites you to come to Him with all your burdens," she calmly explained, "and He promises you 'I will refresh you.' He invites you to come away with Him for a little while so He can soak you in His peace."

"Do you spend ten minutes talking to God?"

She nodded.

"How do you find ten minutes to pray with three kids?"

We drove a full block in silence. Finally she said, "I need my prayer time to help me juggle my responsibilities. I would be totally overwhelmed with the baby, the kids' schoolwork and after-school activities, cooking, shopping, working part-time, and taking care of my in-laws without God's help. My prayers keep me centered and peaceful. It's the only time I get for me, and it helps me see God's love in every event and experience of my day."

"How do you possibly find time to pray with all that to do? You're busier than I am!"

"When Julio first talked to me about it, I felt the way you feel. When he talked about God's love I thought he was crazy. But I saw the transformation in him. He was courageous and joyful in spite of his pain. I wanted his joy."

She had a way of capturing my attention. I listened intently as she said, "Once I decided I wanted the same peace Julio had more than anything else in the world, I found the time to pray. I started with ten minutes, then 15, then a half-hour. Now I spend a half-hour every morning alone with God, and I love every minute of it."

"How could you spend 30 minutes praying?"

"It's like spending time with your best friend. It's the most precious time of my day," she explained. "I have better control over my day when God is my center. Prayer also helps me focus on what's really important and what isn't, and I get more done in less time, with less stress." She smiled and shrugged. "I couldn't manage my responsibilities without God. It's that simple."

She spoke with such conviction. I wanted to try her method but I didn't know where to begin. "What do you say when you talk to Him?"

"I praise and thank Him for my day, my family and friends. I read and reflect on this prayer." She held up her notes with the prayer neatly written on it. "Then I talk to Him about my family and my needs. I ask Him to guide me, and I listen to His inspirations."

It sounded so easy but I couldn't imagine God being interested in me. I asked her, "If there is a God, don't you think He has more important things to worry about than you and me?"

She shook her head vehemently. "Nothing is more important to God than you and me. He loves you. He wants to help you. Could you try it for six minutes?" she persisted.

I wasn't sure. "Will it work in six minutes or will God be mad at me for not spending ten minutes?"

We were driving down her street when she asked me, "Do you see God as an angry God?"

"I only know the God that's punishing me right now."

She asked me why I thought I was being punished. I didn't tell her. She didn't press me.

"Try this." She handed me her notes just as I pulled up in front of her house. "You can do this in four minutes."

I examined the carefully written instructions.

"<u>First</u>: Commit to four minutes, and find a special time and place to pray.

Second: Close your eyes and slowly inhale through your nose to the count of three – hold your breath – then slowly exhale through your mouth. Do this three times.

Third: Ask the Holy Spirit to still your heart and fill you with God's love.

Fourth: Open your eyes; read and reflect on the scripture. Try to imagine Jesus speaking to you."

Next she had written:

> "'Come to me all who labor and are burdened,
> and I will refresh you.'
> (Matthew, 11:28)"

"I praise and thank you, Jesus, for soaking me in your peace... and washing away all my fears and frustrations... and washing away the hurts my fears and frustrations have caused others.

"I praise and thank you, Lord, for soaking me in your peace...and helping me embrace your peace in every moment of this day as your precious gift to me."

Maria then said, "Imagine that you are being soaked in God's peace, as He is washing away your fears and frustrations. Recognizing your fears and letting go of them will help you gain inner peace. Ask Him to help you to recognize and let go of your fears. Thank Him for helping you."

I had one more question: "Why would I praise and thank Jesus for soaking me in His peace when I didn't have peace?"

She laughed warmly. "God wants you to have His peace in every moment. He instructed us to have faith in Him. Everything you ask and pray for, believe that you have it already and it will be yours. When you praise and thank Him for soaking you in His peace, you are acknowledging that you need God and you believe He will bless you. Try it, you'll see."

I had to think about what she was saying. "So I praise and thank Him for something I don't have as if I already have it?" I wanted to believe Maria, so I agreed to try it.

She assured me, "God is always available. Pick a time that will work for you." As she was getting out of the car she added, "Don't worry about what you're going to say. Prayer is a very personal thing. Reflect on the prayer, and then talk to God like you're talking to a friend who loves you and wants to help you. Tell Him all your concerns and ask Him to help you. He'll do the rest."

Chapter 19

It's Me, Oh Lord

"When the spirit of truth comes, He will guide you into all truth."

(John 16:13)

Kitty placed the book face down on her lap, closed her eyes, and repeated the first sentences of the prayer.

"I praise and thank you, Lord, for soaking me in your peace, and washing away all my fears and frustrations. Lord, how can I talk to you as a friend? I'm scared. Are you really here, God?" The words poured from her. "Why are you letting all these terrible things happen to me? I want to believe that you love me and you will help me, but how can I believe it when you're letting all these bad things happen to me?" Exhausted, she leaned back to rest her head, and closed her eyes.

She had a flashback. She was six years old, sitting in Sunday school, dressed in her white organdy dress with a big bow in her hair. She was singing with all the other children:

"It's me, it's me, oh Lord, standing in the need of prayer,
Not my father, not my mother.
It's me, oh Lord, standing in the need of prayer."

She opened her eyes and wiped tears from her cheeks. "It *is* me, oh Lord. I'm scared; I need prayer. Is this book your answer to my prayer?"

Kitty wept until she fell asleep. Later she woke with a sore neck, and for a brief second she wasn't sure where she was. She gazed around the dark paneled den, then looked at her watch. It was 2:30 a.m. She picked the book up from her lap. *Whatever made me think of Sunday school and that song? That was so long ago.* Holding the book in her hand she stood up, stretched, and decided to read a few more pages before going to bed. Jenny Solomon's story continued:

> That night after my children went to bed, I finished the laundry and retreated to my room. I loved this time of the night: quiet house, sleeping children, time for me to watch TV and forget my problems. It would be a good time to pray but I didn't feel like praying. I needed TV to get me through the long, frightening night.
>
> As usual, I went into the bathroom and counted my sleeping pills, then put my sleeping pill for that night into my bottle of saved pills. I had 14; I needed only 16 more.
>
> When I turned on the TV, I thought about Maria and her prayers. I told myself I'd pray tomorrow, but when I hung up my blouse, her instructions fell out of the pocket. I picked them up, read them again, and reluctantly decided to try them.
>
> I climbed into bed, propped my pillows up against the headboard, and followed Maria's instructions. At first I had difficulty breathing the way she suggested. I tried again. By the third breath I was feeling clear and relaxed. I read the prayer slowly, closed my eyes, and rested my head back against the pillows, trying to visualize God soaking me in his peace. I took another deep breath. Then I thanked God and nodded off to sleep. When I woke I saw that I had slept for four hours, and couldn't believe it. I hadn't slept for four hours without a sleeping pill since Jon left.
>
> I started to get out of bed to go into the bathroom when I noticed Maria's written instructions had fallen onto the floor next to my bed. I picked up the paper and read the instructions again. I wondered if saying the prayer again would help me fall back to sleep. I took three deep breaths, and slowly read the prayer again. This time I didn't fall asleep, but I did think about the things that scared me.
>
> I felt a little awkward talking to God about them. I told Him I was scared I would lose the house and have no place to

live. I thanked Him for placing Maria in my life, and I asked Him to help me believe He loved me. I dozed off again, slept for two more hours, and woke up feeling rested.

Maria and I had lunch together two days later. I told her about my experience. I wanted to know if prayer always made you feel so relaxed, almost light-headed.

"Sometimes we feel more relaxed than other times." She added, "If you're faithful to daily prayer, you'll start seeing God's miracles all around you. That is one of the benefits of following the peace principles; often times what appears to be a bad thing turns out to be a blessing in disguise."

"How can something bad turn out to be a blessing?"

"Well, take Julio's cancer. When I first found out about it, I was devastated. I was angry. It was one of the worst things that could happen to my friend and me. But it turned out to be one of the most wonderful blessings in my life."

"How can losing your best friend turn out to be a blessing?"

"It was through his cancer and death," Maria said, speaking very slowly, "that I discovered God's love for me." She cleared her throat. "It's likely you and I wouldn't even know each other if it weren't for Julio's cancer. See what I mean?"

"I understand that you discovered God's love through Julio's illness. But what does that have to do with us knowing each other?"

"I probably would have told you 'buzz off' when you stopped to help me."

"I can't see you doing that."

Maria laughed. "Jenny, believe me, that's what I would have done. I would have thought you were being nosy and stopping just so you could tell everyone about my broken down car."

I was taken aback. "Why would you think that? I didn't even know you."

Maria laughed. "When you're angry at the world, you're suspicious of everyone."

I told her, "I'm amazed Julio's cancer didn't make you nastier. When bad things happen to good people it usually makes them angry and bitter."

"I *was* bitter and angry about Julio's cancer," she confessed. "But he was able to help me see the blessings in his illness."

"Then you'll understand why I'm bitter." I took a deep breath. "I didn't tell you why I feel so desperate, but believe me, there are no blessings in my life. My life is a disaster. My husband, Jon, walked out on us two years ago. He left me with four kids, a mortgage, and no income. He just disappeared." I could feel a lump in my throat but I had to tell her about my situation. "Until you and I met, I couldn't sleep. My situation is no blessing. I'll never see it that way." I tried to control the anger in my voice.

Maria looked at me with so much compassion. "Jenny, I had no idea. I'm so sorry. I guess I'm talking about things I know nothing about."

"You don't know what it's like to be totally alone, broke, and responsible for four kids," I agreed. She didn't say anything. I felt my rage escalating, so I stopped talking. We both were lost in our thoughts.

When I glanced at Maria, her eyes were misty. She lowered them, and I could feel myself softening. I told her, "You've helped me a lot. You can't imagine how much you've helped me." I wiped tears from my own eyes. "For the first time in two years, I felt a ray of hope when I reflected on your prayer. I felt very peaceful when I went to bed. I slept through almost the whole night. I can't remember the last time I had a full night's sleep. I thank you for that."

She spoke in her calm, reassuring voice. "Maybe Jon leaving you is not a blessing, but there are blessings in your situation. For example, do you think you would have tried praying last night if you weren't in this situation?"

I told her there was no way I would have.

"God places gifts in the midst of our pain," she assured me.

"That's a bit much; I'll have to think about that."

She smiled. "Try this when you're worried about something

like your finances or your children: Tell God your fears, then praise and thank Him for taking care of them for you. Continue doing this, even though you don't see an immediate solution. If you do this, you'll begin to see God's little miracles all around you."

That was the second time she mentioned God's miracles. I told her, "I guess it's hard for me to really believe God cares about my problems."

"Faith is like a delicate flower. Be faithful to daily prayer and the peace secrets, and you'll start to believe God cares about you and your family. Your belief and trust in God's love will grow."

"But I don't know the peace secrets. How can I be faithful to them?"

Maria started to laugh. "You've already learned the first two secrets."

"No, I haven't. You never told me any secrets," I insisted.

"The prayer you've said for the last few nights contain the first two secrets for finding peace," she said gently.

"You're kidding. What are they?"

"The first is praise and thank God for all things. Last night you thanked God for soaking you in His peace and washing away your fears. Praising God is the first peace secret."

"You're kidding. Is that why I felt so peaceful?"

"Praising God in all things is a path to finding inner peace."

I laughed. For the first time in two years, I laughed. "What's the other one?"

"Embrace the moment. You asked God to help you embrace every moment as His gift to you."

"I'll be honest, I had difficulty with that one." I shook my head. "That's reaching: Embrace every moment. There are too many bad moments in my life."

"Well, how did you sleep the last two nights?"

I admitted to her that I had slept well two nights in a row. I didn't tell her about my sleeping pills. "But it's hard to believe that's all there is to the first two secrets. What are the other ones?"

"I'll teach them to you as we go along. It's best to learn one at a time."

"When will you teach me the next secret?" I asked eagerly.

Maria laughed. "Not so fast. We haven't finished the prayers for embracing the moment."

"I thought that was last night's meditation."

"There are two meditations for each secret. All the meditations begin with the first secret: Praising and thanking God."

I wanted to learn the next meditation but I was more interested in learning how to breathe. I asked her to show me how.

"We'll practice breathing together, then I'll teach you the second prayer for enjoying the moment."

We finished our lunch. Then Maria told me to close my eyes and to put both of my hands on my abdomen. "Now, slowly breathe in through your nose to the count of four. Do you feel your abdomen expanding?" she asked.

"Yes," I told her.

"Now hold your breath till the count of four, then very slowly let your breath out through your mouth to the count of six. Do you feel your abdomen receding?"

She guided me through three deep breaths. It felt wonderful.

"Deep breathing helps relax our bodies and our minds," she explained. "When we inhale, we fill our body with clean oxygen. When we hold our breath, we give the clean oxygen time to sweep through our brain, relax us, and empty us of anxious thoughts. When we exhale we get rid of the old, pent-up air. It also helps release any tension we may be experiencing."

She advised me to always try to take at least three deep breaths before I began praying. Then she handed me a piece of crisp white paper with the words to the second meditation on it.

"First I'll read the prayer and I'll explain it as I read it to you. Then we'll say the prayer together."

Maria slowly recited the prayer.

"I praise and thank you, Jesus, for soaking me in your love and washing away all my angers and anxieties."

She paused. "Stop after this verse. Let Jesus soak you in His love. Ask Him to speak to your heart." Then she explained that when we are soaked in God's love, He washes away our anger and anxiety. "After we pray for ourselves, we pray for the people our anger and anxieties have hurt."

She continued:

"I praise and thank you, Jesus, for washing away all the hurts my anger and anxieties have caused others.

Maria told me that our angers and anxieties are like weeds with long thorns that touch and hurt others. We don't even realize we're hurting people. "I ask God to help me be more aware of how I hurt others so that I won't hurt them again."

She finished the prayer.

"I praise and thank you, Jesus, for soaking me in your love and helping me embrace every moment of this day as your precious gift to me."

We were quiet, reflecting on the prayer in the silence of our hearts. Suddenly I felt a profound sense of being loved and appreciated. I wanted this moment to last forever. When Maria spoke, I was relaxed and content.

She told me that she usually wrote in her journal at this point, and suggested that I ask God to help me recognize and let go of my anger and anxiety, then write my thoughts in my journal. She also suggested I ask God to help me see how my negative emotions hurt others, especially my family.

"I have a surprise for you," she said with a mischievous smile. She pulled out a thick spiral notebook with multicolored blank pages inside. "I bought this journal for you."

A lump appeared in my throat. I hadn't cried in almost two years, yet I'd cried several times since meeting Maria. I held the book in my hand and examined it. It was beautiful. I hugged her and thanked her, wiping my eyes. She was so thoughtful I couldn't imagine her hurting anyone.

"Maria," I said, "will you give me an example of how you hurt someone with anger or anxiety?"

"Oh," she said, "that's a good question." She thought for a moment. "Well, the other night I was preparing dinner and thinking about all the things I had to do: cook, do the laundry, and get the kids in bed. My in-laws were there, and my mother-in-law was telling me how I should cook, my father-in-law was yelling at the kids, and I was getting more and more frustrated when José called to say he wouldn't be home for dinner. He had to work overtime. I exploded. I gave him a tongue-lashing. I treated him like it was his fault that I was so overwhelmed."

"How did you calm down?" I asked.

"Sometimes I don't. But if I catch myself, I try to stop and take three deep breaths-- that definitely helps-- and then ask God to help me see His peace in this moment. Or I say, 'Praise and thank you, Lord, for calming my spirit and filling me with your peace in this moment.' I say this over and over again until I'm calmed down. When I collect myself, I apologize for my angry behavior."

I shook my head, amazed. "The situation you're describing would make anyone upset."

Maria agreed. "That's why the peace meditations are so powerful. They heighten our awareness of our anxieties and God's power to eliminate them."

"How can anyone be soaked in God's peace at times like that?"

"I can remain calm if I approach the situation with a positive attitude, or take a deep breath as soon as I feel myself getting uptight. If I let my negative thinking take over, I'm done. Once the 'poor, mistreated me' recording starts playing in my head, it's hard to turn it off. The more I think about it, the more irritated I get. I ruin the moments for myself and everyone around me. Last night I destroyed the peace of the moment with my children and my in-laws. I missed the opportunity to let José know I love him and appreciate how hard he works to support us."

"You're kidding, aren't you? You had a right to be upset. He should have told you how much he appreciated you."

She took a deep breath. "I can only change *my* behavior. Last night was an opportune moment to spread peace instead of conflict. I missed it; however, being aware that I missed it will help me be more peaceful the next time I'm in a similar situation."

"You had a right to be upset," I insisted.

She looked directly at me. "Have you ever felt good about yourself after lashing out at someone?"

I frowned. "I don't remember." But I was pretty sure I hadn't.

"I don't like me when I'm nasty and mean to other people," she confessed. "The peace principles help me pause and be mindful of this present moment and the people I'm interacting with at this moment. When I embrace this moment my life is easier and more fun."

Up until that moment I didn't see a connection between finding peace and embracing the moment. But the light bulb went off in my head when I listened to Maria explain how she'd missed an opportunity to spread peace.

"Do you think that's why Julio thought embracing the moment was one of the secrets to peace?" I asked.

She thought for a second. "He pondered and prayed about how he could live the peace prayer of St. Francis. He decided that to live the prayer in the core of his being he had to do it one moment, one person at a time – every moment and every encounter was important. He realized he could never do this on his own. He had to totally depend on God to help him.

"Julio used to get uptight and irritable when he was waiting for his treatments, until his friend suggested they use that time to pray for the other patients. He began enjoying the peaceful moments waiting for his treatment. He loved the opportunity to sit quietly, praising and thanking God for soaking him and the other patients in his peace. Embracing this present moment and not worrying about the moments to come was a revelation for him. Thus he wrote the first meditation."

She asked me if I had any more questions. When I said no, she suggested we say the mediation on love together. Before we went back to work, Maria suggested I say this second meditation for the next few evenings and write down my thoughts.

That night after the children were asleep, I climbed into bed and began my time with God. I took deep breaths and reflected on God soaking me in His love and washing away my angers and anxieties. I wrote my feelings down.

Several nights later, I wrote three pages in my journal. It was like someone had opened the floodgates of my heart. I wrote things about my anger and anxieties that I wasn't even aware of until I wrote them down. I really enjoyed the experience. It was wonderful. I had another good night's sleep without a pill.

The next time we met, Maria planned to teach me the third peace secret: appreciating your abundance. I felt my whole body stiffen when she talked about abundance. I told her I didn't have any abundance to appreciate. I couldn't pray about abundance. I just couldn't be that much of a hypocrite.

Then she asked me about my children. I had to agree they were precious gifts. She asked me about my job. I told her I needed more money but I was glad to have the job. She asked me how I felt about meeting her, and learning the mediations on peace and love. Finally, I admitted I did have some things to appreciate.

She laughed that warm, caring laugh of hers. It wasn't mocking. Her laugh always seemed to portray understanding. The she asked, "Do you want to learn the prayer for the third secret or do you want to wait?"

She had a way of throwing the ball back into my court. I was curious to learn the prayer because I wanted to see if it would have the same effect on me as the other two did. But I wasn't ready to buy into the abundance fairy tale. I didn't answer.

Maria always seemed to read my mind. She came up with another suggestion.

"I've been thinking about you supporting four kids without any help. I thought that before we go on to the next secret, Psalm 91 might help you."

I vaguely remembered Jon's parents talking about the Psalms, but I had never read one.

"When I'm scared, I like to read and reflect on Psalm 91, verses 9-16. I began reading this psalm after I read a story about the actor Jimmy Stewart. His dad slipped a piece of paper into his pocket when he was leaving to go overseas to fight in the second World War. He told Jimmy to keep it in his pocket and to read it when he was scared. It helped him get through the war, and it has helped me get through many personal challenges. I think it will help you, too."

She handed me a folded piece of notepaper. "Wait until you're alone with our Lord. Take your three deep breaths and read this instead of the other prayers."

"Let's read it now," I suggested.

"It's better if you wait and read it alone."

We had to go back to work anyway, so I put the paper in my bag and ran back to my office.

On my way home from dropping off Maria, I thought about my life since I'd met her just 10 days ago. Things at home did seem to be better. The kids weren't fighting as much, I hadn't heard from the bank in several weeks, and I felt better. I was beginning to think maybe there was something to these peace prayers – until I walked into my house that Friday afternoon.

Rachael and Sara were crying. J.J. was calling them names. "J.J. took my cracker," Sara cried.

"J.J. pushed me!" Rachael screamed. "I hate you. I hate you. I hate you, J.J. You're the worst brother."

"You're just a fat pig!" J.J. screamed back.

"Mom, make him stop."

I tried to break it up. J.J. started yelling at me. He said I was a rotten mother and he wanted to find his dad.

I pushed him away from Rachael and told him he better not talk to me that way. He raised his fist to me. I grabbed his wrist. He twisted his arm loose from my hold, as he is much stronger then I am, and ran out the door, slamming it behind him, cursing me as he went.

"I hope he never comes back," Rachael sobbed.

Sara started crying again. "Please don't send J.J. away."

I hugged Sara, reassuring her J.J. would be back. I held her tight as her little body shook. Rachael came over and put her arms around both Sara and me. Finally, she said, "Come on, Sara, let's go watch TV."

There were dishes and glasses everywhere. An orange liquid was dripping down the side of the counter, and my shoes stuck to the sticky floor. Everywhere I looked was a mess. I sat down and stared and wondered, *where do I begin?*

I dragged myself out of the chair and cleaned up the kitchen. Then I took hot dogs from the freezer and prepared dinner. Hot dogs and baked beans, or pizza, were the only dinners I could afford.

Rebecca, my oldest, came in just as I was putting dinner on the counter. She poured the milk. "Hot dogs again?" she said, making a face. "Isn't there anything else? I'm sick of them."

I didn't say anything. She looked over at me. "I'm sorry, Mom. I know you're doing the best you can." She brightened up. "Sunday night, I'm going to treat us to macaroni and cheese. I have my babysitting money." She smiled and put her arm around my shoulder. "Do you think that's a good idea?"

I sighed. Rebecca was the one shining light in my life. She seemed to understand. I thought of what Maria had said about abundance, and I thanked God for Rebecca. *She is my abundance.*

"It's your turn to drive to basketball tonight," she reminded me. I had forgotten it was Friday, my night to drive Rebecca and her friends to their basketball game.

I was so tired and didn't feel like going to the game, but we gulped down our dinner without J.J. and left the dishes in the sink. Rebecca and her giggling friends always lifted my spirits; I enjoyed listening to their chatter as I drove. But the minute I walked into the game, I was attacked with overwhelming loneliness. The same couples were always there, laughing and kidding. Although they were very friendly toward me, our conversations were strained. Jon and I used to be one of those couples. Now I felt like a fifth wheel. I hated it.

When we got home, I was relieved to see a light in J.J.'s room. I was too tired to have another encounter with him and I was too tired to clean the kitchen, so the girls went to bed and I went to my bathroom. Weekends were very painful. I counted my pills. *Why am I waiting? Why not take them all tonight and end it?* I don't know how long I gazed at that pill bottle, wrestling with myself. I knew Rebecca would always watch out for Rachael and Sara. But somewhere deep inside me I knew it wouldn't be fair to her. I sighed and put the bottle back.

I turned out the light and tried sleeping, but my mind was racing. I was uptight and anxious. I got out of bed and turned the TV on. I was channel-surfing when Sara screamed. She sometimes had nightmares. I dropped the remote and ran to her room. She was tossing, turning, and screaming. Rebecca was already there, ready to pick her up when I came in. I told Rebecca to go back to bed. Sara was sound asleep and still screaming. I held her and rocked her, stroking her hair. At first she punched at me and squirmed to get out of my arms, but she finally calmed down. "It's okay, honey, it's okay," I sang to her.

She woke up and looked up at me. "Mommy, are you going away?" she asked between sniffles.

Fear shot through me like an electric bolt. It was as if Sara had caught me counting my pills. "No, honey, I'm not going away," I lied. I rocked her, afraid to ask her why she had posed that question.

Her round, freckled face looked up at me again. "Please don't leave me, Mommy, please don't."

I held her tighter. "Mommy won't leave you. I'm right here." I rocked her until she fell asleep, and then tucked her in. Finally

I went back to my bathroom. I opened my medicine cabinet and took out the sleeping pills. I held the bottle in both hands and stared at it. *What am I going to do?* I asked myself over and over. *What am I going to do?*

Where was the psalm Maria had given me? I rummaged through my purse to find the piece of paper.

I kissed it and held it close to my heart. I prayed, "God, if you are all the things Maria says you are, then speak to me tonight. Show me the way." I opened the neatly folded paper, and slowly read.

> "You have made the Lord your defender,
> and no disaster will strike you,
> no violence will come near your home.
> God will put his angels in charge of you
> to protect you wherever you go....
>
> God says, I will protect those who love me,
> And I will protect those who acknowledge me as Lord.
> When they call me I will answer them;
> When they are in trouble I will be with them.
> I will rescue them and honor them.
> I will reward them with long life;
> I will save them."

I cried and cried. It felt like God was speaking right to my heart. Then I prayed, "Thank you, Lord, for speaking to me, thank you for being with me, for protecting me, thank you for sending your angels to protect us. I have nothing to fear. Oh Lord, you said you would rescue those who love you when they are in trouble. Rescue my children, rescue me." I jumped up and started dancing around the room. I felt free, lighthearted. God loved us and was with us. I laughed, I cried. I was excited to read the words again.

I repeated the last sentence several times: "I will reward them with a long life; I will save them." Then I asked God to give me the courage to trust Him.

I read the psalm several times over the weekend. Every time I read it, I felt like God was speaking directly to me. That psalm was written for me.

I had a wonderful weekend. As Rebecca promised, she treated us to a dinner of macaroni and cheese, garlic bread, and salad. Rather than everyone grabbing their dinner and running off to watch TV like we usually did, each child took his or her plate and instinctively sat down at the kitchen table. We were eating dinner together for the first time in months.

All through dinner I thought about God's promise, "When they are in trouble I will be with them. I will rescue them and honor them." He had used Rebecca's babysitting job and generous nature to rescue us from hot dogs and pizza. We talked and kidded about how wonderful it was to eat something else. Even J.J. thanked Rebecca several times.

Sunday evening I reflected on Psalm 91 again and made a list of all the things I could praise and thank God for. I wrote three pages of things I was grateful for. Then I slept six hours without a sleeping pill. Praise and thank you, God.

**

Two days later as I drove her to work, Maria taught me the prayer for the third secret: appreciate your abundance. As usual, we began with three deep breaths and asked the Holy Spirit to speak to our hearts. "Relax and let the words seep into your heart as our Lord immerses you in trust and hope," she prompted. We said the Prayer of St. Francis together and then Maria recited Psalm 28: 7-9:

> "The Lord protects and defends me.
> I trust in Him and He gives me help."
> (Psalm 28: 7-9)

The words were similar to Psalm 91. Again I was sure this psalm was for me and I told Maria so.

"It's powerful, isn't it?" She smiled. "Shall we go on with the meditation or do you want to think about the psalm?"

"How does it work? Are we supposed to stop and think about the psalm or are we supposed to go on?"

Maria laughed her wonderful laugh. "We're in relationship with our Lord. We can stop and think about what He just said to us in this psalm or we can move on to the prayer. God's in no rush."

I laughed, too. I was always in a hurry. I wanted the magic formula. She handed me a piece of white paper with the meditation neatly written on it. We read it together:

> "Do not let your hearts be troubled.
> Trust in God, trust in me."

She paused. "God is speaking to us. Let us thank Him."

"O holy One, O glorious One, I praise and thank you for soaking me in your trust, and washing away any sense of loss or loneliness I may feel in my heart."

She continued:

> "And for washing away any hurts my sense of
> loss or loneliness may have caused others."

She paused again, then went on:

> "I praise and thank you, Lord, for soaking me in your
> trust,
> and helping me appreciate and use my
> blessings for your honor and glory."

She was silent. I thought about how lost and lonely I felt. I thought about how hard it was to trust God when you've lost everything. I asked Maria, "Why did you pause after you read about loss and loneliness?"

She explained she always stopped to reflect on the pain that she might be experiencing, and to write about it in her journal. "Sometimes we're so busy just trying to hold on, we're not in touch with our feelings."

"Do you ever feel lost or lonely?" I asked her.

She nodded. "Yes, sometimes I feel lonely, and sometimes I feel a deep sense of loss."

"Is it Julio's death? Is that the loss you feel?"

"I miss Julio. I don't feel a loss any more. I feel very close to him, like he is always with me. My feelings of loss have to do with my family."

"Tell me about it."

Maria explained that her father-in-law had been a construction worker. He fell off a roof and now had permanent brain damage.

"He looks normal, but he's confused. It's like he has Alzheimer's, but it isn't Alzheimer's. It's like he isn't there. He was such a dear man, the rock of our family." She wiped her eyes. "He's had a complete personality change, and gets angry, even violent sometimes. He wanders off and we can't find him. Two weeks ago he disappeared for two days. The police picked him up downtown."

I was surprised when her tone of voice changed from sorrow to anger.

"It's too much for my mother-in-law but she won't even discuss the possibility of putting him in a home." Maria admitted she was struggling with her anger over their family situation. She spent her days off helping her mother-in-law, and her husband devoted most of his weekend to helping his parents.

"It's very hard," she sighed. "We're Hispanic. In our culture, we don't put our family in homes. We take care of our own."

I told her I was sorry and asked if there was anything I could do. She smiled and thanked me. I wanted to hear more about the situation with Maria's in-laws but I had a feeling she didn't wanted to talk about it. I suddenly realized that whenever we're together, in spite of all her problems, Maria spends her time trying to help me.

"Are you ready for the third secret?" she asked. I nodded and she explained that in every meditation there is a scripture and psalm verse that relates to that peace principle. She repeated the next verse from scripture, which was Psalm 62:5.

> "I depend on you, God, alone:
> I put my hope in you."

Maria sat very still, her eyes closed. I was thinking about her father-in-law rather than the psalm. I felt disappointed: Maria was so enthusiastic about God, it wasn't fair that she had this problem. If God was taking care of her like she claimed He was, why didn't He take care of her father-in-law?

She brought me back to reality when she said, "Lots of times we're distracted during our prayer, and it's hard to focus on what we're doing." She kept her eyes closed. "When I get distracted, I go back to deep breathing."

I asked her how she knew I was distracted. She laughed. "I didn't. I'm feeling uptight about my father-in-law. So from a selfish point of view, I'm glad you're distracted. Some deep breathing will be good for both of us."

"Maria," I asked, "why do you continue praying when God lets you and your family suffer?

She looked at me. "Suffering and loss are a part of living. Prayer helps me appreciate God's love for me. It helps me know that even in my loneliness I'm not alone. Jesus said suffering is a blessing: 'Blessed are those who mourn for they shall be comforted.' The best way to find comfort is to reach out and comfort others." She smiled and went right into deep breathing.

We took three deep breaths. It relaxed me and seemed to do the same for Maria. We were able to focus on the next meditation.

> "I praise and thank you, Lord, for soaking
> me in your hope, and washing away any
> doubts or despair I may feel in my heart,
> And washing away any hurts my doubt
> or despair may have caused others,
> I praise and thank you, Lord, for soaking me in
> your hope, and helping me appreciate and always
> use my abundance for your honor and glory."

When we finished we let the words seep into our hearts in silence. I thanked God for giving me Maria and the peace mediation. I asked Him to wash away all my doubts and sense of loss, and fill me with trust and hope in Him.

Maria spoke first. "Now is a good time to ask God for anything you want. Ask, and then listen and write what you think and feel."

I told her I had written some of my thoughts down the other night but wasn't sure I was doing it the right way.

"There really isn't any right or wrong way. Just write what's in your heart," she explained. She looked at her watch. "Oh, we're going to have to go back to work. Next time we'll talk about journaling."

"What am I supposed to do now?" I asked her. "Do I meditate on these prayers for four minutes like I did the other ones?" She nodded and went right into the closing prayer.

"I praise and thank you, Lord,
for lighting our way and helping us this day
spread your love wherever we go and whatever we do,
one moment, one heart at a time."

"Sorry I have to run," she said, as she hopped out of the car. "Remember, God holds you in the palm of His hand. He loves you and He never lets you go." She headed back to her office.

I watched Maria disappear. We had been meeting for four weeks and I was just beginning to realize that she had problems I would never be able to handle.

She had suggested I meditate on the abundance prayers for seven nights, so every night after the children went to bed, I gathered my prayers, propped myself up in bed, and began praising and thanking God for soaking me in His trust and hope. I always felt better after my meditation. I could feel the doubts washing out of me and I believed things would get better. For the next few days I felt more peaceful and things ran rather smoothly.

**

On the fourth day, I was hit with reality and I panicked. I received a letter from the bank threatening to foreclose on my house. The kids were fighting and miserable. I couldn't take any more.

That night I counted my sleeping pills and forced myself to meditate on my abundance. I began praising and thanking God for Maria, Rebecca and the other children, and my job. By the time I finished my prayer, I felt a ray of hope that maybe everything would work out. But I couldn't imagine how that could possibly happen.

I felt guilty about the sleeping pills. I went back into the bathroom and mentally battled between saving the pills and putting them back into the original pill bottle. When I prayed, I believed things would work out, but when I considered all my problems, I was scared and thought about ending my life.

Panic over losing my house consumed me. I was uptight and irritable. I later told Maria I couldn't appreciate my abundance and asked her why Julio picked that as a peace secret.

She laughed. "You're doing great. You're persevering in your prayer. You'll see, things will start to change; life *will* get better."

I told her I just didn't see any hope for my future. I always felt a little better right after my prayers, but it didn't last. I reminded her that in spite of her praying, her in-law situation was also getting worse.

"That appears to be true," she agreed. "Remember, I told you that Julio realized that his fear stemmed from the things he projected would happen. I get angry about my father-in-law when I project all the terrible things that could happen to him and us." She paused to make sure I was paying attention. "But I'm worrying about something that may never happen, and if it does, I don't have any control over it. I'm ruining the precious time I have with him today by worrying about tomorrow."

I just didn't understand her. "How can you say that, when you admit you're angry about your father-in-law?"

"I *do* get angry when I think how my family is inconvenienced by his illness." She looked at me intently with her big brown eyes. "One thing I know from personal experience is that misery is a choice. I make my own happiness or my own misery. It all depends on how I perceive the situation, and the messages I repeat over and over again in my mind."

"So you're saying we create our own world by the way we think?"

She replied in her usual thoughtful way, as if she didn't notice my doubtful tone. "My boss talks about the power of our thoughts. He claims we become what we think about all day long. So when I think about how miserable I am because of my father-in-law, I *become* miserable. But when I think about how precious my father-in-law is, and I treasure the time I'm with him, I'm happy-- I'm actually joyful! And I see many blessings from his illness. I observe my mother-in-law's devotion, and I'm inspired.

"I love my father-in-law and sometimes I really enjoy helping him. I enjoy every minute with him as a precious moment, a gift from God, and I am overwhelmed with gratitude. That's why I say little prayers or affirmations all day long to help me appreciate him."

"What kind of prayers?" I asked.

"I praise and thank God for my father-in-law just as he is, and I ask God to soak both of us in His peace."

"You do what Julio did."

She nodded. "Yes, like Julio, I'm realizing that thoughts are the driving force behind our emotions."

I wanted to believe what she said but instead I felt irritated. "Talk about pie in the sky," I told her. "You do have your head in the clouds." I was angry at her suggestion that we choose to be happy or miserable. "I didn't choose for Jon to desert us and leave me with four kids and no money. I did *not* choose that."

Maria shook her head. "I'm not suggesting you had a choice about Jon any more than I had a choice about my father-in-law. But we do have a choice in how we perceive our situations. Prayer gets us in touch with God's love. It helps us see that a greater power is watching over us even though we can't see it or feel it. We can't do it alone, and we don't have to."

I'm not sure why I was so irked by what Maria was saying. I guess I couldn't see the relevance between her in-law situation and my life.

"It's easy for you to say we choose happiness or misery. *You* have a husband. You have relatives who help you out. I don't have anyone."

Maria looked at me with such love that I felt badly for being so defensive. I told her, "I'm trying. But it's hard when I can hardly feed my kids and the bank is threatening to take our house."

Maria raised her eyebrows. "The bank is threatening to do that?"

I nodded.

"Did you call them?"

"No, I'm afraid to."

She thought for a moment. "Let's praise God for taking away your fear and showing you what to do." We took three deep breaths and then she praised and thanked God for soaking me in His peace. When she finished the prayer, I felt so much better that I couldn't believe it. Then Maria advised me to call my banker. She told me the same thing had happened to them several years ago, and that their banker was very kind and helpful.

"Jenny, you're amazing." She added. "God will help you conquer these challenges. I don't know how, but I know He will." Her voice was very encouraging.

Then she asked me if I was writing my thoughts down. I hadn't written anything down the last two nights. I explained to her I was kind of rushing through my prayers, making sure I finished in four to five minutes.

She laughed. Then she told me, "There's a simple exercise I can give you to help you find more abundance in your life that only takes a few minutes. Will you promise me you'll do it, even if you think it's stupid?"

"How can I promise I'll do something if I don't know what it is?"

"I don't want to share it with you unless you promise you'll do it, because I know you'll think it's dumb. But if you do it every day for a week, you'll be amazed how much better you'll feel."

I agreed to try it, so she pulled out her notebook and scribbled something on it. "This is part of your journaling to help you discover all the abundance you don't even know you have. Perhaps you'll even discover solutions to your problems."

"I doubt that," I said. "I know you believe in miracles. I try to believe. I get hopeful for a miracle, and then the bank sends me a letter about foreclosing on my house. I have no money. I can't imagine any kind of miracle that would help me."

She sighed. "That's a tough one. But God will help you. This exercise will help strengthen your belief, and it might help you find a way to pay your mortgage." She handed me two blank pages. The first page had "I can" written on the top. The second had "I am" written on the top.

She suggested that I make a list of all the things "I can" do, and a list of all the things "I am."

"Why would I do that?" I asked, looking at her skeptically.

Her big brown eyes looked straight into mine. "Because you promised to do it and you are a woman of your word."

We both laughed. "Okay, I'll do it for at least two nights. I feel foolish, though."

That night I praised and thanked God and felt better until I got to the appreciating my abundance part. Reluctantly I looked at the blank paper with "I can" written on the top. I thought about Psalm 91: "I will rescue them." I started writing.

"I can: walk, talk, eat, yell, be angry, cry, hate." I looked at it. I erased hate and be angry. "I can sing, I can sew, I can cook, not very well these days but I can cook. I can drive. I can love, I can be a friend, I can sing if I want to, I can bathe, I can dress myself, I can sew, I can make beautiful clothes."

The list was silly, but I did feel better about myself. I even laughed to myself.

The next night I worked on the "I am" list. "I am tall, I am funny, sometimes, I am kind, I am hardworking, I am responsible…"

Every night for the next four nights I looked over my lists. I'd usually add one more thing to each page. By the end of the week I was feeling pretty good about me. One thing on the "I can" list caught my attention. *I can sew.* I used to be a very good seamstress. When I showed Maria my list she noticed I had written down "I can sew" several times.

"Have you ever thought about doing alterations or making clothes for people?" she asked.

"Funny you should mention that. I've been thinking about it." I hesitated and plunged ahead. "Maybe I could do it at night and on the weekends. I've thought about getting a second job, and I love sewing. But where would I get my customers?'

I had done all my mother-in-law's alterations, but I hadn't talked to her since Jon left. I was sure they knew where Jon was. They could have made him come home, but they didn't.

Every time I thought about Jon's parents, I felt rage. We used to be so close. How could they take his side when he deserted his children, their grandchildren?

They used to call but I wouldn't let the children talk to them. They offered me help but I refused it. I hated Jon's parents as much as I hated Jon.

I resolved to think about the sewing idea later. So much had happened since I met Maria four weeks ago, and I was feeling better about myself. I had glimmers of hope. Maria even knew a man who worked at the bank where I had my mortgage, and he assured me the bank didn't want to take the house away.

Again I thought of Jon's parents. Meanwhile, Maria encouraged me to focus on learning the last two peace secrets. She thought they might help me find the courage to do whatever I had to do to solve my mortgage problem. I told her if she was thinking the secrets would help me ask Jon's parents for help, that was not an option.

But I agreed to learn all the secrets. I was hoping the next two would be easier, and I promised Maria that I would continue the meditations for 30 days.

That night I journaled, "There are three things I must do: Learn the last two secrets, contact the bank and place myself at their mercy, and find customers for my seamstress business."

Chapter 20

Kitty Experiments

"If you ask me for anything in my name, I will do it."

(John 14:14)

Kitty put the book down and looked at her watch. It was 4 a.m., but she wasn't tired. She walked over to her desk, took out a yellow legal pad, paused, and wrote "I can" at the top of one page and "I am" on the top of another.

Lord, I thank you and praise you for helping me find what I can do. She paused again. She began writing, "I can walk, talk, read, write, ride, give parties, raise money for charity, play bridge, play golf, help abused women, swim, play, laugh, cry, love." She wrote 20 things she could do.

She put the pen down and looked over her list, giggling to herself. *I can do more things than I realized.* She turned to the next page and began writing: "I am kind, smart, funny, intelligent, organized." She amazed herself with 18 items.

She turned to the next page and began writing her feelings. She wrote, "Everyone thinks that I think I'm perfect, but I don't; that's why I try so hard. I'm afraid if I don't strive for perfection, I'll fail.

"But when I read my 'I can' and 'I am' lists, I'm surprised at the talents I do have." She put her pen down and thought about what she had just written. She read what she had written out loud. She sighed.

She picked up *The Peace Way* and flipped through the pages until she found the meditation for the first secret: enjoy the moment. "Lord," she prayed, "I don't think I've enjoyed many moments. I was always busy trying to do everything right."

She wrote the meditation for peace on the yellow legal pad. She read it. She also wrote the meditation for love. Then she took three deep breaths and prayed and reflected on both the mediations. She read them quietly to herself. She thought about them, then she wrote about her fears and anxieties. She wrote two more pages. She stopped and read them, and praised and thanked God for the night, for Caroline, and for the book. Kitty resumed reading.

**

I was hoping the fourth secret would be easier than the first three. Maria had said the fourth secret was probably the most important one for finding peace in my heart. "Choose to forgive. That is the fourth secret."

"Choose to forgive!" I shouted. "If you mean I have to forgive Jon or my in-laws, it's out of the question. I have every right to hate Jon. He deserted me. He left me with four children. I'll hate him until the day I die."

Maria didn't say a word while I stared out the car window. Finally I said, "Well, let's hear this meditation. I'll try it, but I can't forgive."

Maria didn't comment; she just reminded me about breathing. We did this three times. We said the prayer to St. Francis. Then Maria began the meditations for the fourth secret, choosing to forgive.

> "If you forgive others...your heavenly
> Father will forgive you."
> (Matthew 6:14)

> "Oh my holy one, my glorious one, I love you
> and I praise and thank you for soaking me in
> your mercy, and for washing away any sins
> or selfishness I may hold in my heart."

Maria paused.

> "And washing away any hurts my sins or
> selfishness may have caused others."

She paused again.

"I praise and thank you, Lord, for soaking me in
your mercy, and filling me with forgiveness and love
for myself and all those who have ever hurt me."

I was taken off guard when she started praising and thanking God for "soaking me in His mercy and washing away my
sins and selfishness." The words struck a chord deep in my
heart. I felt uncomfortable. I felt the same way I did when Sara
asked me not to leave her. Until now I had been thinking only
about myself and *my* misery. I didn't really think about the
children and their pain.

I suddenly felt very selfish. When Maria prayed that God
would wash away the hurts our sins and selfishness caused others, I realized many of my actions were selfish and hurt my
children. I suddenly realized God was my children's only hope.

I had a lump in my throat. Tears rolled down my cheeks
and I wiped my eyes quickly. If Maria noticed, she never let on.

I silently repeated in my head, "Lord, help me forgive myself and all those who have ever hurt me." I told our Lord that
I wasn't ready to forgive Jon. I wasn't even ready to forgive myself, but I would throw myself on God's mercy. My mind was a
thousand miles away when Maria softly read Psalm 25:9,

"He leads the humble in the right way,
and teaches them His will."

Once again she paused. I didn't say a word. The chirping
birds, a slight breeze, and the traffic in the distance added serenity to the moment and soothed my inner pain. I felt a deep
sorrow for my children. I could feel the anger oozing out of me.

Maria broke the silence with the next meditation, but she
changed the "I" to "we."

"O Holy One, glorious Lord, we praise and thank you
for soaking us in your humility, and washing away

any pride or prejudice we may have hidden in our
hearts, and that may have caused harm to others."

Maria didn't speak for a moment and then went on:

"We praise and thank you, Lord, for soaking us in
your humility and filling us with forgiveness and
love for ourselves and all those who ever hurt us."

This prayer also hit home. I realized in an instant that I was
guilty of pride and prejudice. Immediately in my mind I tried
to justify my right to be hurt, my right to be angry about my
bruised pride. I was lost in my thoughts when Maria said,

"I ask God to lead me. I listen quietly and write my
thoughts in my journal. Then I close with the same prayer:

"I praise and thank you, Lord, for lighting my way and
helping me go through this day forgiving myself and others
while spreading your love wherever I go, whatever I do, one
moment, one heart at a time."

She concluded with, "I plan my day and go on my way. It's
really very simple. Simple but powerful."

I was relieved when Maria looked at her watch and said she
had to run back to work.

That night I was anxious to get to my prayers. I tried to
rush the children through their homework and get them off
to bed, but they weren't going to be rushed. Sara and Rachael
just couldn't get themselves together. I resisted Sara's pleas for
a story until I thought about the prayer I was rushing to say,
"Wash away my sins and selfishness." I reluctantly agreed to
read to Sara, and I was glad I did.

When I was finally alone, I went into the bathroom for my
usual ritual with the sleeping pills. I pulled the two bottles out
of the medicine cabinet. As I started to take the top off the first
bottle the words of the prayer went through my mind again. "I
thank you and praise you, Lord, for soaking me in your mercy

and washing away my sins and selfishness." I gave a large sigh and put the bottles back in the medicine cabinet.

Then I read the meditations and reflected on the words. When I began writing in my journal, I tried to justify my desire to end it all and leave my children with my parents as the thoughtful thing to do. But I couldn't. I asked myself how I would ever support these children. My parents had offered to help me, but they were barely making ends meet themselves, so I always assured them I was fine. Jon's parents had offered me a job with their company, but I definitely refused that offer.

I wrote all these thoughts in my journal, then put it down and read the second meditation. When I read the words "wash away my pride and prejudice and the hurts my pride and prejudice causes others," I started to cry. I sobbed. I couldn't ask my parents for help. I was ashamed. I was humiliated. I was too embarrassed. I wrote my feelings in my journal. "Lord, help me. I am embarrassed. Is this pride?"

Every night that week I read and reflected on the forgiveness meditations. I didn't talk to Maria about it; I was too embarrassed. I was glad when the week was over to move on to the fifth peace secret.

By now, Maria and I met for lunch every Monday, Wednesday, and Friday. I had been reflecting on forgiveness for the last four nights when she told me there was a special journal exercise that went with the forgiveness meditation. But I realized I didn't want to hear it. The forgiveness secret had unmasked a lot of hurt buried in my heart. I couldn't take any more.

Peg with Mary DeCarlo

Peg's brothers and sisters and their spouses

Peg leading a meeting about the Courage of One campaign

Peg attending a business luncheon for Courage of One

Peg on her 75th birthday

Peg and Alice O'Neill

*Peg and Frank O'Neill with their sons, spouses, and
grandchildren (Not pictured is Frank, Jr.)*

Peg speaks at the end of her 75th birthday Mass

Peg and her husband, Frank

Peg and Frank with their six sons

Chapter 21

Kitty Reflects on Forgiveness

"Blessed are the merciful, for they shall be shown mercy."
(Matthew 5:7)

Kitty reread the exercise on forgiveness. She related to Jenny's embarrassment and understood why Jenny didn't want anyone to know about her desperation. Then, thinking about her children and Matt and their situation, she wondered if she was being selfish. Quickly she assured herself she wasn't. She began praising and thanking God for her children. She even praised and thanked God for Matt. Then she went into the kitchen to make some coffee. It was 5:30 a.m.

When she saw the time, her first instinct was to put the book down and get to work. Then she remembered it was Saturday, so she decided to give herself a break. *I've been up all night and I'm not tired. I'm going to relax and finish this book. Caroline is right; it isn't long.*

She sliced peaches, strawberries, and oranges, and put the fresh fruit in a crystal long-stem compote. The sun was rising over the hill as she carried her fruit and coffee out to the breakfast room, bringing the book with her. Through the bay window, she watched the orange sun ascend into the sky, praising and thanking God for this beautiful sight. When it was full daylight, she picked up the book and continued reading Jenny's story:

**

Right from the beginning, I found that the best time for
me to pray was in the evening, after the children went to bed.

There were nights I didn't feel like praying, but Maria encouraged me to give it 30 days. I longed for peace, the kind of peace Maria had. I looked forward to practicing her prayers for 30 days. The 30 days were over and I hadn't learned the fifth secret. I decided to try her peace secrets for another 30 days.

I couldn't wait to learn the prayers for the fifth secret. Maria began as she always did, "Let's take three deep breaths and ask the Holy Spirit to lead us in this prayer so we can be steeped in God's presence." After our deep breathing we said the Prayer of St. Francis together. I liked that prayer better every day. I guess I liked it better because I was beginning to understand it. When we finished the prayer, Maria read the scripture passage John 13:34,

> "Love one another, as I have loved you."

She paused and then read Psalm 30:11,

> "You have changed my sadness into a
> joyful dance. You have taken away my
> sorrow, and surrounded me with joy."

She then began the first meditation.

> "I praise and thank you, Jesus, for soaking
> me in your joy – and washing away any
> sadness or sorrow in my heart."

At first I was distracted. I didn't think about what she was saying. She continued the prayer.

"And washing away any hurts my sadness or sorrow may have caused others."

I heard her the second time she mentioned sadness and sorrow. I was sad and full of sorrow. It was interesting that this meditation came right after the forgiveness one. It was very appropriate.

"I praise and thank you, Lord, for soaking me in your joy and filling my heart with a desire to encourage others to be the person you created them to be and not who I want them to be."

"I need the meditations for the fifth secret," I told Maria. "This prayer might be just for me. I'm always trying to make my children the way I want them to be."

"Jen," Maria said, "that's the curse of being a parent. I think all parents struggle with this one. This next psalm is a big help to parents."

"Indeed, Lord, you love truth in the heart.
Then in the secret of my heart teach me wisdom."

For a moment we both thought about the words. I repeated the words out loud and told Maria, "They are beautiful, consoling words. I need a lot of wisdom. I'm not very good at encouraging others.

"This next and last meditation is on wisdom," she said.

"I praise and thank you, Lord, for soaking me
in your wisdom and washing away all desires
in my heart to control or contradict others."

She paused.

"And washing away all the hurts I have caused
others by trying to control or contradict them."

She was still for a moment.

"I praise and thank you, Lord, for soaking me
in your wisdom and filling me with a desire to
encourage others to be who you created them
to be and not who I want them to be."

Maria gave me her big smile. "You now have all the secrets."

I reviewed the peace secrets with Maria. "The first secret is **P**raise God in all things. The second is **E**njoy the Moment. The third is **A**ppreciate Your Abundance. The fourth is **C**hoose to Forgive, and the fifth is **E**ncourage Others."

Like a proud teacher, Maria was all smiles. "You've got it."

I had one more question. "I understand why Julio wrote the

first meditation, but I really don't understand how he came to pick these five secrets as the key to peace." As usual, our time was running out. Maria said we'd have to talk about this the next time, and closed with the usual prayer.

"Praise and thank you, Lord, for lighting my way as I go through this day spreading your love wherever I go and whatever I do, by encouraging others, one heart, one moment at a time."

**

I decided I would practice the meditations and the peace secrets for another 30 days, and as time passed, so much happened. Maria's car was fixed, so we now drove to work together only once a week. We did manage to have lunch together many days.

The more I practiced the principles, the more I realized the wisdom behind them. The principles are the opposite of turmoil and confusion. We need the virtues in the meditations in order to live the peace principles. The big obstacles to inner or outer peace are the faults we ask God to wash away, such as fear and frustration, anger and anxiety.

When I felt I had to control everything and everyone, I became very uptight. But when I turned the children and my situation over to God, I felt better just knowing someone other than me was watching over my family and my affairs. That's why the meditations for the fifth secret, encourage others, is one of my favorites. I loved the words "wash away my desires to control or contradict others."

One day when Maria and I were having lunch, we began talking about the obstacles to peace. We both agreed that fear and frustration were chief among them. She told me, "We get frustrated when we can't control a person, thing, or situation. That frustration often turns into fear because we think we're being deprived of something we have a right to. When we get into this frame of mind, we miss the blessings in this moment."

Then she said something that got me very upset.

"It's difficult for us to embrace the present moment or appreciate our abundance when we have an illusion that our life will be better after we get a raise, or a new house, or more money, or a vacation, or when the child support check arrives," Maria explained. "These unrealistic expectations set us up for misery.

I just stared at her. Then she said, "For example, you think and hope your financial problems will go away when Jon starts sending you child support. But you don't know that if and when he starts supporting your family things will be better – " Maria suddenly stopped talking and looked at me. "I shouldn't have said that. I'm sorry. I'm talking too much."

"You surprise me. You're usually so gentle."

"I'm sorry. I stepped over the line," Maria apologized.

"Yes, you did, but I probably needed to hear it. You're right. I do blame our financial problems on Jon, and it doesn't make things any better. But if you were in my position you would do the same thing."

"I'm sure I would."

I suddenly felt enraged – not at her, but at Jon. "He has a responsibility to his children. He's their father. I have every right to expect him to support us," I told Maria. My voice kept getting louder. "We made vows. I kept mine. It's not fair. I'm stuck with all the responsibility while he's off drinking somewhere. I'll force him to pay child support if it's the last thing I do."

Maria spoke calmly. "Yes, Jen, he does have responsibilities and he should pay child support. But you can't control his behavior no matter how much you want to. You can only control your behavior. Putting your hopes on him is hindering you from appreciating what you *do* have, and from making your blessings work for you. Do you even know where he is?"

"I don't have a clue, the bastard. I can't believe he's doing this to us. It's not fair. Why should I have to carry this burden alone?" I screamed.

"It isn't fair," Maria agreed. "But life isn't fair. Don't you see, Jen, you can't control his behavior. In principle you're right, but your anger isn't hurting him. It's only hurting you. You're missing the joy of this moment waiting for something to happen that you have no control over; you're hoping that Jon's financial support will change everything. And even if he did come through, it probably wouldn't be enough. You'll still have financial burdens, and you'll still be hurt and angry."

I sulked. "You don't know that."

"No, I don't. I only know from my experience. When I get mad at my mother-in-law for not putting my father-in-law into assisted living, I start thinking she's the cause of our problems. When I think this way, I project on our current misery and wonder how much better we'll be when Papa's in a home. I get so angry. I make myself and everyone around me miserable. When I get into this frame of mind, I'm the loser because I lose the joy of this moment by wasting precious time on something I have no control over."

Maria looked at me. "I know it's not the same as being a single mom with a deadbeat husband," she said with empathy. "But the principle is the same."

I shook my head. "That's easy to say, Maria. But you can't know what it's like for me. I'm scared. I hate Jon for deserting us. At least you have a husband who loves you and cares for your children. I have nobody but me to support and take care of my children."

"You're right," Maria sighed. "And if I was in the same situation, I don't think I could handle it as well as you're handling it. There's no comparison between taking care of my in-laws and being deserted by your husband with no money and four kids to support. I'm sorry if I seemed presumptuous."

I knew she was right but I didn't want to hear it. We didn't speak for a few minutes; then Maria said she probably should go back to work.

As she started to get up, I touched her arm. "Don't go just yet," I pleaded.

She looked at me. "Jenny, I didn't mean to hurt you. I hope you know that."

"You don't have to apologize, because everything you said is true. I guess I just didn't want to face it." I looked at my hands. "I know in my heart I have to move on, but it's so hard. And you're right that when I focus on God's love for me, I feel better. I feel confident that he's taking care of me. It's amazing, the peace I feel. But when I think about Jon, I get angry, uptight, frightened. How can I enjoy the moment when I'm scared?"

"Did the 'I am' and 'I can' exercise help you?" Maria asked.

I thought she was changing the subject, but I told her I got a lot out of it. As a matter of fact, I had two dressmaking jobs from two women at work. "Why do you ask?"

"There is a good journaling exercise for forgiveness, and it might help you be less scared."

I was willing. "If it works like the 'I can' and 'I am' list, I'll try it. What is it?"

She told me to turn my journal sideways and make three columns, then write the word "Hurt" as the heading for the first column. Then I should head the second column "What are my blessings" and the third column "What did I do to hurt others?" She suggested that I list all the things that Jon did that hurt me, and to leave lots of space between the hurts. In the second column next to each hurt, I was to write a blessing I received *because* of this hurt.

I stopped her. "Where are you going with this?" I asked. "It sounds like a wacko idea."

She laughed. She said it was wacko but very powerful.

"What do I write in the last column?" I asked.

"You reflect on your hurt. You reflect on your blessings, then you reflect on what you did to someone else that hurt them the way Jon hurt you."

I was indignant at her suggestion that I'd hurt people the way Jon hurt me. I told her I'd never deserted anyone, never shirked my responsibilities. As usual she ignored my resistance. She encouraged me, "It really helps to free us from all the hurts that are imprisoning us." I didn't like the words she was using, but I did feel imprisoned.

Maria's ideas had all helped me, so I reluctantly tried the exercise. I listed all the hurts Jon inflicted on me. But I just couldn't think of even one blessing, and I'd definitely never done to anyone what he did to me. I put the exercise aside and didn't go back to it until several months later.

I practiced the peace process for more than eight months and had noticed that there was a formula to the meditations. I praised God, then I asked Him to help me by washing away the obstacles to peace, and then I listened for his inspiration and wrote it down.

I called it PAL: Praise, Ask, Listen. I put aside special time every day to spend with God. I was so excited I couldn't wait to tell Maria. She hadn't picked up on the formula, and she was as excited about my discovery as I was. From that time on we talked about our PAL method when we talked about the peace secrets and our prayer time.

**

My life changed so much in those eight months. I finally got the courage to ask my parents for help with my mortgage payments, and they did it in a way that I didn't feel like I was mooching off them.

I began cooking better meals for the children, and I insisted we sit down at the kitchen table and eat dinner together. At first the kids resisted, but they accepted it. I was also getting a strong urge to share the peace principles with them. Finally one night I suggested we go around the table and everyone share one thing in his life that he was grateful for.

J.J. rolled his eyes and gave me a totally bored, disgusted look. He made a crack about me trying to force him to pretend everything was okay. Rachael did the same, but Rebecca and Sara were enthusiastic. They were so cute. Sara said she was grateful for all her family. She asked J.J. if he was grateful for her. He reluctantly said, "I guess I am."

I couldn't wait to share my progress with Maria. One day when we were having lunch, I was so overjoyed with all the things that were happening in my life, I had to share them.

"Maria, when we first met and I was complaining that God never listened to me, you said that maybe our meeting was His answer to my prayer. I now know He did hear my prayer and He sent you to help me. I am so grateful to you and your friend Julio and your friend at the bank where I have my mortgage. I praise and thank God every day for all three of you."

Maria reached over and gave me a big hug. "I do the same thing for you," she said. "You'll never know how much you've helped me."

We both started to laugh. "Thanks to you, Maria, whenever I feel inadequate, I get out my gift list and quickly review it, and thank God for each gift," I said. "Every morning I lift my talents and gifts up to God in prayer. I review how I can use them to bring peace and love to my family and everyone I meet this day. It makes everything I do so much easier."

I told her, "This is my eighth month. I'm seeing a difference in my life and in the way people treat me. Even the kids are seeing a difference; my boss, too. He's given me more responsibility and a raise."

"That's wonderful," Maria giggled. "Isn't God marvelous? He's constantly showering us with miracles."

"Yes, God is wonderful, " I agreed. I told her I'd initially had trouble accepting the fact that our behavior stems from either feelings of love or fear. I told her I now know that it is so true. "Remember several months ago you told me I was so obsessed with getting Jon to meet his obligations that I was missing opportunities to help my children become more self-reliant? You were right. We never sat down together for a meal.

"Now we have dinner together every night. At first the children didn't like the discipline but now they enjoy it." I was so excited telling her this I had to giggle. "Every night we talk about the peace principle of the week. This week we're talking about appreciating our abundance and our gifts. Last week I asked each of the children to talk about a precious moment that had taken place during their day and how they enjoyed the moment. This week I'm asking them what gift they experienced and how it helped someone else. It's exciting to hear what they say."

"That's a great idea," Maria said beaming. "I'm going to try that with my children. They're younger than yours, but this is a good thing for little children to learn."

I admitted to her that the kids had difficulty with the abundance idea. "But they're beginning to see," I added. "Some nights are better than others. J.J. thinks I'm a Pollyanna. I try to send him love but sometimes I'm seething inside." I could feel my jaws clench when I talked about J.J.'s attitude. "He sounds so much like his father it scares me."

Maria shook her head. "You've come so far. I don't have teenagers but I can just imagine their attitude about appreciating their abundance."

"That's when praising and thanking helps," I said. "You were right; it's not easy. Lots of times I'm so angry I don't want to praise and thank God. Teenagers can really push you to your limit." We both laughed.

"But I've promised myself that I will praise God for everything. At first I was sure I wouldn't pray or praise after the first 30 days, and now I'm at the end of my eighth month. I do see a difference in my outlook on life. And, thanks to you, Maria, I do feel better about myself – and I might even try the forgiveness exercise."

I surprised even myself with the last comment, but I realized it was true.

Chapter 22

Decision

"You will have pain, but your pain will turn into joy."

(John 16:20)

Kitty put the book down. She rested her head against the chair and thought about Jenny. *She is such a Pollyanna. With all her problems, how could she possibly think she had abundance? It's misleading to let children think everything is okay when it really isn't. I've got it much better than Jenny, but at least Jenny had a job.* Kitty looked at her watch. She couldn't believe it was almost 6:30 a.m.

She took her empty dish into the kitchen, washed it, and put it away. Then she took a long-stemmed wine goblet out of the freezer and pushed it up against the water dispenser on the refrigerator. She placed a lemon wedge on the side of the glass and went back to her book.

**

Maria and I continued meeting twice a week for lunch. I was now into my eighth month of practicing the PEACE principles. Passion for God's presence within; Enjoy the moment; Appreciate your abundance; Choose to forgive; and Encourage others.

Meanwhile, Maria found herself having some difficulty implementing the courage-to-forgive idea. Her father-in-law's condition was growing progressively worse. Her mother-in-law wouldn't even discuss the possibility of putting him in a long-term-care home. Maria's husband, José, and his brothers and sisters took turns spending the night with their parents. José's father was usually agitated. He roamed the house at night, yelling and cursing. The children were concerned for their mother's safety and health.

One day Maria asked, "Jen, how are you making out on forgiveness? I was doing great for a while," she continued, not allowing me to answer, "but I'm having a real hard time with forgiveness. I'm so angry at my mother- and father-in-law. They're selfish. We're all exhausted. My father-in-law takes off and disappears for hours. This last time he got on a train and went into town, and we didn't find him for two days. This is the third time he's disappeared like that, and he's getting violent. The frustrations are so great, and he doesn't want my mother-in-law handling the money or telling him what he can or can't do."

"That's a tough one," I agreed. "It's harder to forgive when the person irritating you is always around doing the same thing over and over again. I think our situations are very different."

"Tell me what you do," Maria requested. "You seem more at peace, and you have a lot to be angry about."

Her words made me think. "It's funny, but I'm just realizing how angry I really am. I think we have to identify with our anger in order to forgive. I'm really working on the forgiveness secret. I did what you told me to do. I followed the forgiveness exercise and it works. First I praised and thanked God for Jon and our relationship. Then I listed all the ways that Jon hurt the children and me. Then I went back and looked for blessings from each of those experiences. I'm still working on it." I got a little weepy telling her about my experience.

"Let's not talk about it," Maria suggested.

"No, it's okay," I said as I wiped my eyes and got myself under control. "I want to talk about it. You won't believe how much this exercise has helped me forgive."

"Do you think that listing all the things he did to hurt you helped you?" Maria asked.

"That was the first part. It was the second and third parts

that were hard but really helpful. Have you tried the forgiveness exercise yet?" I asked her.

Maria admitted she'd skipped it. "Up until now, I wasn't feeling enough anger toward any one particular person," she confessed, "so I couldn't make a list of painful experiences. I guess I wasn't being honest with myself."

I had to laugh. "You were so forceful about me doing it and you never did it!"

Maria looked a little sheepish. "I was forceful because I thought it would help you move on. I knew if I told you I had never done it, you wouldn't either."

"I put it aside for a few months after you explained it to me," I admitted. "I don't like to leave things unfinished, but I just couldn't do it. I almost quit the whole program because of it, but I finally began making my forgiveness list in the fourth month."

Then I started to giggle. I told her about when I first tried to focus on having the choice to forgive. "I changed the word 'choose' to 'courage' because it does take courage to forgive. I looked at the list of hurts Jon had caused me. I looked at the "blessings" column. It was empty. That's when I got the idea to review my "I can" and "I am" list. I realized a lot of the things on that list were a result of me having to take care of my children without Jon. I began thinking about all the things that the children are now doing and that God is able to bring good out of the bad things that happen to us.

"And I was filled with gratitude. I praised and thanked God for my sight, health, the order in my life, and my ability to read and comprehend things, my ability to make beautiful clothes. The more I praised and thanked God for these gifts, the more I began to realize that they were blessings I never appreciated before Jon left."

"That's awesome," Maria said.

"I started to write. I couldn't stop listing all the blessings the children have received over the past year. J.J. is a busboy at the Roadhouse. He's met two wonderful businessmen who are mentoring him. One sweet man wants to hire him for the summer.

"He's proud of himself. He wouldn't have this job if he didn't need the money. Rebecca has a babysitting job with the Scott family, and they've taken her on two trips. She loves the children and she's learning so much about art and music. The two younger children are learning the joys of being grateful for all they have. The best part is the family dinners. My family is much closer since I started working on my inner peace. We discuss the steps to peace every night at dinner. It's fun and it gives us something very positive to discuss."

"You do seem much happier than you were when we first met."

I nodded. "Before you taught me the peace principles, I felt sorry for the kids so I didn't ask them to help around the house. That was a mistake. Now everyone helps. The older children cook one night a week." I had to laugh. "Sometimes it's horrendous, but we have fun. I have to bite my tongue, turn my perfectionist nature over to God, and let them do things their way. It's killing me, but I'm determined. And J.J. and Rebecca give me 15 percent of their earnings every week. It really helps. I'm not struggling like I was. For the most part, I manage to juggle all my responsibilities with a calm and peaceful heart."

"Jen, that's so exciting," Maria exclaimed. "The shoe's on the other foot. When we first met, I thought I was helping you. Now you're helping me. Tell me more about the third part of the exercise."

"Oh, yes," I said wryly. "Listing all the ways I hurt people the same way Jon hurt me – I hate that part. It's hard because I have to be honest with myself. That's why I changed the name from 'choose to forgive' to 'courage to forgive.' I always believed I would never cop out on my responsibilities or desert anyone. But I began to recognize that, although the circumstances were very different, I too deserted people in my life."

Maria looked at me with a puzzled look. "How did you possibly hurt other people like Jon hurt you?"

"I realized I'd deserted my friends. I have three close friends who I never see or call anymore. I'm too busy with my own problems. I assumed they had happy, well-ordered lives, but in reality I don't know if that's true. I really deserted them," I confessed to her.

"Wow," Maria piped in, "that's profound. I never thought about that. Maybe I'm cutting my mother-in-law off when she needs me most."

"You might be," I said. I told her I was beginning to realize I'd also unintentionally hurt my parents: I didn't keep in touch with them as often as I should, so we had planned a trip to visit them. "They were excited, but at the last minute I decided not to go." I was choking up just thinking about it.

"Are you okay, Jen?" Maria asked, reaching for my hand.

I nodded. "Just give me a minute," I said as I wiped my eyes. Then I exclaimed to her, "I didn't go because I didn't have any money, and I was embarrassed. I convinced myself I wasn't going because I didn't want to worry them, but I was too proud to tell them I was broke. I was ashamed. They're helping me with my mortgage now, and I didn't want them to feel I needed any more help. To save my own pride I hurt my parents."

I never told anyone anything about my personal life, and I didn't know why I was baring my soul to Maria.

"Did you get all these insights about yourself from doing the forgiveness exercise?" Maria asked.

I told her I felt that these insights about me are also gifts from Jon's behavior. Even the forgiveness process was a gift. "Self-discovery and self-honesty are extremely painful, but when I follow through and persist, I find it is an adventure in love. It's unbelievable how freeing it is."

Maria was pensive. She looked at me. "It's amazing how much you've grown in a few short months," she said.

I squeezed her hand. "Maria, I owe you so much. I had hit bottom when I met you. I was depressed. I didn't know what to do or where to turn; I dreaded getting up. I was frightened for my children. But I see everything differently now. And the kids are getting so much out of this. I don't have to struggle to juggle all my responsibilities like I used to." I was even tempted to tell her about the sleeping pills, but I decided not to.

Maria looked at her watch. "Time's up," she announced. "We have to go." We hugged each other and rushed back to work.

**

The more I practiced the peace process, the more I realized that enjoying the moment, appreciating blessings, choosing to forgive, and encouraging others are interrelated. Each secret reinforced the others, and praising and thanking God is the key to living the secrets. I was excited watching my children grow closer to God and to one another. They had more confidence in themselves and they were happier.

At first I didn't realize how much I was energizing them by encouraging them to focus on the weekly peace secrets. Although I was open and honest with them about the secrets and prayers, I didn't share with them the most important secret: praising and thanking God in all things.

I kept praising God and asking Him to give me the courage to teach my children the power of praising Him. I'd listen for His inspiration. I kept writing in my journal, "Be not afraid, I am with you." I knew that was true because I wasn't struggling like I used to. I was juggling all my responsibilities with confidence. I was making enough money to pay my bills and my mortgage. I watched my children blossom, and I was happy, really happy, for the first time in years. But for some reason I was afraid to mention praising God to my children.

Finally one night I mustered up the courage to suggest to the children that they praise and thank God for their father. I was nervous. I'd start to say something about praise and I'd change my mind. Finally I blurted out, "I have an idea."

The kids had been chatting to one another, and they stopped talking and looked at me. J.J. gave me his usual disgusted look, but I kept on.

"Why don't we go around the table and everyone praise and thank God for your dad?" My heart was racing, my palms were sweaty. I took a deep breath.

I was shocked when they all agreed it was a wonderful idea, except J.J. "Me first," Sara piped in. "Praise and thank you, God, for my daddy and the way he used to carry me on his shoulders. Dear God, if you know where Daddy is, put him on your shoulders and carry him home to us."

The girls and I all had tears in our eyes. Each child praised out loud. Like Sara's, their prayers were deep and very touching, though J.J. sort of grunted his.

From that night forward, we spent the first few minutes before dinner praising and thanking God for our abundance and for Jon. The children praised and thanked God for taking care of their father, even though they couldn't see it. I was deeply touched. Their prayers were beautiful, simple, and loving.

One night, several weeks after the children began praising and thanking God for their father, I was in bed thinking about our family's dinner routine. I felt a wonderful warm glow flow through me. Somehow I knew everything would work out. I was deep in thought when J.J. came into my room.

"Mom, are you asleep?" he asked.

"Come in, honey," I answered. "I'm just lying here thinking."

J.J. was still intolerant of me and everything I did. I tensed up when I saw him. He seldom wanted to talk to me. When he did, it was usually to tell me about all the things I did wrong.

"Can we talk?" he asked. Asking for permission to talk wasn't like J.J. He usually blurted out what was on his mind without any thought of the consequences. His sharp tongue cut right to the heart.

I praised and thanked God under my breath as I sat up and wrapped my arms around my knees. I motioned for J.J. to sit on the side of my bed, an invitation he usually declined. Much to my surprise, he came over and sat next to me without any hesitation.

He looked down at the floor and started mumbling, having a hard time trying to say what was on his mind. "Mom ... um ... ah ... I'm proud of you," he blurted out while looking at the floor. "I'm proud to have you for a mom. We're lucky kids. I just had to tell you." He raised his head and looked into my eyes. His blue eyes were red and swollen. It was obvious he had been crying.

We stared at each other. I didn't know what to say. This was so unlike J.J. Instinctively I stretched my arms out to him and he fell into them. We squeezed each other. He sobbed and sobbed. I just held him. Finally he said,

"Mom, I was furious with Dad for leaving us. But I was more furious with you. I blamed Dad's leaving on you. I didn't want to think Dad deserted us. Whenever you got upset about not getting your child support, I hated you. I couldn't wait to get out of here. I was trying to find Dad so I could move in with him."

I didn't say a word. I held him and let him talk.

"I'm sorry, Mom. I'm so proud of you. You had the guts to stick to your peace secrets. I was embarrassed every time I heard you talk about peace secrets. But it works. You helped us see what a wonderful life we have. When you asked us to praise and thank God for Dad, I couldn't believe it. I thought, 'Here she goes again. When is she going to stop doing this to us?' But tonight when we started thanking God for Dad, I got such a warm feeling for him. I never felt that way about anyone." He lifted his head and looked at me.

"When I went to my room," he continued, "I couldn't stop crying. I was overwhelmed with admiration for you. I kept thinking, 'Yeah! She's got what it takes. Thank you, God, she's my mom.' You had the guts to share all this stuff with us, even though we made fun of you and gave you a hard time. I hate to admit it but it's changed me, Mom." He started to cry again, but he kept talking.

"You know, Tom Finnegan's dad deserted them," J.J. shared. "He and I bad-mouth and complain about our dads. I don't want to do that anymore. I know everything is going to work out for us. It sounds crazy, but I know it inside. Dad will be okay, I just know it."

J.J. and I talked for almost two hours. He asked me many questions about his dad. He wanted to know how we met, what he was like then, when he changed, why he was the way he was. I tried to answer him as honestly as I could, explaining that I didn't have the answers to all of his questions. The moment was precious, until he asked me why Jon's parents, the Solomons, never called or came to see us anymore.

I tensed up. I was feeling so good about our talk until he asked me that. I just shrugged my shoulders like I didn't know why. I knew if I told him that they tried to call but I wouldn't answer, I would turn him off. I was a coward. I didn't want him to turn against me again.

I gave him a goodnight hug. "I love you, Jonny. I know you don't like me to call you that, but you'll always be Jonny to me."

He laughed. "I love you too, Mom. You can call me Jonny; you deserve to call me anything you want."

When he got to the door, he turned around and looked at me. "By the way, Grandpop and Grandmom Solomon and I e-mail back and forth several times a week. They always ask for you." He ran off to his room.

I panicked. I wonder if they told him that they sent him birthday cards. Did they tell him they tried to call and I wouldn't let them talk to the kids?

I thought about the last two hours with J.J. and began praising and thanking God and asking Him to help me do the right thing about Jon's parents.

I hoped J.J. was right about his father. The first few years of our marriage, Jon was a wonderful husband. Then he began drinking heavily. He'd probably had a drinking problem when we were in college but had kept it hidden. He was also diagnosed as bipolar, which worried me about our children and heredity. It's funny, I had not even thought about the possibility of one of the children being bipolar since I started my peace program.

I sighed, smiled, and said aloud, "God, that's one more thing you'll have to take care of. You'll have to work out this grandparent thing." Then I fell asleep.

**

Kitty put a bookmark in the book, stood up, and stretched her arms toward the ceiling with the volume in her left hand. She switched the book to her right hand and stretched again. She put it on the table, did a few more stretches, stood up straight, and again picked up *The Peace Way*. Holding it, she thought about Caroline's words: "If you get to the point that you have nowhere else to turn, you might try the secrets for 30 days."

And with that, Kitty repeated to herself her decision. *What do I have to lose? I might be as lucky as Caroline. This time I'm going to persevere.*

She put down the book and went up to shower and dress.

Chapter 23

Kitty Receives a Miracle

"Your heavenly Father knows all that you need.
Seek you first His kingdom over you, His way of holiness,
and all those things will be given you beside."

(Matthew 6: 33-34)

Kitty kept her commitment. She faithfully woke up a half hour earlier and praised and thanked God for her life exactly as it was. She followed the peace secret meditations in the book, practicing one secret a week and saying the prayers for that secret every day. She focused on the words and how they related to her life. Although she found it difficult at first, she praised and thanked God for every situation she encountered, and it worked. She felt better about herself and her situation.

She also followed Caroline's advice and praised and thanked God for finding a place to live. Whenever she started to panic about where she was going to move, she praised and thanked God. Her children and friends were impressed with her calm demeanor.

She cheerfully dove into managing the move while making light of her situation. Every evening she scanned the apartment rental ads, searching for something affordable. Two weeks remained before she and Matt had to be out of their home.

Kitty and Susan helped separate Kitty's things into three categories: boxes for storage, things to give away, and the items she'd need to use on a daily basis.

"I really can't make these decisions until I know where I'm living," Kitty said with a sigh. She was standing in the living room amidst boxes when the phone rang. "Susan, be a dear and answer that, please," she said to her daughter. "If it's for me, I'll call them back."

Kitty could hear Susan talking on the phone; she couldn't help but wonder who was on the other end of the line. Then she heard Susan say, "I know Mom will want to talk to you. Let me get her." Kitty clenched her fists and mumbled, "I praise and thank you, Lord, for Susan. I told her I didn't want to talk on the phone." She sighed. "Oh well, praise and thank you, Lord."

Susan came running into the room. "Mom, you'll never guess what's happened. Mrs. Frenche is on the phone. She just heard you got a great offer on the house and you have to be out by the end of July. The Frenches are going to Italy for six months and she was wondering if you'd consider living in their townhouse until they return. She's waiting on the phone."

Kitty looked at her daughter. "You're not kidding?"

"Mom, she's on hold!"

Kitty picked up the phone. "Hello, Elsia," she said in a warm voice. "Susan said you're going to Italy for half a year. That's wonderful. No, we don't have a place to live. We didn't expect to sell the house so soon. That's very sweet of you. Your call's an answer to my prayers. Yes, we'd love to stay in your townhouse till you get back. That gives us time to find our own place."

When Kitty hung up, she and Susan hugged. They danced around the living room. "Praise and thank you, Lord," Kitty kept saying. "Susan, this is like a miracle. Their townhouse is gorgeous."

"Call Dad and tell him," Susan urged her mother.

Kitty stopped dancing. "Yes, I should call your father. I wonder what he'll say. It's funny that it's Mr. and Mrs. Frenche helping us through this, even though they don't know it. I first met your dad at a frat party. When he shook my hand, I got goose bumps all over. He was a big football hero and I was a lowly high school junior. It was a quick introduction," Kitty reminisced.

"I didn't see him again until Christmas, when I met him at Mr. and Mrs. Frenche's annual Christmas party. They were close friends of my parents, although they were younger. And Mrs. Frenche was your Grandmother Murphy's best friend. That was the night your dad asked me for a date."

Kitty sighed, then smiled. "It's funny, Susan, I never expected to meet your dad at the Frenches' house. He was from West Philadelphia. I thought he was really cute, but I didn't think my parents would approve of me going out with an Irish Catholic. But when they met him at the Frenches', they never gave a thought about him being a city kid or Irish Catholic. They liked him from the first moment they met him. The rest is history." She sighed.

"Mom, why don't you call Dad now?" Susan persisted.

"I'd rather wait," Kitty replied. "It all happened so fast. I need to think about it. Don't be disappointed, I'll tell him tonight. It's getting late and we still have to decide what goes into storage and what doesn't. We'll only need our clothes and a few personal things to move into the Frenche's townhouse."

Matt hadn't said anything more about divorce, and Kitty was hoping he might change his mind now that the Frenches' townhouse was available. She wanted the opportunity to discuss it with him face-to-face. In her heart she knew they probably needed a break from each other. Their relationship was volatile. But she was hoping they could live together.

Kitty was delighted at Matt's reaction to moving into the Frenches' home. He thought it was a good idea. "We can both live there," Kitty added.

"Let me sleep on it," was his response. But the next morning, he told her he was getting a place in town.

She watched wistfully as her husband exited the driveway. She prayed, "Lord, help me get through this. I praise and thank you, Lord, for this sad moment." Tears rolled down her cheeks. She gazed out the window. *I must get myself together.*

She wiped her eyes and moved toward the phone. *I'll call and get my plane reservations for California,* she decided. She had promised her Uncle Chip she would visit him in California at the end of the month. Kitty had never purchased an airline ticket; Matt's secretary, Terri, always took care of that, but she didn't want to call Terri.

She got the number for the airline from information, and realized she'd be traveling clear across the country alone – something she'd never done. She got very nervous.

Making an airline reservation was much more tedious than she had anticipated. Waiting on hold while the agent looked up different flights irritated Kitty. Holding the phone to her ear, she straightened things around the house. By the time the agent came back to the phone, Kitty's patience had worn thin and she gave her a tongue-lashing. The woman calmly tried to explain to Kitty what kept her, but Kitty slammed the phone down before she finished. She immediately regretted her behavior.

She again dialed the airline and started the entire process over. The agent gave her several choices. Once Kitty decided on a flight, the rep asked for a credit card number.

Kitty's attitude switched from arrogance to panic. *Is my card any good? I can't live without my American Express.* She and Matt hadn't discussed any of this.

She felt a chill run through her body. Until now she hadn't thought about credit cards. *You can't do anything without them. What am I going to do? Damn Matt! He has to help me.*

Then she caught herself. She took three deep breaths and repeated to herself, "There's peace in this moment." She thanked God for the gift of this moment and His unconditional love. She repeated to herself, "I am growing and prospering in this moment."

As she repeated her affirmation, the airline representative patiently waited. Finally she asked, "Mrs. Murphy, what type of credit card will you be using?"

"Just a moment, I have to find it," Kitty muttered. "Thank you, Lord, for my credit card. Thank you for the peace in this moment. Thank you for taking care of me," she whispered to herself. She rummaged through her purse for her wallet, pulled out her gold Amex card, took a deep breath, and gave the number to the woman. Her heart pounded while she waited. It seemed like hours. Then the agent thanked her, reviewed her reservation, and asked if there was anything else she could do. Kitty was triumphant. *You did it! You made your own reservations. That wasn't so bad.*

Kitty planned a special dinner for the family's last night in their home, but Matt didn't join them. Kitty, Doug, and Susan ate by the pool. "Mom," Susan said, "you deserve a pat on the back for the superb way you've handled this move. I can't believe how calm you've remained in spite of some very upsetting things. I'm impressed."

"I second that," agreed Doug.

Kitty almost told them about her peace book, but she decided against it. She thanked the children and served dinner. It was a bittersweet moment. They reminisced about all the fun and celebrations they had in the house. There were long moments of silence, each of them lost in private memories. Finally Kitty told them, "I've decided to go to California and visit Uncle Chip next week. I'll be settled in the new house. The break will be good for me."

Susan and Doug agreed. "It'll give you a chance to visit Ken," Doug said. "I'm sure he's a little homesick." They tried to be cheerful.

Matt arrived just as they were finishing dinner. He tried kidding around, but the moment was obviously painful for him. He finally said goodnight and went to bed. Doug and Susan helped their mother clean up before they left.

The next morning, the movers arrived at 7:00 to take the furniture and items going into storage, while Kitty, Sadie, and Susan packed Kitty's things in Doug's SUV.

Susan stayed at the house with the movers while Doug and Sadie helped Kitty move into the townhouse. Matt had taken most of his belongings that morning. Doug took the rest of his father's things to his apartment later that day.

Sadie stayed at the Frenches' townhouse getting things in order, and Susan went out to get some lunch for everyone while Kitty and Doug did a last-minute check on the house. It was 2 p.m. and the house was completely empty. Kitty and Doug took one more walk through the vacant house. It looked so different. It was empty, eerie, and cold. Doug put his arm across his mother's shoulders.

"It's a new chapter in your life, Mom," he said. "You'll see; it's going to be exciting." He hugged her and they shed a few tears.

Kitty gently pushed away. "I'm sorry, honey; it does hurt." She took a handkerchief from her bag and wiped Doug's eyes. "Yes, you're right," she said softly. "It's a new chapter. I'm not sure how exciting it'll be, but I've learned one thing: God does have a plan for all of us. I don't know what it is, but I do know it'll all work out for the good."

They walked out the front door of their home for the last time. Mother and son said good-bye, turned in opposite directions, and walked to their cars.

Chapter 24

A New Beginning

"Blessed are the poor in spirit, for theirs is the kingdom of heaven."
(Matthew 5: 1-3)

When Kitty returned to the townhouse, soft music was playing and freshly made sandwiches were on the kitchen counter with a note signed, "Love you, Mom. ~Susan."

Sadie was vacuuming one of the bedrooms. Kitty praised and thanked God for all her blessings, especially her children.

She suddenly felt empowered as she looked around her new home. She had always run a well-ordered household, but these past six weeks had been trying. It was different from anything she'd ever done before.

The sudden rush of joy she felt took her by surprise. She praised and thanked God for helping her handle the pressure of the move. She felt good about the way she organized everything to make the move smooth and quick. She felt good about making her own plane reservations. And most of all, Kitty was proud of the way she felt about herself. And she was equally proud of Susan.

Thank you, Lord, for taking care of me. I appreciate it. She felt good about Sadie, who was more than a housekeeper; she was a dear friend. "Sadie, what would I ever do without you?" Kitty said as she put her arms around her and gave her a kiss. "Thank you for being here. You made this move so much easier."

Sadie's eyes filled with tears. "Kitty, child, you know I'd do anything for you. You're my family," she responded. They hugged and laughed.

Sadie and Kitty walked around the elegant townhouse. "It's beautiful!" Sadie gasped. "It's beautiful, just like you, Kitty."

Yes, it's beautiful, but very different. Classical music played softly in the background. "Well, Sadie, it's home for now."

Sadie was quiet as she looked around. Kitty had never told her that she and Matt were separating. But Sadie, who didn't miss much, asked, "Where are Matt's clothes?"

Kitty suddenly felt deflated, frail, and frightened. "We're separating for a while," she whispered. This was the first time she had spoken about it as an absolute. She felt as if she were talking about someone else. She was relieved when Sadie acknowledged her with a quiet, "Oh," and didn't say anything more about it.

"Well," Sadie suggested quickly, "let's unpack these last two boxes." They worked side by side, lost in their own thoughts and saying little to each other.

The townhouse was already furnished with the Frenches' furniture, so emptying the boxes was fairly simple. Kitty placed her books, pictures, and a few precious china pieces around the living room and den. It was 4:30 in the afternoon when the last item of clothing was hung up in the closet. By 5:00, the townhouse looked very *Kitty.*

When it was time to take Sadie home, Kitty felt lonely. She didn't want to see her leave. She wrapped sandwiches for Sadie to take with her.

"Are you going to be all right here by yourself, Kit?" asked Sadie. "Let me call Susan and Doug and tell them to come over tonight."

Trying to hold back tears, Kitty looked at her, straightened up, smiled, and reassured Sadie she'd be fine. "I'm having dinner with Caroline tonight," she told Sadie. "She's bringing something over to celebrate my first night here. That's why I want you to take the sandwiches."

Kitty drove Sadie home, and when she arrived back at her new house there was a vase of multicolored roses-- just like she had in her garden-- at the front door. *How sweet.* She assumed they were from Matt. She opened the card.

> "I hope these roses from the garden at your house
> brighten your spirits as well as your new home. If I
> can do anything for you, please call me. – Sophia."

"How thoughtful!" Kitty exclaimed, as she wiped her eyes. She tried to call Sophia but as usual she got her answering machine and left a message.

Then she turned on her favorite Mozart CD, *The Symphonies*, and the music filled the townhouse. *Great. They have the music wired throughout the entire house. It's really cozy.*

She took out her mother's favorite cream linen tablecloth and hugged it close to her heart. Her mother had given her the tablecloth when she and Matt were getting married. She could still see her mom caressing it while telling Kitty the story behind it.

"My mother gave me this cloth when I married your father," Kitty's mom had told her. "I save it for romantic dinners with just your dad and me." She kissed Kitty, telling her how much she loved her and how thrilled she was that her daughter was marrying Matt. "Whenever you and Matt have a romantic candlelight dinner and enjoy the luxurious feel of this cloth, think of your dad and me."

Kitty held the cloth closer to her cheek while she thought about her mother. "I miss you, Mom. I hope you're with me now. I need you," she said out loud. She carefully placed the cloth over the rosewood dining table. She set the roses in the middle of the table, laid two places, lit the candles in the living room, sat down on the big wing chair, and tried to enjoy the peace.

In spite of the music and the beauty all around her, Kitty was alone and lonely. *Oh Lord, thank you for this special moment with you. Thank you for the courage to face this new chapter in my life. Thank you for your presence. I know you're with me.* She opened her notebook and wrote down all her blessings.

Chapter 25

Compassion

"His heart was moved with pity for them because
they were troubled and abandoned."

(Matthew 9:36)

The doorbell startled Kitty from her thoughts. Wiping the tears, she slowly moved toward the door.

"Hello, Miss Independent," Caroline announced. "I'm honored to be your first guest." She hugged Kitty. "How are you?" She looked into Kitty's eyes. "It hurts, huh?" she said sympathetically.

"A little," Kitty admitted. "I can't believe this is me. God and me." She tried to smile but her spirits were low.

Caroline held up a takeout bag from Kitty's favorite restaurant. "Well, I have your favorite grilled salmon salad and this wonderful bottle of white wine," she said, hugging Kitty again. "We're celebrating a new beginning tonight. I have good vibes about it. I think you and Matt will be entering into a new phase that'll be more wonderful than before."

Caroline raved about the beautiful roses, and Kitty explained that Sophia had gathered them from Kitty's garden and left them at her front door.

Caroline nodded her head. "Sophia is a very compassionate woman. She hasn't had an easy life."

"I feel badly I gave her such a hard time."

"She understands," Caroline explained. "When people have to sell their house but don't want to, they often take it out on the realtor."

"I guess I better praise and thank God for Sophia; she did do a wonderful job."

During dinner, they talked about the PEACE process and their personal growth. "Tell me, Caroline," Kitty asked, "do you regret giving up your work?"

Caroline laughed. "At first, I felt lonely, almost like a failure. Not now. I'm happier than I've ever been. And I don't miss the guilt. I'll never forget missing Amy's Christmas play or Chuck's state championship game or Malcolm's derby race. I was a prisoner to my business. I sacrificed my family for my career."

"I never thought about that," Kitty said.

"I doubt I would have discovered God's love for me if I hadn't quit working," Caroline said. She sighed. "You know, Kit, Malcolm talked me into quitting my job. He's such a good kid. He's never given us an ounce of trouble. He put me wise to Chuck's problems."

"Malcolm's always been very mature," Kitty noted, taking a bit of salmon. "And he knows just how to handle Nick and you."

"It's funny how things turn out, isn't it, Kit?" Caroline looked out the large bay window. "I wanted to be a success *for* Malcolm. When he was born, I promised myself he would never be poor. He'd be rich. He'd call the shots. People would cater to his wishes. No one would ever take advantage of him. Then, after 22 years, I find out he hated me working and never being home."

Kitty glanced at Caroline. She had never heard her friend talk this way. She'd always felt there was a secret story behind Malcolm and Caroline's life before Nick, but Caroline never talked about it.

"Don't worry about Malcolm. He doesn't seem to be worried about anyone taking advantage of him. Nick loves him like he is his own son," Kitty commented.

Caroline gave a small smile. "I know that now. But when he was born, I was terrified that he'd end up being treated like me. I was treated like I was nothing," she confessed. "That's why I called him Malcolm, after Malcolm Forbes."

"Malcolm Forbes!" Kitty gasped. "How clever. I assumed Malcolm was his father's name. But, Caroline, everyone loves Malcolm. He's gracious and smart. He's a very special person."

"Oh, I don't worry about him," Caroline acknowledged. "I'm so proud of him." She took a bite of salad and chewed thoughtfully. "Kit, have you ever wondered who Malcolm's father is? You know, I've never told anyone about my life with Malcolm's father."

"I'd be lying if I said I haven't wondered," admitted Kitty. "The thought has crossed my mind a few times. Do you want to talk about it?"

"I was the perfect child growing up," Caroline said laughing. "I was a tomboy. I could outplay the boys in street hockey and outwit them in gin rummy. I was a good student, too. I won a scholarship to New York University, but there was a part of me that wanted to live on the cutting edge. I kept it in check during high school, but that urge for excitement got me into big trouble in the middle of my freshman year at college.

"Unfortunately, I met a 43-year-old bachelor playboy who swept me off my feet. He wined and dined me with champagne lunches at the Ritz and dinners at Le Cirque. He took me to the theater, opera, and Club Fifty-Six. We had a passionate love affair.

"I threw caution to the wind, quit school, and moved in with Mark. I was traveling with the rich and famous. He introduced me to cocaine. We drank and partied all night and slept most of the day. He had a penthouse on Park Avenue. I thought I was set for life."

Kitty listened intently, her dinner forgotten for the moment. She looked at Caroline with amazement.

"At first, everything was exciting and glorious," Caroline continued. "Then I got pregnant. That was the first hint of Mark's vicious temper. He threw me across the room; he cursed me and insisted I get an abortion. He threw a thousand dollars on the floor and told me not to come back until I was 'fixed.' I was devastated. But I couldn't stand the thought of losing him.

"I was confused. I thought he loved me. I did what he wanted. But we never recaptured our passion. Reality set in. We had violent fights. We would throw things, yell and scream at each other, and then we'd make passionate love. I got pregnant again. But this time, I refused to have an abortion." Tears welled in her eyes.

"He threw me out like I was garbage. He wouldn't take my calls. I had no money, no place to live, and no clothes. He changed the locks.

He wouldn't even let me come back and get my things. I had to live in a woman's shelter in New York City. Fortunately, I was able to get a job as a clerk in an advertising office." She wiped her eyes again. "It was so many years ago. I don't know why I'm getting upset. I guess it's because I never really talked about it to anyone, until now."

Kitty reached out and touched Caroline's hand. "Don't talk about it if it's too upsetting," she offered.

"I want to talk about it, if you don't mind listening."

"I'm fascinated," Kitty said warmly. "It helps me to understand you better."

"Malcolm was the light of my life," Caroline said with a glow. "But I was too ashamed to tell my family about him. I always made excuses why I couldn't come home. My parents couldn't afford to help me. They had their own financial problems. Malcolm was a year old when I finally told my parents about him."

"Oh," Kitty said, shaking her head. "You must have felt so alone. I can't even imagine the fear and pain you must have experienced."

Caroline smiled. "Malcolm is God's special gift to me. That's really why I began my career. I was determined to be rich and never to be dependent on anyone, ever. I wanted Malcolm to have every advantage I never had."

Kitty shook her head and said, "It's only natural to want the best for your child."

Caroline sighed. "I lost all perspective. I saw my job as the only means of security for my family. To tell the truth, if Malcolm hadn't forced me to admit Chuck's drug problem, I never would have quit my job. I never would have bothered with the peace principles. When Malcolm finally forced me to open my eyes, I suddenly became desperate for new solutions. All my know-it-all theories for controlling my life and my children didn't work."

"Your new perspective doesn't erase all the good you accomplished," Kitty said firmly. "This is probably a time-out for you. Do you think you'll go back to work when everything is straightened out?"

"Probably," Caroline answered. "I don't think I'd go back into the same field, though. I don't really know what I'll do, but I do know I'll approach it differently."

Caroline looked down at her dinner. "I hated Malcolm's father after being hurt so badly by him, and poor Nick took the brunt of my bitterness toward men. I went into our marriage with a lot of baggage. My one goal for working was to be better, more successful, and richer than any of the men in our company. I was driven by hate and revenge."

Kitty shook her head. "I never had a clue. When we first met, you seemed so carefree and full of fun."

"I knew how to act carefree and fun. I honed that act into a fine art when I lived with Mark. He wouldn't tolerate anything else."

"But you and Nick were always the life of the party," Kitty protested. "You never appeared bitter, until the past several years."

"It was always there just below the surface, ready to erupt at any moment," Caroline admitted, swirling the wine in her glass. "I managed to keep it under wraps for a long time. Do you remember when we first talked about the peace principles and you got so angry at Nick?" Caroline focused her eyes on Kitty. "Believe me, Nick got the short end of the stick in our marriage. I'm just now realizing it. Following the exercises on forgiveness has helped me recognize my demons."

They were both silent for a moment. Then Caroline asked, "Kitty, have you tried the forgiveness exercise in the book?"

"No, I haven't," Kitty admitted.

"I didn't do it at first either, but then I started to make a list of all the ways Mark hurt me. That was easy. He hurt me in more ways than I had realized. The hard part of the exercise was making a list of the blessings I received through that pain. I could only think of one – Malcolm. But I kept working on it, and slowly I began recognizing other blessings. I'm amazed at all the blessings I've received as a result of that experience." Caroline hesitated and then laughed.

"It took me a while to make the list of the ways I hurt others. When I began working on it, I realized that I was doing to Nick what Mark did to me. I deserted Nick and the children for my career; really, for my revenge. I'm so grateful to be free from all that hate and revenge. It's a cancer." She took a deep breath. "Sorry. I'm doing all the talking."

Kitty looked at her friend. "I thought I knew you, and I didn't know you at all," Kitty admitted. "You're amazing. You've suffered so much pain and rejection, yet you still survived. My life's been a cakewalk compared with yours. I feel foolish complaining about my petty problems when you've been through so much."

Caroline looked into Kitty's eyes. "What you are going through is every bit as painful as what I went through. It's your pain and it hurts. It's not the situation that hurts; it's the pain that the situation causes that makes us hurt."

Kitty stared at the candles on the table. "I appreciate that. It does hurt. But your story is helping me get some perspective and hope. Thanks. I'm still amazed we were so close and yet you had another life I never even suspected."

Caroline shrugged. "We never had any reason to discuss it until now."

"You have so much wisdom. I think you'll end up going back to work, maybe not just for money. You'll be successful and you'll probably make a lot of money in spite of yourself," Kitty laughed.

"Perhaps I will go back when all the kids are grown," Caroline responded thoughtfully. "I've also learned that money is a good thing when it's used properly. I want to use my wealth and talent to help others discover the peace secrets – to grow love and peace in the world. I'd like to find a way to teach businesspeople that success and spirituality go hand in hand." She hesitated, her face glowing in the candlelight. "You know, Kit, it's funny; you and I always seem to end up on the same path."

"Not always," Kit answered. "I got married several years before you. You had a magnificent career. I haven't done anything but run a house and raise a family, and I did a pretty poor job at that. Look at me. What do I have to show for the past 25 years?"

"You have a lot to show for it," Caroline insisted. "True, you're going through a tough time now, but you and Matt are still very much in love. I watched you that night at the country club, Kit. He's crazy about you, and I think you're still crazy about him."

"I miss him," Kitty admitted, sipping her wine. "I can't imagine life without him. But I have to move on, and I have to get a job. What do you think I can do?"

"There are a lot of things you can do," Caroline reassured her.

"You're a master fundraiser. Every organization needs a good development person. What do you think you want to do?"

"I don't know," Kitty answered. "I'm good at raising funds for charities, but I don't know how good I'd be working for a nonprofit organization."

"Well, do you enjoy it?"

Kitty smiled. "I'm not crazy about asking for money but I've realized charities need money to fulfill their mission. In that way, I found it challenging. I enjoyed helping St. Julian's and the breast cancer organization get the help they need. I know a lot of people." Kitty looked at Caroline. "But do you think people will donate money to a charity I'm working on when they find out we're broke? We're no longer in a position to give large donations ourselves."

Caroline thought for moment and offered, "Like you, I've worked on a lot of charities, and I've served on several nonprofit boards. I learned the secret to fundraising, Kit, is engaging people in the mission of the charity. You raised more than half a million dollars for an insidious disease because you watched your mom die from breast cancer. You have a personal passion for a cure, and you know the urgency of finding that cure. You engaged people in a mission to cure cancer. Of course, your social position got you in the door, but it was your passion and belief that inspired people to contribute such large amounts."

"I always thought people gave because of who I was, not because they wanted to fight cancer."

"It was because of you," Caroline suggested, "but not because of who you were. Your passion and enthusiasm inspired them to want to give to the cause."

Kitty laughed and couldn't stop.

Caroline looked puzzled, then started to giggle even though she didn't know what she was laughing about. "What's so funny?"

"All these years, I really believed I was able to raise big donations because I was Kitty Bradshaw Murphy. I took pride in that." Kitty shook her head. "I don't know why I'm laughing."

The two women finished their dinner in companionable silence. Then Caroline perked up.

"Maybe you should even consider getting a paying job with the

American Cancer Society," she suggested. "On the other hand, you could work for one of the local colleges, or a private school."

Kitty liked both ideas but felt overwhelmed. "Where should I begin? How do I find a job? I don't know. I'm 46. Who wants to hire an inexperienced 46-year-old? Oh well," she sighed. "I'm not going to think about it right now. I'm going to California to visit Uncle Chip for a few days. I leave next Wednesday. I'll start looking when I return."

"Are you going alone?"

"Yes. It's the first time I've ever traveled that far alone. I'm a little apprehensive flying by myself."

Caroline smiled. "Well, I can understand how you feel, but it's actually a wonderful flight. I think you'll enjoy it. You have five hours to yourself to pray, read, and think. Focusing on God's love and protection will help you."

"You'd be proud of me," Kitty interjected with a smile. "Every morning I get up and open my scriptures and read psalms of praise. I'm amazed at how peaceful I begin to feel. Sometimes my mind wanders and I get distracted, but I pull myself back to thanking God for all his blessings. To tell you the truth, I'm amazed at myself. God is becoming my friend. It helps a lot."

"Are you reflecting on the meditations in the book?" Caroline asked.

"Every day I reflect on one peace secret and the two meditations for that secret. I'm on the third week. I'm getting a lot out of it."

"I'm glad," Caroline said as they both got up to clear the table. "I hope someday you'll tell me what changed your attitude about God."

"It wasn't anything earth-shattering," Kitty responded, smiling. "I wasn't getting much out of universal love. So I asked God, if He really exists, to help me believe in Him. And He did. It's as simple as that."

"Let's praise and thank God for our friendship and the many blessings He's bestowing on us and our families," Caroline suggested, and they did.

Susan called just as the women finished cleaning up.

"Tell Susan I said hi," Caroline said, giving Kitty a hug. "I'll let myself out."

Chapter 26

Apprehension

"I prayed to the Lord and He answered me.
He freed me from all my fears."

(Psalm 34:4)

Susan wanted to know how Kitty liked the townhouse. "I'll be there for breakfast tomorrow," she enthusiastically told her mom. "Are you all right?"

"Yes, of course." Then she relented. "Well, it's a little lonely without Dad, but I guess I'll get used to it."

"Don't give up so easily, Mom," Susan encouraged. "I'm proud of the way you've handled this. You're one great woman," she said, affirming her mother. "I can't imagine you and Dad not being together. After 25 years, he's like your right arm."

"You're right," Kitty answered. "Maybe we don't appreciate our right arm until we lose it. I'm getting all teary-eyed. I'll be looking for you at breakfast. I love you, Susan."

Susan stopped by her mother's place every day until Kitty left for California. The night before the trip, Susan and Doug took Kitty out to dinner. "See if you can get Uncle Chip to come home for Christmas," Doug suggested. "He hasn't been home for a couple of years. Tell him we miss him."

Kitty slept fitfully. She really didn't want to fly to California alone. She finally fell into a deep slumber and dreamed she was lost in California and couldn't find her way. She bolted up in bed, unsure where she was. The room was strange. Once she realized it was a dream, she took a deep breath and tried to go back to sleep, but it was no use. Finally at

4:00 a.m. she got up and made herself coffee. She sat in the living room and randomly opened her Bible to Psalm 34.

> I will always thank the Lord;
> I will never stop praising Him.
> I prayed to the Lord and He answered me;
> He freed me from all my fears
>
> Find out for yourself how good the Lord is.
> Happy are those who find safety with Him.
> Honor the Lord, all his people.
> (Verses 1, 4, 8, and 9)

As she reflected on God's love for her, Kitty began to relax. She felt an overwhelming desire to pray for Chip. She began thanking God for Chip. *Thank you, God, for Chip's friendship. Thank you for his love. Take care of him, Lord. Help him in any way he needs help.*

She wrote in her diary what she was thinking and feeling, noting her apprehension about being alone. But she felt reassured that she would not be alone and everything would be fine.

Kitty showered, dressed, looked over her tickets, rechecked her bags, and put everything by the front door. Susan arrived just as she was taking a last look at herself in the mirror.

When Susan dropped her mother off outside the baggage check-in, she asked, "Are you sure you don't want me to help you?"

"I'll be fine, honey," Kitty replied. "You run along and go back to sleep."

Susan got her mother a skycap and gave her a hug. "Have a great trip, Mom. I love you." She quickly ran back to her car and jumped into the driver's seat. Then she was gone.

Chapter 27

Praise Works

"Even all the hairs on your head have been counted.
So do not be afraid."

(John 10:30)

As Kitty watched the first-class passengers board the plane before everyone else, she couldn't help but think, *I should be in first class.* She
walked up to the desk and inquired if it were possible to get a first-class
seat. She learned she needed upgrade certificates, or pay an additional
$2,200. "Forget it," she told the agent.

Once on board, Kitty tried to calm down as she buckled herself in
to a seat in the middle of a crowded row. She'd never thought to ask for
an aisle seat, and she tried to control her frustration, but snapped at the
flight attendant when she couldn't get a blanket. *Caroline would tell me
to thank and praise God for this moment, but I have a right to be angry. I
should be in first class with a blanket to warm my feet.*

She tried to get comfortable in her seat but she had a headache,
a backache, and her neck ached. Halfheartedly she consoled herself.
*There is peace in this moment, there is peace in this moment, there is peace
is this moment.*

She folded her arms, pouted, and intoned the words to herself like
a spoiled child doing what she was told, against her will. But the words
gradually relaxed her and she rolled into praising and thanking God
for soaking her in His joy, and for the grace of this moment. Little by
little she felt the tension ooze from her. Her aches and pains seemingly
vanished.

When she realized how much better she felt, she started laughing to herself. *Kitty, you're a spoiled brat.* She apologized to the flight attendant. She began praising and thanking God for the woman, and a few minutes later she returned with a blanket. When she walked away, Kitty sighed. *It's easy to send peace to another when I focus on it. I feel so much better about me. That attendant was nice to me because of me, not because of what I have. I turned the situation around by accepting God's peace in this moment. It's amazing.*

Kitty relaxed, said the Prayer of St. Francis, took three deep breaths and read her meditations for choosing to forgive. When she finished her prayers, she took out her copy of *The Peace Way.* She had only a few more pages to read of Jenny Solomon's story:

**

Every time I looked at my forgiveness exercise, I thought about how cruel I had been to Jon's parents. I assumed they knew where Jon was, but maybe they didn't know any more than I did. I was having difficulty being honest with myself regarding the way I treated them.

As I grew closer to God, I realized that the Solomons, Rebba and Ben, didn't deserve my cruelty. They had always been kind to me. They treated me like one of their own children; I never once felt like an in-law. I actually enjoyed their company more than that of my own parents. I love my parents, but they still treated me like a child. The Solomons always treated me like an adult. We laughed and joked together, sharing feelings and experiences as equals, as peers.

I missed my long heart-to-heart conversations with Rebba. But I was sure she and Ben knew where Jon was, and I didn't understand why they didn't make him face his responsibilities.

Ben and Rebba had four children – three boys and one girl. They were a tight-knit family. I used to love to visit the Solomon house when I was in college. Their house was full of laughter and love, and I was fascinated with the stimulating conversations.

Jon and I were married just shy of eight years when tragedy struck the Solomon family. Jon's younger brother, Alan, was in a serious automobile accident. He was driving on the beltway when a drunk driver's car jumped the median and smashed into Alan's car. For six months he was comatose before dying from a lung infection. After that, a gray cloud hung over the Solomon family. Anger and bitterness transformed the fun-loving family into a group of revenge-seekers. Jon and I were as bitter and angry as the rest of his family, and we fed on each other's venom. Then the family was hit with another tragedy: Rebba was diagnosed with breast cancer.

Prior to Alan's death, Rebba and Ben Solomon were business partners in their own consulting company – Solomon & Solomon. It was a motivational company specializing in sales training. They taught people how to work with their customers and become high-achieving sales professionals. They trained the employees of large companies like IBM and AT&T. They also franchised their training program. They wanted Jon to join the company, but he had bigger and better ideas. He didn't want to work for his parents.

Everything changed after Alan died. The Solomon family was obsessed with getting revenge. They wanted the driver who killed their son, and every other drunk driver, to get the death penalty. Anger and rage consumed their every waking moment. This man had robbed their son and brother of his life and he was going to pay for it.

The stress and pain of the extended trial took an additional toll on the family. Their once-fun family gatherings turned into angry and bitter disputes. At first Rebba was vocal, but she grew quieter and quieter. She'd sit and stare for hours without talking. When the children tried to bring her into the conversation, she retreated to her room.

When Rebba was diagnosed with breast cancer, the family went into a tailspin. She was the maternal strength. After she learned she had the disease, she distanced herself even more. She didn't want to hear anything about the trial. Instead she threw herself into her disease, reading everything she could on breast cancer. She got several opinions before agreeing to a mastectomy.

Initially her children tried to advise her on what she should do, but she ignored them. She would discuss her options only with her husband, Ben. She had surgery, chemotherapy, and radiation. A spiritual woman, she turned to meditation and prayer to help her through her journey.

Finally Rebba recognized that the family's rage over Alan's death was a far greater malady than her breast cancer. Their rage had turned inward. It had become a family cancer. She slowly changed her attitude.

At its onset, Rebba's cancer robbed her of all energy. She was constantly fatigued. When she started to regain her energy, she began attending AA and Al-Anon meetings to understand alcoholism. She was more concerned about Alan's killer being rehabilitated than she was about him going to prison. Ben was puzzled. How could she even entertain the thought of forgiving Alan's killer? But he slowly came around to her thinking. Both Ben and Rebba focused more on helping drunken drivers become sober, contributing members of society than trying to incarcerate them.

The Solomon children lashed out at their parents for being disloyal to Alan's memory. The parents' stance on alcoholism created a family division. I went to visit the family once after Jon left me, but I couldn't handle their attitude toward alcoholics, either.

During that visit, I had a big fight with Rebba. I told her she was a wimp. I lashed out at her. "Your son was robbed of life by an irresponsible, selfish drunk out on a joyride. Doesn't that mean anything to you? This kid killed your son, and you're trying to help rehabilitate him?"

Rebba looked directly into my eyes and responded, "Jenny, honey, two wrongs never make a right. Yes, this young man took my son's life. But cancer taught me that life is very short, and I'm grateful for a second chance to live my life more fully. That young man, too, deserves a second chance."

"So he can kill someone else?" I retorted. "Is that what you're saying? Is that what you want?"

Rebba gently explained, "He paid a greater price than Alan. Alan's at peace. This young man has to live with Alan's death for the rest of his life. He's a smart, talented young man. He has stopped drinking. He's in AA, and he has the ability to keep hundreds, maybe thousands of other kids from making the same mistake he made. His tragedy may save hundreds of other lives."

"You're crazy, Rebba," I accused. "I can't stand listening to this rubbish. No wonder Jon is an irresponsible alcoholic. You encouraged him." Rebba's eyes filled up but I didn't care. I grabbed my children, packed their things, and left.

I hadn't seen or talked to them since. They tried to help me but I refused to talk to them. I cut them out of my life. But they never missed sending a birthday card with money to the children and to me. I put the children's money in the bank-- the only good thing I did for my children. No matter how tempted I was to borrow that money, I never did. But I didn't give the children their cards, and I returned anything the Solomons sent me.

I shudder when I think about how cruel I was to the Solomons. I had begun praising and thanking God for them, but I was afraid to call them; I was sure they were angry with me. I felt an inner longing to reach out to them, but I was afraid.

Finally I began praising and thanking God for the courage to do the right thing and call Rebba and Ben. One day I took a deep breath, asked God to help me, and dialed their number; my heart was pounding and my hands trembled.

"Hello," Rebba's pleasant voice answered. I was tempted to hang up. I opened my mouth but nothing came out. Finally I muttered,

"Hello, Rebba, this is Jenny."

"Jenny! How are you?"

To my surprise, she acted like we had just talked yesterday. We talked for 20 minutes. She asked all about the children, and I promised I'd bring the kids to visit them the following weekend.

Rebba and Ben welcomed us with open arms. They never questioned me about the way I'd treated them after Jon left. I realized what a fool I had been to cut these two dear people out of my life and out of my children's lives. I resolved to heal the breach that had nearly destroyed my family.

Rebba and I had a wonderful time catching up on the past two years. She was even dearer than I had remembered her. I kept asking myself again, *Why did I ever push this woman, who's been such a mentor to me, out of my life?* I realized it was because she lived a life of peace, and I didn't want to hear it. I wanted to be angry. I wanted to hate Jon. I really felt badly when Rebba told me, with tears in her eyes, that they'd not heard from nor seen him since he'd disappeared almost three years ago.

I felt very comfortable sharing the peace secrets with them. They were as excited about the power of praise as I was.

When I first went to work, Rebba and Ben had offered me a job. I turned it down. But this time, Ben had an idea I couldn't turn down. He suggested that I design a workshop based on the peace secrets.

"Jen, you can work from home. Just think, you'll be helping others do something you love doing. You could keep your current job and give your workshops on the weekends. We have the resources to help you get started. What do you think?"

I had goose bumps all over. "Oh, Dad," I said, "I'd love that, but I can't give workshops. Who am I to teach others what to do?"

"Honey, you're the perfect person to help people find peace in their lives," he encouraged me. "Look at you! You're a different young lady. Let's at least look into it."

I told him about Maria, who would be the perfect leader for a workshop. "She's the expert, and she's very outgoing. I'm just a beginner."

"You can pool your talents. You have the materials and the passion. We have the resources to help you put it together."

The more Ben talked, the more excited I got. "Where would we give the workshops? How would we get people to come?"

"If we approach it right, you'll get more bookings than you can handle. People are searching for ways to juggle their over-scheduled lives with peaceful and calm hearts. We'll help you with the design and marketing. I know some ministers and rabbis who would love this program for their congregations. You think about it."

I couldn't wait to tell Maria. She was as enthusiastic as I was, and we met with Ben and Rebba a few weeks later. Maria told Ben all about Julio and his journey to peace. Over the next few months, we formed a nonprofit company: Our mission was to inspire people to find God's love in their hearts and spread it wherever they go. Rebba suggested we call our company Courage of One and make "Finding peace in a chaotic world" our tag line. Maria and I loved it.

Ben helped us design five workshops on the peace secrets: Passion for God's presence within; Enjoy the moment; Appreciate your abundance; Choose to forgive; and Encourage others. Later we designed a daily journal book following the peace secrets and a study guide for weekly study groups.

That's my story. That's how *Courage of One* study groups began.

No one has ever heard from Jon. I flushed my sleeping pills down the toilet and love spending 45 minutes every evening talking with God. My children still say the peace prayers together every night after dinner. Praying together has created a spiritual bond between us. I believe a family that prays together stays together.

I am now financially independent. J.J. is the man of the house and has become very protective of the girls and me. We love it. He is living the St. Francis peace principles. Rebecca works part-time for the school, and she's still babysitting for the Scott family. She and I don't always see eye to eye, but she is growing into a beautiful young lady. Rachael is my challenge right now. She's 12, she likes the boys, and they like her. That's one I'll leave to God. Sara hasn't had a nightmare in more than a year. I quit my job, but I still sew and I teach workshops full time.

I learned through prayer that the secret to finding joy in your work is love. I love my work, I love my God, and I love the people I'm blessed to serve, and I love you, my reader. Now you know my story. I pray you will find God's love in your heart and spread it wherever you go, whatever you do, one moment, one heart at a time. Until we meet again, farewell.

Kitty wiped her eyes and read the note on the bottom of the page: *Stop by and visit our website: www.courageofone.com. Tell us about yourself and your experiences with the peace principles.*

She closed the book and thought about the Solomons and Jenny. She jotted a few notes in her journal and then fell asleep. Caroline was right. The flight was exceptionally pleasant.

PEACE

Don't leave home without it.

"The fruit of silence is prayer.
The fruit of prayer is faith.
The fruit of faith is love.
The fruit of love is service.
The fruit of service is peace."
Mother Teresa's business card

Chapter 28

Encourage Others

"Teach us how short life is, so that we may become wise."

(Psalm 90:12)

At first, Kitty didn't see Chip waiting for her at the baggage carousel. "You've lost so much weight!" she said, giving him a big hug. "I didn't recognize you."

He grasped her hands and stood at arm's length looking at her. "Let me look at you, Kit. You're an eye-catcher. How many men tried to pick you up on the flight?" he laughed.

They talked all the way to Chip's apartment, a small but elegant two-bedroom apartment in Santa Monica with a beautiful ocean view. Large baskets of red and white impatiens hung from the deck railings. Classical music played softly in the background.

"Do you like this CD?" he asked Kitty.

"It's beautiful," she replied. "Sounds like Puccini."

"Isn't it great?" He closed his eyes. "I just love it. I wanted everything to be perfect for you: soft music, ocean breeze, sunshine, the smell of fresh-cut flowers."

She gave Chip a big hug. "I'm so glad to be here with you and your music. Whenever I listen to classical music, I think of you." She took his hands. "Let me look at you. You look wonderful, but you're so thin. Are you okay?"

"I watch my weight," Chip said, passing it off as nothing. He wanted to know about the kids, the move, and Matt.

Kitty told him about Ken, Doug, and Susan.

"I see Ken often," Chip told her. "He's going to make it as an actor.

I'm sure of it. He has perseverance." He grinned. "He'll be joining us for dinner tonight. He's eager to see you."

Although Kitty wanted to see her son, she was always apprehensive about being with him. He was a little too self-righteous for her comfort. She didn't have the same relationship with Ken that she had with Doug and Susan.

But she told Chip, "I'm looking forward to seeing him, too."

Chip changed the subject. "How are things with you and Matt?"

Kitty sighed. "Not good, Chip, not good. We're headed for bankruptcy and divorce."

"Divorce, you and Matt?" Chip was clearly shocked. "You're so in love. How can you be getting a divorce?"

"*Were* in love is more like it."

Chip looked at her silently for a moment. "Kit, people don't just fall out of love, not when their love is as deep as yours and Matt's."

Kitty fought back despair. "Do you mind if we don't talk about it right now?"

"Why don't you freshen up," he suggested. "We'll go to lunch. I have a surprise for you."

He took her to the Beverly Wilshire, where everyone knew him. Kitty was proud to be his niece. For the first time in months she felt important. But they didn't get a chance to talk because people constantly stopped at their table to say hello. Chip introduced Kitty as his niece. The women were gracious but the men dubiously checked her out, while kidding Chip, "Your niece? That's a good one!"

Chip enjoyed showing Kitty off. She was elegant and today she looked exceptionally beautiful. There was a warm glow about her; her recent disappointments and hurts had uncovered a depth she had hidden in her self-assured days of money, social position, and love.

In spite of the interruptions, they had a few good laughs sharing old family stories. They finished lunch and were drinking coffees when Chip gave Kitty a small gift.

She carefully opened it. "Oh! It's wonderful," she whispered, gazing at a framed picture of Chip, Kitty, and her mother and father in Paris, taken the summer between Kitty's junior and senior years in college. "Thank you!" she whispered, holding the picture in both hands. "You're so sweet." She leaned over, kissed him on the cheek, and held the photo close to her heart. "You know I'll treasure it. We had such a wonderful time that summer. Remember the dinner cruise down the Seine?"

Chip laughed. "I remember. You complained all night because Matt wasn't there."

"Well, you have to admit it was very romantic. Of course I loved being with you and Mom and Dad. But it would have been perfect if Matt had been there. It was a glorious night." She sighed. "Oh, Chip, I wish we could turn the clock back and put everything back the way it was."

Dinner that night with Ken went better than Kitty had anticipated. They were both so glad to see each other, and it was obvious that Chip and Ken had grown very close. The three of them laughed and kidded about different family members and situations.

Then the conversation led into a discussion about how family members unwittingly hurt each other. Ken and Chip joked about pain they'd received and dished out. They shared ideas about love and forgiveness.

Kitty, although uncomfortable with so much raw honesty, was intrigued. Chip and Ken had an open and honest dialogue about their frailties and shortcomings. In her world, people never admitted deficits.

But she was most in awe of Ken's ability to weave the most serious subjects into humorous stories that kept her spellbound. She listened intently, finding each story more interesting than the previous one.

The next morning, Kitty woke up at 4 a.m., stretched, and lounged quietly in bed. She smiled to herself, thinking about how interesting and fun Kenny's stories were. *I really don't know him.* Underneath his self-righteous façade was a self-effacing, humble, caring young man who needed reassurance and encouragement rather than criticism. It was a side of Ken that Kitty didn't know. Last night was probably the first time she really relaxed and enjoyed her firstborn's company.

She stretched again and said a quick prayer. "Thank you, God. Thank you for Ken and Chip. Thank you for loving all of us and bringing us together."

She got out of bed and went to pull back the curtains. The twinkling lights on the Santa Monica Pier pierced the darkness. When Kitty slowly slid open the glass door, a rhythmic wind whirled into the room, catching the drapes and Kitty by surprise. She stepped back. For a brief moment, she'd forgotten she was at the ocean. Pulling her silk robe up around her neck, she stepped out onto the terrace, took a long, deep breath, threw her head back, and let the salt air penetrate into her soul. *Thank you, God, thank you.* Tears rolled down her cheeks.

She was at peace with herself when regrets about Ken crept into her thoughts. *Was he always an interesting storyteller? How come I never recognized his sensitivity? When did he develop a sense of humor?* She was glad to be alone. She needed time to think and pray about her relationship with Ken. *What kind of mother am I that I know so little about my own son? Where have I been all these years?*

She went back inside to get her prayer card and journal.

She prayed, "Thank You, God, for loving Ken and protecting him. God, You are so good. You are a power in our lives. You are watching over me in spite of my selfishness. Thank you, God, for Chip and Ken. Thank you for Matt. Thank you for Doug and Susan. Thank you for Caroline. Lord, thank you for this trip."

Kitty took three deep breaths and began reading the meditation for the fourth week: "I praise and thank you, God, for soaking me in your joy and washing away any self-righteousness and selfishness I may have in my heart; wash away the hurts my self-righteousness and selfishness may have caused others. I praise and thank you, Lord, for helping me encourage others to be as you created them, and not as I want them to be."

She slowly read and reflected on being soaked in God's joy and wisdom. The words welled within her. Love and gratitude poured from her heart, and Kitty lost all sense of time. Twenty minutes passed, but it seemed like two. "Lord, help me. Show me your way. I want to be kind and compassionate. I don't want to control and contradict people. Help me.

"Lord, thank you for removing my dark glasses and showing me the real Ken. Thank you for this time with Ken and Chip. Lord, help me to be a better mother. Help me find a job. Help me straighten out all our finances. Help me talk to Matt about our situation. Help me demand that Matt tell me everything about our financial situation, and what he's going to do about it."

Suddenly, Kitty realized she was only praying for herself and the things she wanted. Her thoughts turned to Matt. *Dear Matt. What is he feeling? I wonder.* For the first time since their financial problems began, Kitty wondered if her husband was worried. She had just assumed he was doing what he wanted to do, that he was being selfish and only thinking about himself.

She wondered if he was scared. *I wonder if he doesn't want to talk about it because he doesn't know what's going to happen. Oh my Lord, I'm trying to control Matt, Susan, and Ken. I praise and thank you, Lord, for changing my heart and washing away all my desires to control and contradict others.*

She was lost in thought when she heard the apartment door close. She jumped up and went to see who closed the door. Chip's bedroom door was slightly ajar. The room was dark and Chip was gone. Kitty couldn't help but wonder where he was going at 5:00 a.m.

She wandered into the kitchen to make coffee. She watched the coffee drip into the pot as the wonderful aroma of fresh brew filled the apartment. Carrying her coffee outside, she pulled her robe up around her, took a deep breath, and slowly sipped her coffee.

It's just you and me, God. She looked up into the dark sky. The stars were slowly fading as the darkness gave way to the morning light. *Oh, I'm so glad I'm here. I didn't realize how uptight I've been. Thank you, God, for this time to rest. Thank you.* She put her head back, closed her eyes, and listened to the waves lapping against the beach.

Chip pushed the sliding door back, causing Kitty to jump. "I must have fallen asleep. What smells so good?" she asked.

He grinned at her. "Come in and enjoy my favorite morning delight."

Chapter 29

Rejoice

"Rejoice, rejoice in the Lord always."

(Philippians 4:4)

They sat in the small dining area and had delicious muffins Chip had brought in from a local bakery. At first their conversation was the usual, covering what was happening in the news.

Then Chip asked, "Kit, you seem very calm in spite of all your challenges. Tell me what you're doing to help you get through this." He spoke slowly, as if he chose his words carefully.

She looked into her coffee cup. "It's a long story, but I think it'll make you happy."

Chip waited patiently for her to continue.

"Don't laugh or faint." Kitty felt a little silly. "I start every morning praying."

"Kit, why would I laugh?" Chip asked.

"I don't know. I just thought you might."

"Quite the contrary, I'm thrilled for you. It shows in your face. You look younger and more radiant than you've looked in years. You were always beautiful, but your face seems softer, more relaxed. You glow. I'm curious about what prompted you to start praying in the morning."

Kitty told him about Caroline's transformation from a cynical, negative person she hated to be with to a delightful, joyful person she loved to be with. "In spite of all her problems, she's always up and positive." Kitty explained. "A friend gave her the book *The Peace Way* and it changed her life. She spends a half hour every morning visiting with our Lord and following the peace principles in the book."

"And how did all this help you?" Chip inquired.

Kitty laughed. "She was determined that I would try her peace process. I definitely wasn't up for anything religious, but she persisted. One day she suggested I try it for 30 days and see what happened," Kitty explained. "She wore me down.

"Finally, I was desperate. I was in so much pain. It couldn't have gotten much worse. So I decided to start praising and thanking God for taking care of me and finding me a place to live. I was skeptical, but it worked."

Chip looked puzzled. "Praising and thanking God for taking care of you – is that the peace process?" he delved, leaning over the table to hear more. "That's interesting."

"Well, there's more to it than praising and praying. I've never tried to explain it to anyone. I just started practicing it a month ago. Let me try to explain it to you." She took a deep breath. "It's like discovering some hidden secrets to having more fun and getting more done."

"Oh, it's about time management."

Kitty laughed. "That's a good one. It's not about time management but when you practice these principles you – how do I say it? – you look at things differently. As a result, you do have more fun, more time, and less stress. For some reason, it's easier to juggle all your responsibilities with less struggle."

Chip nodded. "This sounds like something I could use. Tell me about it."

"It's simple," Kitty said, excited that he was interested. "You follow five peace principles. The principles can be remembered with the acronym PEACE.

"First, P stands for a passion – for God's presence within. You get in touch with God's presence in your heart through praising and thanking Him."

"Just how do you do that again?"

"Every day you commit to spending several minutes visiting with God. You start by praising and thanking Him for loving you and protecting you. You take a deep breath, hold it, then let it out. You do this three times. Deep breathing slows you down and helps you enter into a prayerful state. You ask the Holy Spirit to lead you in your prayer. Then you reflect and meditate on the peace prayer for that day."

"That's very simple. Is there a peace prayer for each peace principle?" Chip asked.

Kitty nodded. "Sort of. The first principle, a passion for the presence of God within, is included in all the meditations. There are two meditations for each of the other principles."

"What are the other principles?"

"Well, the E in PEACE stands for embracing the moment. The first week of the month, you focus on embracing the moment and seeing God's plan in the moment. The idea is to focus on enjoying this moment rather than worrying about the future."

"You mean, live in the now," Chip suggested.

"Yes, that's kind of it. I remind myself that God has a plan for me in this moment, a plan full of hope. When I take the time to stop and think about God and His plan for me, I calm down and get so much more out of the present moment."

Kitty hesitated. "I have a long way to go on this one. I usually start out okay in my morning prayer, but as the day progresses and pressures build, I tend to fall back into my old habits. I get uptight and panic because things aren't going according to my plan, and I'm miserable. I push to get things done. Everything is a struggle."

She laughed. "When I let God run the show, and I enjoy the moment, I struggle less, and enjoy what I'm doing more. It makes everything so much easier."

Chip looked at her. "That's interesting," he said. "I've been trying to live in the now. But it sounds like your prayer takes it to a higher level – embracing the now. I'm going to think about the word *embrace*," Chip added. "I have difficulty staying focused on the moment. Maybe if I try embracing it, it will be easier to stay focused on the present."

Kitty agreed with Chip and went on to explain that the letter A in PEACE stands for appreciating one's abundance.

"This is the second meditation. You focus on appreciating all the abundance God places in your life. God gives you everything you need, and you decide how you'll use it. When you focus on abundance rather than scarcity, you become more aware of all the blessings you do have.

That way, you're grateful and confident that God loves and provides all that you need always, wherever you go, and whatever you do."

She stopped and gazed out the window. "Why do you think it is so difficult to embrace God's love and appreciate our abundance?"

Chip looked at her, his fingers folded in the prayer position leaning against his lower lip. He didn't say anything for a few seconds. Finally he spoke slowly and thoughtfully. "To tell you the truth, I'm amazed, Kit. You sound so much like Fran." Fran was his late wife.

Chip looked at her and smiled as if he had just understood her question. He repeated her query. "Why do I think it's so difficult to believe God loves us and provides us with everything we need for this moment? Fran used to ask me that very question. She used to say, 'Chippy, when you know God works everything out for your good, why do you fret and storm around trying to make everything go your way?' "

He laughed and shook his head. "I never understood what she was talking about. But I'm learning. It's funny you bring this up now, because lately I've been thinking a lot about God's love. I think it's difficult to trust God because we don't really grasp the meaning of love."

He shook his head. "I don't know the answer to your question. I think our perception of love may be one-sided. We see love as giving to another, and we don't see the value in being a gracious receiver." He looked at Kitty. "Does that make sense? The older I get, the more I realize it's easier to be the giver than it is to be the receiver. I'm not a gracious receiver," he confessed. "I want to control everything."

"You know, you're right." Kitty agreed. "I love giving gifts, but I'm uncomfortable receiving them. I do expect people to give me presents on certain occasions, like my birthday and Christmas. But I seldom appreciate the gifts I receive." She paused. "I do love the picture you gave me yesterday, and I didn't think I deserved it." She laughed. "This is heavy stuff."

"I think one reason I don't trust that God is taking care of me," Chip said, "is because I don't know how to love. I want to control everyone and everything in my life, and that isn't love. When we truly love someone, we accept them as they are, not who we think they should be."

"That is so true. I never thought about it that way."

"When you think about it, Kit, love drives us to new heights. True love is not an emotion. It's a depth of caring and giving, rising from a wellspring within our hearts. Nothing we do for the beloved is a burden. It is pure joy. When we love, we long for the best for our beloved. No sacrifice is too great. Not even the sacrifice of letting go." Chip took a deep breath and looked out the window.

"God's love is total, unselfish, and all giving," he added. "If we really grasped His love for us, we wouldn't just enjoy every moment, we would be *in* joy in every moment." He looked at Kitty and took a deep breath. "God's love is all-encompassing, and that kind of love is foreign to our human behavior. It's difficult to comprehend. Does that make sense?"

Kitty nodded. "It makes a lot of sense. It's difficult for me to fathom that someone could love me so completely." She looked pensive. "Chip, do you think that we're afraid to embrace God's love because we want to be in control, and letting someone love us so completely makes us too vulnerable?"

Chip looked intently at Kitty. He thought for a few minutes before answering, "I think that's a good point." He nodded his head.

"When you talked about passion for the presence of God within, you really touched a nerve. Fran definitely had passion for God's love, and she radiated it daily – not in words but in her actions."

"I'm not in Fran's league," Kitty corrected. "I'm a beginner."

"Still, the way you talk reminds me of her." Chip looked out the window.

Kitty sat back in her chair and observed him. He looked so much like her father. He had always been stockier than her dad, but now that he had lost weight, he was tall and lean like her Dad had been.

Chip still looked toward the window. As if talking to himself, he said, "She loved life so, and life loved her back." They sat in silence for a few minutes. "Fran had a favorite quote from Confucius that describes your peace process: 'To know something is not as good as to love it. To love something is not as good as rejoicing in it.' Your peace process is all about rejoicing in the moment, rejoicing in your abundance, and rejoicing in your relationships with others. There's a lot of wisdom in it." He thought for a moment.

Then he started to laugh. "I used to think I controlled my life. In reality, the only thing I control is how I perceive life. You would think that after all I've experienced, I'd realize God has a plan for me, and if I place myself in His hands and let Him work His plan through me, I'd be a happy guy. And I do realize God has a plan, but I'm constantly taking things into my own hands. My ego gets in the way."

Kitty laughed. She threw her head back and laughed till she almost cried.

"What's so funny?" Chip asked, half laughing.

"I do the exact same thing! I sound like I have it all together. Believe me, Chip, I'm the same control freak I've always been. Occasionally I get glimmers of God's love in special moments like today. I really feel wrapped in His love, but a lot of that has to do with you and this apartment."

Kitty thought for a moment. "You don't realize it, Chip, but you're a perfect example of embracing God's love and spreading it wherever you go, and whatever you do. When I talk to you, I feel loved and cared for. I feel God's love for me through you. You're serene." She placed her hand on his and looked him in the eye. "I thank God every day for you. You're His special gift to me."

Chip's eyes filled up. "Thanks, Kit; you know I feel the same about you. But don't canonize me. I have a lot of baggage I need to let go if I want to be free in God's love."

Kitty was surprised to hear her uncle talk this way. She didn't know what to say. "Try praising God for yourself exactly as you are. It helps," she encouraged him. "I tell you, it's amazing how prayers of praise still your heart and calm you down, and it builds your trust."

"Do you praise God?" he asked. "Is that how you pray?"

"All the peace prayers begin with praising and thanking God. The more I praise, the more I realize it's the secret to entering into relaxed prayer."

"Relaxed prayer?" he repeated, a little surprised. "Is that more like a reflection or meditation?"

Kitty laughed and shrugged her shoulders. "I don't know, Chip. I don't know anything about meditation. This is all new to me. I just follow the book." "Tell me about week three," Chip prodded.

Kitty sensed that for some reason Chip was uncomfortable, but she went on. "Well, week three is the c in PEACE, which is courage to forgive. After we praise, we ask God to show us who we need to forgive. I've only done this once. It's kind of stupid, because when I pray about forgiving, I keep thinking about forgiving myself for the things I didn't do but wish I had done. So I'm obviously missing something." She looked at Chip. "I can't believe I'm telling you all this. What're your thoughts about forgiveness?"

"We're all on a journey, I guess," Chip said. "Some days we travel better than others. We do things that hurt ourselves and others. It's hard to forgive ourselves." He sighed. "I guess we can't forgive others if we can't forgive ourselves. I have a lot of self-forgiving to do."

Then he looked at his watch and jumped up from his chair. "Oh, Kit, we'll have to continue this conversation later. I made an appointment with a close friend of mine, Jeffrey. He's going to give us a guided tour through the Getty Museum. You'll love it. Ken is meeting us at the museum."

Kitty was a little disappointed that he'd cut the conversation short. Normally she would leap at the opportunity to have a personal tour through the Getty. But right now, she was surprised to realize, she would have rather talked to Chip about forgiveness.

Chapter 30

Relax

"Let us go off by ourselves to some place
Where we will be alone and you can rest awhile."

(Mark 6:31)

It was a sunny, breezy California day, and Kit and Chip enjoyed the drive in silence. Chip finally spoke up. "You never told me what the last E in PEACE was for. I assume you do that the fourth week of the month."

"Yes, I'm working on the fourth week now," Kitty told him. "E stands for encouraging others. You said it this morning when you said true love is accepting a person for who they are, not who you want them to be. You encourage people to recognize their unique gifts and use them to spread peace wherever they go." Kitty looked at Chip and grinned. "Come to think of it, you're a perfect example. I just realized that I've never known anyone so open and enthusiastic."

Chip cocked an eyebrow at her. "Me?"

"You've helped me see that everything isn't always black or white. It's something I need to learn. I need to be less predictable, more spontaneous." She thought a moment. "I need to try to be more like you."

"We have to talk more about this later," Chip said. "I'd like to read that book. You surprised me when you said I help calm you down. I don't see myself that way. I see myself more impatient and impulsive. I appreciate what you said back at the house." He turned the car into the museum parking lot. Ken and Jeffrey were already there.

After their tour of the Getty, Chip had an appointment. They ate a quick lunch and went separate ways. Ken took Kitty over to see his apartment.

"Mom, you look great. I'm amazed at how calm you are under the circumstances."

Kitty didn't say much. She was thinking about how strange it was for her to be there with Ken and without Matt.

"Mom, you okay?" Ken asked. "You're so quiet."

"I'm just enjoying the ride and thinking about how nice it is to be here with you. You've been here two years, and no one's come out to see you."

"Everyone is pretty busy with their own lives," he said, making light of it. He asked about Doug, Susan, and his dad. They discussed the family without getting into the awkward matters of finances or the divorce.

It was 5:00 when Ken dropped off Kitty. She was tired and glad she and Chip were having a quiet dinner at home. They had a delightful evening talking about friends. The conversation about forgiveness never came up, and Kitty was too tired to bring it up.

She was dying to know what Chip was going to say about forgiving yourself. But she didn't want to open old wounds unless he wanted to. She remembered back four years ago when Chip had told her he was taking his family to Mexico for the New Year. He was so excited. It was a surprise for his wife, Fran, who loved Mexico. She was sure that Chip had many regrets about that trip. Fran and their 6-year-old son, Grant, were killed in a car accident during that vacation.

They went to bed early. It was still dark when Kitty woke up the next morning. She was lying there, trying to decide whether to get up or go back to sleep, when she thought she heard the front door close. She sat up and wondered what time it was.

It was 5:00 a.m. She threw her robe on and stepped out onto the terrace. She took a long, deep breath, and took in the fresh sea air. *Ah, I love it.* Chip's room was dark. *I wonder if he goes out for a run this early? But he doesn't get back until 9:00. I wonder what he does for four hours.*

She made coffee and gathered her journal and *The Peace Way,* then went back on the terrace to enjoy her prayers with the lapping of the waves as background music.

Like yesterday, Chip arrived home with steaming hot French pastries. They enjoyed breakfast, but Chip didn't resume yesterday's conversation. Kitty wanted to ask him where he went every morning, and she usually wasn't shy about asking direct questions. But today she decided to let it go. *If he wants me to know, he'll tell me.*

Chip apologized that he had to work most of the day, but he promised to spend the weekend with her. He had arranged for his friend Buddy to take her wherever she wanted to go. "If you want to get your hair done or get a massage, a friend owns Perry's Day Spa. He said he'll work you in. We can call him right now. Their massages are the best, and it's my treat."

Kitty spent the morning at Perry's Spa, and then Buddy took her to his favorite restaurant for a fresh fruit salad. She shopped on Rodeo Drive and got back to the apartment shortly before 5:00 p.m. She and Chip had a quiet dinner at a restaurant around the corner, watched a movie, and then retired for the evening. The subjects of forgiveness and peace never came up. Kitty still hadn't adjusted her sleep pattern to Pacific Time, so she welcomed another quiet night.

Chapter 31

Healing Memories

*"Come to me all you who are labored and
burdened and I will give you rest."*

(Matthew 11: 28)

On Saturday morning, she heard Chip go out again. *I've got to ask him where he goes.* As usual, he was back at 9:00. This time, however, he didn't bring any pastries. "Come on," he announced, "I'm taking you to Shutters for breakfast. It's Saturday, and we should celebrate a day off."

They sat right by the window overlooking the ocean. Breakfast was delicious, and Chip suggested they take a walk along the beach afterward.

"Let's talk about your peace program," he said in between bites. "We were talking about forgiving ourselves when we had to cut the conversation short."

"I was afraid you weren't going to bring it up again," Kitty admitted. "You know me; I'm dying to know what you were going to say. I like to get all the details. I was very frustrated the other day when we ended the conversation so abruptly," she scolded. "I'm not like you, Chip. I can't move from one thought to another without closure."

"I'm glad you came out to visit, Kit. I want to talk to you about some very important things I haven't told you before."

Kitty's face glowed. "I love hearing your stories."

"This is a little different from my stories about celebrities and art," he told her as they got up from their table.

It was a perfect morning to walk. The fresh salt air, the gentle waves, and the clear blue sky with large puffs of white clouds set the scene for a perfect day.

They strolled for a few minutes before Chip broke the silence. "I want to tell you about Fran. Do you mind?"

"I would love it."

"Where do I begin? Let's begin with God. I didn't have much time for God until I met Fran." He smiled. "She loved her God and she was filled with His love for everyone and everything."

He looked straight ahead. He seemed to be groping for the right words. "I think she made me a better person. You know, by example. She slowly convinced me that God was a loving God and He had a plan full of hope for us."

He sighed and continued, "Kit, I'm glad you're here. I haven't really talked about Fran and Grant. It's been too painful. I need to talk about them. You're sure you don't mind listening to me rattle on?"

"Of course not. I'm all ears," Kitty reassured Chip, as she locked her arm into his.

"I met Fran at an art show at the Beverly Wilshire. The moment I saw her, I knew I wanted to marry her." He stopped, looked at Kitty, and smiled. "Life was beautiful! I couldn't take my eyes off her. I couldn't believe she could possibly love me as much as I loved her. But she did."

"You were made for each other," Kitty agreed.

Chip smiled. "I guess we were, because my whole life changed when I married her. I stopped drinking, my business grew, and I found my true self through Fran. Then Grant was born. I never dreamed I could love a human being the way I loved Grant. He just brought out every morsel of goodness I had in me. Kit, for seven wonderful years my life was perfect. I couldn't wait to get home at night just to play with Grant and talk to Fran. Then in one brief second I lost it all. I've said to myself over and over again, 'If only I hadn't taken them to Mexico, if only we had stayed at the resort.' We wouldn't have had the accident." He walked a few more steps without saying anything.

"Sometimes I torture myself with 'if only.' I guess that's why enjoying the moment is one of your peace principles, because regrets eat us alive." He looked out at the Pacific. "You know how Fran always

wanted to go to Mexico. We promised each other we'd go someday."
He stopped talking and hastened his pace.

Kitty was tempted to console him but she didn't. She sensed he was
searching for the right words to express himself and she didn't want to
distract him.

He slowly began speaking again. "The trip was my Christmas present to her." His voice broke. "She was like a little kid when she opened
the envelope with the tickets. She hugged me and danced around the
house like an angel. We were both excited just anticipating the fun we'd
have – the three of us in Mexico, with no responsibilities. We would
just enjoy each other for ten wonderful days."

He sighed and then continued, "We had a glorious time. We had a
breathtaking suite overlooking Mismaloya Bay at the La Jolla de Mismaloya in Puerto Vallarta. For five days we chilled. We went to the
beach, we played in the water; Grant loved it. He'd run to the water's
edge and as soon as the water covered his feet, he'd giggle and tear back
to the beach carrying his little bucket. I could have watched him all
day. He was so cute." Chip started to cry. He wiped his eyes and continued talking. "We fished, snorkeled, ate, took long naps, and sat on
our terrace talking for hours after Grant went to bed. We giggled and
laughed. We just enjoyed each other."

He paused and walked in silence.

Kitty waited for him to continue. She already knew the rest of the
story but she'd never heard him talk about it.

"By the sixth day, we were rested and ready to leave the resort life
behind and experience Mexico's natural paradise," Chip deliberately
explained.

His voice began to quiver again but he continued. "We planned to
drive down the coastline to explore lagoons and secluded coves. Fran
loved nature and she loved wildlife. We wanted to get a feel for the
country and its people. We headed south on Route 200 for Barra de
Navidad. It was one of those glorious summer days, something like
today. We were laughing and singing Grant's favorite song, *Michael
Row the Boat Ashore*. Out of nowhere that truck came straight at us. It
happened so fast. I remember screaming, 'Fran, Grant, hold on!' I tried
to swerve." He started to sob.

Kitty directed him over to a bench. He sobbed and his chest heaved. "I'm sorry, Kit," he gasped.

"It's okay, Chip. Let it out." She sat, putting her arms over his slumped shoulders and offering him a handkerchief. She sat beside him quietly and let him sob. He finally wiped his eyes and blew his nose. "The next thing I remember was waking up in the hospital," he explained, as they got up and began walking along the beach again. "I didn't know how long I'd been there. I just wanted to see Fran and Grant. The first words I heard were, 'Mr. Bradshaw, your wife wants to see you. Do you think you're well enough to be pushed into her room?' I was confused. I still wasn't sure what happened. I just knew I had to see Fran and Grant. I wanted to hold them, tell them how sorry I was." He began sobbing again. Kitty walked silently beside him.

"The doctor pushed my wheelchair into Fran's room. On the way down the hall, he told me we were in a very serious accident. I had a concussion. Grant had serious internal injuries, and Fran was critical, but he didn't prepare me for how she looked. I couldn't wait to talk to her. I knew she'd be able to tell me exactly what happened. She was much better at explaining situations than I was. I expected to see her sitting up in bed with that big smile, eager to talk about the accident and how we'd get home." He started to sob again.

Kitty put her arms around him. He tried talking.

"I gasped when I saw her," he choked out. "She had tubes coming out of her head, her arms, and her side. Her face was all distorted. She opened her swollen eyes and reached out for my hand. She was weak but determined to see me." He started to cry again.

Kitty watched him bend over in wrenching sobs as she tried to control her own tears. "Maybe we should talk about this later."

Chip gestured with his hands. "I need to talk. I'll be okay."

He dragged his palms over his eyes then whispered, "She beckoned to me to lean over. She barely had the energy to reach up and hug me. 'Chippy, I love you so much,' she whispered, clinging to me. Her voice was so weak I could barely hear what she was saying, 'Oh, Chippy, did they tell you God took Grant home to heaven?' Tears rolled down her cheeks."

He started to sob again. He leaned over and deep groans came from somewhere deep inside him. Kitty had never seen anyone so distraught.

"I didn't know," he groaned again, "if she was having delusions or if it was true. No one had told me Grant was dead." He sobbed.

Finally he sat up, wiped his eyes, and continued. "She gave me a squeeze and whispered, 'I love you so much, Chippy. I don't want to leave you, honey, but it's time for me to go and join Grant.' " He started to weep again. "I tried to tell her to rest and we'd talk later. She squeezed me tighter. 'We'll always be with you,' she said. 'Don't grieve for us, go on living. Marry again. I love you.'

"Then she let go and fell back on her pillow with this smile on her face. She was radiant!"

He started to sob again. "She …she… lifted her head as if she saw something, and then said very clearly, 'I'm ready!' She gasped a breath and was gone." Chip broke out in moans. He rocked back and forth on the bench.

Kitty wasn't sure what to do. She watched him. She wanted to hold him but she didn't.

"One trip," he managed to choke out. "One car ride, and all that I loved was gone," he hollered. "My life was over."

They sat on a bench side by side until Chip's sobbing subsided. Finally he stood and slowly started walking in silence.

"Chip, I'm so sorry," Kitty whispered, following.

Chip hesitated. He appeared to be having difficulty explaining his next thought. "I hated God for taking Fran and Grant from me," he blurted out. "He stole my family from me. In a passing second, everything I loved was gone.

"No warning … a brief hug from Fran, and it's over. No Grant, no Fran, just emptiness.

"I felt like heavy steel was pushing against my chest. I couldn't breathe. I couldn't move. I was powerless." His voice got stronger and stronger.

"Faces were racing around me, talking and advising me, and I was frozen in this nightmare." He shook his head. He looked at Kitty. "Kit, I wanted to run away. I wanted to put everything back together again like it was. I wanted to turn back the clock, change what happened. I wanted to wake up and find out it was a nightmare." His voice quivered. "I couldn't. I was helpless, trapped in my own skin. I wanted to die. There was nothing to live for. I thought I'd never laugh again."

Chip stopped again, and they sat quietly staring out to sea.

Chip whispered, "I realize now that she held on until she could hold me and tell me everything would be all right." He stopped talking, wiped his eyes, and started to sob.

Kitty put her arm around him. "Maybe you shouldn't talk about it," she again suggested.

"I want to talk about it," he said, squeezing his eyes tightly, as if willing no tears to fall. "Give me a minute to get myself together. I'm all right, honestly I am," he assured her. After a moment, he went on with his story. "Of course, she was right about Grant. He died an hour after he arrived at the hospital."

Chip got up and started to walk. He had pulled himself together and told the rest of the story in a very matter-of-fact way. "The hospital was wonderful. But there were a lot of complications getting the bodies out of Mexico. You know the rest. You and Matt helped me arrange bringing Fran's and Grant's bodies home. I couldn't have done it without you. I was confused and in a daze. I look back now and realize I didn't have a clue what I was doing. Matt handled everything." Then he added, "Kit, he's one hell of a guy. Don't lose him."

Kitty made no comment, just wiped her eyes. The pair walked for at least ten minutes in silence before Chip continued with his story.

"The emptiness, the loneliness – I couldn't bear life without Fran and Grant. I started drinking again, but this time much worse than before I married Fran. I spiraled downward very quickly. I really wanted to die. I didn't have the courage to commit suicide, but I was trying to drink myself to death."

They walked for another long period in silence. Kitty thought about her own loneliness. She couldn't imagine losing her whole family and going on with life.

"Now you're so alive and full of life," Kitty said, breaking the silence. "What changed you from wanting to die? I mean, losing Fran and Grant, how could you want to go on?"

"I didn't want to," Chip admitted. "One year to the day of their funeral, I woke up in a psychiatric hospital strapped to the bed. I had tried to kill myself with booze. I wanted to die, but it was obvious I probably wasn't going to.

"I was just going to be miserable, so I thought maybe I'd better start trying to live again. I tried moving my arms. I couldn't. I struggled to get loose, but I couldn't. I thought about Fran and Grant. I wondered if they could see me." He sighed.

"I was overwhelmed with shame. I didn't want Fran or Grant to ever see me in that condition. I was a disgrace to myself and to them. I was killing them over and over again with my self-pity. I was the only one who could give their lives meaning, by doing things for others in their names. I woke up that day and vowed I'd keep their spirits alive."

He sighed again. "They were dark, dark days. My doctor introduced me to Alcoholics Anonymous."

"You joined AA?" Kitty asked, surprised.

"I'm one of the lucky ones," he told her. "I've never slipped since my first AA meeting. The biggest thing I learned in AA was to forgive myself, and that a power greater than myself was holding me, watching over me, and forgiving me of all my mistakes."

"Oh, that's why you were so interested in forgiveness the other day," Kitty interrupted. "That's part of AA, isn't it?"

"Yes, that's why I was so interested when you told me about forgiving yourself. AA is a spiritual, 12-step program," he explained. "Forgiveness is a big part of it, and you'll be interested to know that forgiving yourself is the first step in forgiveness."

Kitty was surprised. "Are you suggesting that forgiving myself isn't as off-the-wall as I thought it was?"

Chip laughed. "You were right on."

"I'm glad to see you laugh."

He sighed. "I needed to cry, Kit. I needed to get it out."

"I'm glad I was here."

He looked out to the sea and smiled. "I'm glad you're here, too. God has been very good to me. I met wonderful people in AA, and I slowly began living again. My business picked up. My friends encouraged me. I got back on my feet. People were so supportive."

"You seem very happy. I don't know if I could ever get back on my feet if something like that happened to me," Kitty said.

"I became obsessed about doing something in Fran and Grant's memory, so I started an organization in Fran's and Grant's names to help feed street people. Reaching out to others rejuvenated me. It gave me a new meaning in life," he said, smiling.

"I'm glad you found something that makes you so happy."

"Actually Kit, being with the street people is a big help for me. They are like my family; I can't wait to open up in the morning."

"Is that where you go at 5 a.m.?"

He confirmed with a nod. They walked quietly along the beach path. Chip spoke up again. "There is, uh, one more thing I'd like to tell you."

"You seem hesitant. Is it something else about Fran and Grant? You can tell me anything, and it will always be just between you and me," Kitty assured him.

"I want to tell you about a little snag in my life."

"A snag?"

"Remember when I had pneumonia two years ago?"

"How could I forget? You never told me until you were completely better."

"Well, earlier this year a shadow showed up in my chest X-ray. At first, they thought it was nothing – just an aftereffect of the pneumonia. But my cough persisted; it wouldn't go away." He looked out toward the ocean. "And my doctor was getting concerned," he said reluctantly as he walked a little farther.

"Go on," Kitty impatiently pushed for more information.

"It turned out to be more than a shadow. I had lung cancer."

"Lung cancer?" Kitty repeated. She stopped walking and covered her mouth with her hands, stunned. "You never told us. Why?"

"I said I *had* lung cancer. They feel they've gotten it. I didn't want to worry you," he responded.

"Didn't want to worry me? Chip, as close as we are, how would you feel if I did that to you?"

"I would be upset." Chip's shoulders were slightly slumped. "Kit, try to understand. At first, I didn't believe it. How could I possibly have cancer? I was just getting my life back together. I wanted to live. The doctors were sure they found it in the early stages, and I was given a good chance of beating it. I was hopeful and decided not to tell anyone. It was just a blip in my life that would soon be resolved."

"What's the prognosis?" Kitty nervously asked.

Chip turned his head to the sea as he answered her. "I had extensive treatments, and they seem to have worked. It's fine. Everything is fine."

"You're telling me the truth?" Kitty asked.

"Yes, yes."

"You know, Chip," Kitty began, "outside of Matt and my children, you're the only family I have." Her voice quivered. "Please don't keep me in the dark about anything as serious as cancer. It hurts me to think you felt you couldn't share this with me." She discreetly blotted her nose. "You're so thin. Are you sure they got it all?"

He put his hands on her shoulders. "I'm sorry, Kit. I didn't want to hurt you. It just didn't seem that important. Yes, yes, everything's fine."

"You're not convincing me."

He hesitated. "Well, they did find another spot on my other lung."

"Chip!"

"I'm starting treatment next week. It's a tiny little pimple. They're just giving me precautionary treatment."

"You just said everything was fine, and it's not," Kitty said, her voice quivering. "Please, promise me you won't keep me in the dark again. I love you, and I don't want anything to happen to you. Now promise!"

He promised. Then he said. "So, that's the whole story. You're my only family. I wanted you to know the story. But I'm emotionally talked out. Let's just walk for a while, if you don't mind."

The breeze was capricious. It swept across their faces and ruffled their hair. Kitty thought about how gentle God was. *Right now, we need your gentle breeze, dear God. Thank you. Thank you for Chip. How can he possibly be so happy? Lord, please still my curiosity. I have so many questions.*

Chapter 32

Find Your Purpose

*"I alone know the plans I have for you, plans to bring you prosperity
not disaster, plans to bring about the future you hope for."*

(Jeremiah 29:11)

Chip and Kitty walked simply enjoying each other's presence. Kitty welcomed the silence. She needed to think about everything she'd just heard.

She finally spoke. "Chip, you are amazing. Life's hit you with some real struggles, yet you keep going. In spite of all your pain, you seem happy. How do you do that?"

Chip kept walking. He didn't answer for some time, and Kitty wished she hadn't asked him.

He eventually replied, "Kit, grief is like being trapped in a deep dark hole. Then occasional tiny glimmers of light appear. The glimmers slowly grow into brilliant light. I cherish the light of life. I know it is so fragile." He looked at her with his broad smile. "It's the darkness of night that makes daylight so bright, and the pain of sorrow that makes joy so sweet, and the barren winter that makes spring so glorious. Happiness is a choice, and a full life is a roller coaster of joy and sorrow, night and day, spring and winter."

"You think we can choose to be happy even in the midst of pain?"

"Yes, I do. Actually, that's what your peace process is all about."

"I guess so." Kitty put her hands in her pockets. "I'm not sure I understand how the peace process helps us find happiness in the midst of pain."

"Well, when Fran died, I felt sorry for myself. I was the victim of cruel circumstances. That was the darkest time of my life, but also the greatest time of growth. It was in that dark abyss that I discovered a much deeper purpose in life than just living to please myself. I learned the meaning of compassion, love, and understanding, both for myself and others."

"You were always compassionate and understanding," Kitty said.

"On the surface," Chip began to explain. "I wanted people to like me. I had compassion and understanding when it was convenient for me. But I never really put myself out for anyone unless I really felt like it."

Kitty thought about that. The soft breeze blew off the ocean and she pushed her hair off her face. "I'm not following you. How do you find peace in pain?"

"If I understand your principles correctly, you praise and thank God for everything going on in your life both good and bad. Is that correct?"

"That's the gist, but it's hard to do. I don't think I could praise and thank God for the death of my spouse and family."

"You said you're praising and thanking God for being in the midst of your current challenges, even if you can't see Him."

"Yes."

"I guess I sort of did that when I made a commitment to give meaning to Fran's and Grant's lives. AA helped me appreciate the blessings in my life, especially the blessings of Fran and Grant. When I began to think of our life together as a gift from God, and my memories as blessings, I began to move on in my life. I'll always have an empty place in my heart for Fran and Grant. No one can take their place. At the same time, it is that emptiness that inspired me to reach out and help others. That brought purpose and meaning to my loneliness, which brought me joy and peace."

Kitty sighed. "I'm trying to get to that same place."

"Kit, you've come a long way." He told her that he loved a scripture passage from Jeremiah: "I have a plan for you, a plan full of hope."

"I believe God plants in our hearts a desire to fulfill that plan. He lights our way, as you say in your prayer, to help us fulfill our purpose for living. I believe my purpose in life is to help the forgotten men and women on the streets, especially those with AIDS. And God has planted in my heart a deep desire to help and touch these men and women, in Fran's and Grant's names. And that gives me great delight."

"You are amazing," Kitty said.

"It's what keeps me going, Kit. That's why I'm excited for you and what's going on in your life right now. I'm glad you found the peace principles. As you praise and thank God, God will reveal his plan for you. Now that your children are raised, God has something else for you to do. You'll discover a unique purpose in life that only you can fulfill. Whatever it is, it'll be something you love to do."

"I hope you're right. I can't imagine what purpose God has for me. I don't even know how to get a job."

"You're at a crossroads in your life. All the things you held sacred have been pulled out from under you." Chip frowned. "It hurts. But some day you'll look back at this and see how it helped you find the real you."

"What do you mean?"

"Well, sometimes I think you see yourself as Douglas Bradshaw's daughter rather than seeing yourself as Kitty Murphy."

"I *am* Douglas Bradshaw's daughter."

"You are, but you're also a unique individual separate from Douglas and Katharine Bradshaw. You're a wonderful wife and mother. However, I always felt … how can I say this? It's as if Douglas Bradshaw's daughter is a wonderful wife and mother, not Kitty Murphy. Your identity is all tied up in being a Bradshaw, rather than being you. Who is Kitty Murphy?"

Kitty shook her head. "Chip, my parents were my best role models. Isn't that natural?"

"Your parents did a great job raising you. You'd be crazy to forget that. I'm saying that you have to discover who you are, who Kitty Murphy is. Why is she on this earth? You're being called to step out of the shadow of your parents and live your own life."

"It almost seems as if you want me to abandon my loyalties to Mother and Dad," Kitty said, confused.

"My loyalty is to you, Kit," Chip said gently. "That's why I'm telling you that there'll come a day when you will thank God for all the pain you're suffering now. You'll get through this and discover beautiful, wonderful you. That's what life is all about. It's the core of your peace process."

"Chip, you couldn't help what happened to you. And you turned your suffering into joy for someone else. But I don't believe we have to suffer to discover who we are. I'm in this situation because Matt was irresponsible."

Chip hesitated. "Kit, Matt made some mistakes, but he wasn't irresponsible. He's like hundreds of other guys who got caught up in the tech boom. It turned around and bit him. He's there facing it every day, trying to work it out. He hasn't run away. He's just as scared as you are, but he's facing it. I know you don't want to hear this, Kit, but don't forget, you also got caught up in the tech boom."

Kitty frowned. "Yes, but he was the expert. He should have stopped me."

"Kit, let's be honest. He tried to stop you. You were on a roll, and you weren't going to let anyone stop you."

She was silent for a few moments, and then she asked, "How did we ever get into this conversation?" As an afterthought she added, "You know, Chip, I think I did a pretty good job of raising my children and being a good wife up until now, even if you don't think so."

"Kitty, I agree," he said. "That's what I'm saying. I'm very proud of you, and your parents were proud of you."

"You know, Chip, I am a Bradshaw, and you and I are the last of the Bradshaws. I'm not going to let Matt's financial irresponsibility embarrass us and ruin our family name."

Chip raised his eyebrows. "He's ruining the Bradshaw name, is that what you think?"

"I don't think it; I know it."

"Maybe we should talk about this later," he said softly.

"No, I want to talk about it now."

He stopped and looked at her. "Kit, listen to you. You're more concerned with the Bradshaw name than you are with Matt, your children, or even yourself." He hesitated. He started to say something, but thought better of the idea. He walked faster and Kitty trailed slightly behind.

"What were you going to say?"

"I've probably said too much."

"I want to hear it," Kitty said catching up to him.

He slowed. "Kit, doing the right thing will never ruin a family name. Everyone has difficulties in life. When we're down, people will criticize us, but they are not our real friends. Our real friends will stick by us and support us. You know that fifth principle, encourage others? Let me tell you that Matt is doing the right thing. Matt is one hell of a guy, and I hope you wake up and see that before it's too late."

"I get your gist, Chip. Let's just drop this conversation." Kitty felt exhausted. *It's all too much – Fran, Grant, AA, Matt, and peace.*

Chip seemed to understand that she didn't want to talk, and they headed back to the car in silence.

As they walked, Kitty's thoughts raced between Chip, Matt, and her family name. She replayed in her head the events of the past few months. *Matt should have stopped me from buying those stocks. He was supposed to be the smart one. He did try to stop me, but he didn't try hard enough. I have to protect the Bradshaw name. I wonder if Matt is scared? I can't stand this. Lord, how can I praise you?*

Chip stopped walking. "I'm sorry if I hurt your feelings. I hope you know I love you." He stepped in front of her and looked into her eyes.

"You asked me how I could be so happy. I had to find the real me to find happiness. I don't want to see you hurt. But I know you will discover wonderful things about yourself. You'll find strengths you never knew you had. I really believe you and Matt will get back together and you'll have a fuller and richer relationship." He shook his head. "You'll probably experience some more tough times but you *will* get through them. Just keep doing what you're doing and you'll be just fine."

Kitty didn't know what to say. They continued walking in silence. Kitty watched the ocean waves crest and break. The breeze was light and warm. The sand felt good underneath her feet. Although she did not appreciate Chips remarks, she felt the atmosphere was right for this conversation. She finally said, "It sounds to me like you're blaming me for all our problems."

Chip shook his head. "I'm not blaming anyone. I'm only pointing out that you are a person, a wonderful human being with special qualities unique to you. And Matt is a person with unique and wonderful qualities. As humans, you'll make mistakes. But if you're true to yourself, you will get through it and be a better person because of it. That's what life is all about."

They walked on without speaking. Kitty occasionally looked over at Chip. *He is sweet. He's just being honest with me. I don't want to ruin our time together. Praise and thank you, Lord, for this moment and for Chip. Is he right? Am I too concerned about the Bradshaw name? Help me appreciate this time with Chip and this conversation.*

By the time they reached the car, Kitty was feeling a little better. She watched her uncle fasten his seat belt. "Chip," she said hesitantly. He looked over at her and gave her one of his big grins.

"You're probably right about Matt. I haven't thought about how scared he might be, and I haven't thought about him trying to put it all together. He could run away but he hasn't. He probably wants to. But you're not right about us reconciling. Too much has happened between us. We'll never get back together."

Chip seemed to choose his words carefully. "Don't give up so easily. Look at what you've accomplished these past few months. You're taking time every day to get yourself into a peaceful, calm state. You're facing all the unexpected events in your life with trust that God has a plan for you."

"I still can't imagine what kind of plan He has for me, or us."

"Keep doing what you're doing and it will evolve. AA opens its meeting with the serenity prayer: 'Oh God, give me the serenity to accept the things I cannot change, the courage to change the things I can change, and the wisdom to know the difference.'"

"I'm glad we're having this talk," Kitty told Chip. "I need more honesty in my life." She paused. "You're being honest with me, and I need to be honest with you. I'm heartbroken and scared. Sometimes I'm downright petrified, and then there are moments when I have a peace like I've never had in my life. It's weird. I'm scared but not frightened. I do think we're all going to be okay."

He nodded his head in agreement and started the car.

Kitty continued, "But I'm a bit miffed about what you said to me about my sense of identity. It's hard to accept that as a wife and mother

I'm more concerned about my parents than my husband and children. But I will think and pray about what you said."

"I hope I didn't upset you too much," Chip said sincerely.

"You did, but maybe I needed to hear it, and you're the best person to tell me. Chip, you're going to be all right, aren't you?" she asked, anxious to change the subject.

"I'm going to be fine. Let's get some lunch. It's almost 12:30.

They chatted about what type of job Kitty should look for when she got back to Philadelphia, and spent the afternoon sauntering down Rodeo Drive. After stopping into Starbucks for a cappuccino, Chip suggested they go to a 5:00 p.m. Mass. Kitty was taken by surprise. She'd thought Chip was a member of the Unitarian Church.

He explained that he and Fran used to attend the Unitarian Church. But after Fran died, a friend invited him to the Catholic Church. "When I walked into the church for the first time, they were singing the hymn 'Be Not Afraid.' I felt the words were written directly for me. There was an overwhelming presence that I've never felt before. It's the church for me. I love it."

Kitty responded curtly, "You're indeed a complex being. Just as I think I understand you, you throw me another curve. What other surprises do you have for me?"

"Hey, are you upset about the Catholic Church?" he asked. He seemed surprised by her attitude.

"Of course I'm not," Kitty refuted. "If you find peace in the Catholic Church, that's fine. I just never expected it."

"Kit, you certainly don't have to go. It's a beautiful ceremony. The Mass is alive with prayers of praise and thanksgiving. They have a wonderful choir. You love beautiful music; I thought you might enjoy it."

It was 4:15. Kitty stared intently at the bustling barista behind the counter.

"Will you be disappointed if I don't go?"

"No, not at all. I'll go early tomorrow."

Kitty was agitated. Why did Chip have to bring up church? He knew she was, at best, ambivalent about organized religion. *The minute you discuss anything spiritual, people want to drag you into church.* Was he trying to ruin her day, first talking about her parents, now church?

They sat in silence. In her mind, she struggled. *There is peace in this moment. I don't want to feel peace in this moment. He ruined the moment.*

The two of them finished their coffees in silence.

Kitty looked over at Chip. He smiled back at her, and she noticed again how thin he was. *Don't be so selfish, Kit. He's lonely. He just wants you to go with him. It won't kill you. He's been so good to you.*

"How long is the Mass?" she asked.

"About an hour."

"I'll go; it might do me good," she said halfheartedly.

The church was packed. Kitty hadn't attended a church service in years. The flowers, burning candles, and soft organ music calmed her heart and relaxed her nerves. She listened intently to the priest's homily. To her surprise he preached about peace and how peace of heart comes from God's loving presence living within us.

Thank You, God, for loving me. Thank You for speaking to me through so many different people. Help me listen.

When the congregation sang, "Let There Be Peace on Earth," Kitty's emotions exploded and she began to cry. She was embarrassed, and she covered her face with her hands as she wept throughout the rest of Mass.

They drove home in silence. By the time they arrived, they were both exhausted, but Kitty thanked Chip for the day. "It was like a spiritual retreat. I loved it. I enjoyed church, too. Thanks." They both agreed they weren't hungry and retired to their rooms.

The next morning Kitty sat on the terrace and prayed. *I'm going to miss this when I go home.* She praised and thanked God for the wonderful trip. She thought about how much Chip loved and trusted God in spite of all his suffering. She thought about what he'd said about her self-worth. She thought about the priest's homily and the music. She was overwhelmed with wonder at God's love, His goodness, His people, and His world. Then she remembered Caroline's words:

"I can't begin to tell you how many wonderful things have happened in my life since I started praising and thanking God and sending love out to all the painful situations in my life."

Kitty reflected on the prayers for forgiveness. She extracted her journal and made a list of all the hurts she'd experienced. She wrote rapidly.

The thoughts came faster than she could record. Next she made a second list of all the blessings she received from the hurts. These included renewing her friendship with Caroline, making the plane reservation herself, flying to California alone, finding her own place to live, and living on her own for the first time in her life. She also listed facing the electric company, practicing the peace process, finding God, getting to know her own son better, and having honest conversations with Chip. She thought about all the things she'd accomplished in the past few months and everything she learned in the past four days. *It's almost too much to take in. Maybe Chip is right. I have lived in a bubble.*

Lost in her thoughts, she jumped when she heard her uncle. "Oh, Chip, you startled me – but it's a nice way to get scared," she added. Taking him by the hand, she walked into the dining area. "I'm dying of curiosity. When you leave the house at 5:00 a.m., do you go right to the shelter and spend all this time there?"

"Ah, ah, ah," he said smiling, "curiosity killed the cat and satisfaction buried it. Now I don't want to have to bury you, do I?" he teased. The table was set for two with a bowl of fresh sliced fruit and freshly squeezed orange-and-carrot juice, a mixture Kitty had grown to enjoy.

"Chip, tell me. I can't go home without knowing everything you do in the morning."

He smiled. "Come on, eat your fruit," he urged.

"I'll eat when you tell me," she said, pouting.

"Aren't you the spoiled one! You're going to be disappointed. I go out at 5:00 a.m. to run. I run for a half-hour, and then I go to the shelter. I turn on the stoves and get everything ready for breakfast. Sometimes I help bathe the guys they picked up off the street the night before – not very exciting, huh? But I love it. I gave them a big commercial stove in honor of Fran and Grant. It doesn't sound like a lot, but they really needed it. Those restaurant stoves cost about $25,000."

"I think it's wonderful," Kitty gushed. "I admire you. As I said last night, you're a complex man. Every day I'm surprised about what I learn. Do you stay there until 9:00, or do you go somewhere else?"

"I go to the 8:00 a.m. Mass, stop at the bakery, and come home. It's my favorite time of the day. I feel very close to Fran and Grant when I'm at the shelter or in church. I feel I'm helping them live on in the hearts and memories of many people who never knew them."

"You wanted to give meaning to their lives, and you have. You're helping a lot of people."

"They help me more than I help them." He gave Kit his big, broad smile. "I'm going to miss you. I've loved our chats. I know you're going to be fine. Your life may change, things may be very different, but you'll be happier than you've ever been."

"I hope you're right."

"You're on the right track. Don't get discouraged. God has great things in store for you. Relax and go for the ride. It's a blast." He leaned over and kissed Kitty on the cheek.

They had a late lunch, walked the beach, and talked about many different topics. The day ended too soon. Kitty packed her bags before she went to bed. Ken was driving her to the airport the next morning to catch an 8:00 a.m. flight home.

Before she turned in, she gave Chip a big hug. "I love you, Chip. Thanks for showing me such a wonderful time. And thanks for being honest with me. You gave me a lot to consider. God bless, and good night."

Chapter 33

Faith

"Courage, my daughter, your faith has made you well."

(Matthew 9:23)

Kitty had dinner with Doug and Susan her first night home. She told them all about her trip, and how much she'd enjoyed Ken and Chip. Doug and Susan were glad their mother and Ken had gotten to spend some quality time together.

The next day, Kitty started looking at employment ads. She went to an agency and talked to friends. She answered several ads, but the first question they asked was, "How much experience do you have?" Most of them told her to send a resume. She was getting discouraged when one of her friends told her about a local college looking for someone to work in its development office. "I know the head of development," her friend assured her. "I'll recommend you."

This gave Kitty some encouragement. Her friend did get her an interview with the head of development. He was gracious but a little pompous. He used words like *prestigious* and *elite* to describe the college, and questioned Kitty extensively about how she raised so much money for breast cancer. Who were her big donors? How did she woo them? He then had her meet with two other members of the staff. In spite of Mr. Sway's pretentiousness, she felt the interviews had gone well.

But she didn't get the job. They said she was overqualified. "We're not looking for someone to run our events," he told her. "We're looking for an assistant. It's obvious, Mrs. Murphy, that you would be better suited running a development office."

Kitty continued looking, but the responses were the same. She either lacked experience or she was overqualified. *How is it possible that I am overqualified when I've never worked in an office?* She continued her search for two months with no luck. Matt sent her a check every week with a little note assuring her she would find the perfect job.

She faithfully spent a half hour in the morning meditating on the peace secret of the week. "I'm amazed at how calm and confident I am," she told Caroline at Starbucks one morning. "Somehow, I know it'll all work out. Matt and I are getting along better. We have dinner one or two nights a week. I'm worried about him, though. He's so drawn and thin."

She looked at Caroline and said, "Either I'm in complete denial or I've found the secret to inner peace. I only have three months left in the townhouse, and I don't have a clue where I'm going."

That night she fell into a deep sleep, but woke up when she heard the phone ringing. She fumbled for the receiver. "Mom, this is Doug," announced the voice on the other end of the line. "I'm at the University of Pennsylvania Hospital with Dad. He's bleeding internally. Susan's on her way over to pick you up."

"Please, God, don't let anything happen to Matt," Kitty immediately pleaded. She said it over and over again as she rushed to get dressed. The phone rang again. It was Susan telling Kitty she was around the corner. Kitty continued her prayer: "Oh, God, you have a plan. I just have to trust you. I praise and thank you for Matt, and for the doctors taking care of him."

In the car, Kitty encouraged Susan to join her in praising God for her father's health and recovery. They prayed together on the way to the hospital and walked into the ICU at 1:00 a.m. Tubes were attached everywhere to Matt's body, and his gaunt, pale face scared her. He looked so frail and so old.

Kitty took his limp hand and prayed silently, praising and thanking God for healing him. *Thank You, Lord, for touching and healing Matt. Thank you for his doctors and nurses. Thank you for giving them the wisdom to properly diagnose and cure his illness.*

The doctor told Kitty, "He's a lucky man. He got here just in time. He had an enormous ulcer that was just about to burst." He told Kitty that Matt would probably be in the hospital for several days. Numerous tests would be needed to determine if he had any other problems.

Kitty slept in the chair by her husband's bed for two nights. She gently placed warm compresses on his head when he shivered, and cool ones when he was feverish. She continually rubbed his lips with ice and moisturized them with Vaseline. The first night, he drifted in and out of restless sleep, quietly moaning and groaning when he tried unsuccessfully to turn. By the third day, he was feeling better but was still weak.

"Kit, I've had stomach pains for a long time now," he told her. "I thought when we got all our affairs straightened out, they would go away. It's amazing how one minute you're going along feeling fine, and then you collapse. The pain was so excruciating, I couldn't talk."

He looked out the hospital window. He didn't say anything for a while. Then he added, "Lucky for me, Doug was with me. I've learned a lot from this experience." He looked away. He stared out the window again. After a long silence he said, "Kit, will you do me a favor?"

"Of course! What can I get you?"

"I want you to talk to our lawyer. I want you to know what's going on with our affairs. I've instructed him to lay everything out for you, so you understand where we are and what you can expect."

Kitty was horrified at his insinuation. "Don't worry about that now. We can discuss this when you're feeling better."

"Hon, I want you to talk with Jim," Matt urged Kitty. "It's important. Will you promise me you'll talk to him tomorrow?"

Kitty suddenly had trouble getting her breath. She opened her mouth wide to take in some air and felt like something was pushing her chest. *Is Matt dying? Did the doctors tell him something I don't know?* Then she prayed. *Thank you, Lord, for taking care of us. I depend on you, Lord, and I put my hope in you. Thank you for soaking us in your hope.*

She had a lot of questions but she didn't want to burden her ailing husband. He was still weak. She had a strong urge to pray with him, but she was embarrassed. Instead, she leaned over and kissed him good night. "I love you, Matt. No matter what happens between us, I will always love you," she said, trying to hold back tears.

He looked at her. "Thanks, Kit. You'd better go. It's getting late.

You don't want to be driving in this area alone at night." It sounded like he was dismissing her. But just as she got to the door, he said, "Kit, you're a great woman. I appreciate you being here. Thanks."

Kitty cried all the way home, and she talked to God out loud. "God, what are you doing? Since I've been praising you, things are getting worse. Praising is supposed to empower us. My whole life is crumbling." She couldn't stop crying. "He doesn't love me anymore. That's obvious. It's over. Maybe he knows he's dying. Oh my God, what will I do? This praising doesn't work. What will I do?"

Wild thoughts pirouetted in her mind. She was paralyzed with fear. Matt had been in the hospital three days. True, he was doing better, but he still wasn't well. Did he know something she didn't know? *Oh God, is he going to die?*

Kitty's phone started ringing as she put the key in her front door. It was Caroline.

"Kit, I just heard about Matt. How is he?"

"You must be psychic; you always seem to call when I'm at my lowest. I think he'll be okay." Kitty sighed, feeling stricken. "I don't understand why all this is happening to me. Since you taught me to praise God, my whole world has fallen apart. I suppose I was expecting some kind of immediate reward. What's the point of using a cure that doesn't work?"

"You've had a lot happen to you in a short time," Caroline agreed.

"My husband's bleeding to death and I'm back to not having a place to live. I can't get a job. They tell me I'm overqualified but I've never worked. I don't think my experience is a very good advertisement for praising and thanking God." She sighed again. "If you ask me, God needs a better marketing plan if He wants people to praise Him."

Caroline gently laughed at Kitty's remark. Once she started laughing, she couldn't stop. "I'm sorry, Kit, but I can't help it. You're probably right. God does need a good marketing plan. Do you have any suggestions?"

Kitty laughed and calmed down enough to say, "You know I have to blame someone, Caroline. I just couldn't believe it when Matt got sick. But I really can't blame it on God. Matt doesn't take care of himself. He eats a lot of junk food and he's been under unbelievable stress.

I feel terrible. The poor guy was so sick and he was in excruciating pain. But he's feeling much better."

"Nick said the same thing. He said Matt's been under so much stress, he's surprised Matt didn't get sick sooner. Did the bleeding stop?"

Kitty took a deep breath and said, "Yes, he's much better. And to tell you the truth, I think my prayers helped. I had the strongest urge to pray with him but I lost my courage, so I prayed quietly. I don't know whether I was imagining it, but he seemed to calm down and fall into a deep sleep after I prayed for him." Kitty sighed. "Oh, it's all too much."

"I'm sure your prayers made a big difference," Caroline encouraged her. "What can I say? You're angry with God's PR system, so I'd better not say much." She laughed again.

Kitty also chuckled. But the exhaustion and emotion seemed to have caught up with her, and she started laughing and couldn't stop. "I'm a mess. One minute, I'm a crying fool; the next, I'm a hyena."

"I'm glad you can see some humor in all this," Caroline said with levity.

"Let's praise God," Kitty suggested. "He may have a rotten marketing plan, but He does have a sense of humor. And you know what else I'm beginning to realize? God doesn't mind when I get angry with Him. He understands me better than I understand myself."

They prayed together, praising and thanking God for Matt's health, Nick's healing, Kitty's job search, and whatever else they could think of.

Kitty felt much better when she hung up. She kicked her shoes off and fell into a chair where she proceeded to doze. She didn't know how long she had been asleep when she felt someone looking at her. She opened her eyes. Susan was standing in front of her.

"Oh, how did you get in?"

"When you leave the keys in the door, it's easy."

Kitty put her hand over her mouth. "Oh my gosh, that's dangerous."

Susan leaned over and gave her mom a warm squeeze. "You must be exhausted. Let me get you a cup of tea."

"You're an angel. Thanks for coming over."

Susan stayed overnight. She and Kitty both left early the next morning, Susan to school, and Kitty to the lawyer's office.

Chapter 34

Be Not Afraid

"I'm going to put breath into you and bring you back to life."

(Exodus 37:6)

The lawyer told Kitty that he had good news and bad news. The good news was that Matt's once-conservative investing skills were paying off. When he'd purchased an annuity for Sadie in the mid-1980s, he also purchased one for Kitty. It was generating $500 a month, and she already was getting $500 monthly from an annuity from her father.

She stared at him. "That's the good news?" she asked sarcastically.

Her lawyer smiled. "Believe me, Kitty, it's better than nothing. You'll have to get a job."

"Is that the bad news: I have to get a job?" Kitty inquired.

Her lawyer looked a little sheepish. "That's part of it."

Kitty was impatient. "Well, what else?"

"We'll need to cancel all your credit cards, except for your American Express. That's one of the best cards," her lawyer explained. "However, the balance needs to be paid at the end of every month. It's for emergencies only."

"You're kidding, aren't you? You're telling me I have to live on $1,000 a month, and I can't use my American Express card? How can I possibly do that? That's poverty level," she said, trying to control her voice. "What about the proceeds from the house?"

"That's being held in escrow until all the debt against it is paid. We're hoping you'll get some money from the house by the time the Frenches return from Italy. I'm sorry." He explained that he and Matt had been working for weeks to pay creditors, make arrangements for Kitty, and keep Matt in business.

Kitty controlled the rage she was feeling. She wanted to scream out, "There's no way I can live on this! I'll get my own lawyer and fight this." But she didn't. In a soft, controlled voice, she uttered, "You're kidding, Jim. Certainly you're joking."

Jim looked pensive. "Kitty, things will definitely get better," he said, trying to reassure her. "When you get a job, you'll have more money."

"When I get a job? Are you crazy? Do you have any idea how hard it is for a 46-year-old woman to get a job, especially if she doesn't have any experience? Would you hire me? Answer me honestly: Would you?"

The lawyer stared at her. He shifted in his seat. "I don't need anyone right now."

"You mean you don't need an inexperienced 46-year-old woman. You don't even have the guts to be honest. Well, no one wants to hire me." She felt a lump well up in her throat. She took a deep breath, coughed, and regained her composure.

"Kit, this will pass," Jim said. "Matt's doing everything he can to generate income. Matt's an incredible guy, and he's crazy about you." He looked into her big blue eyes. He cleared his throat. "You know that, don't you?"

Jim's probing question didn't even register in her mind. Kitty was too shocked to say anything. She had wanted clarity on where she stood financially, but she hadn't expected it to be this bad. She couldn't possibly live on $1,000 a month. She couldn't believe Jim and Matt were doing this to her.

"Jim, how am I going to live? Have you figured that one out?"

"Kitty, we tried every way we could to get you more income. This is temporary. I'm sure Matt will turn things around. He's a smart guy."

"You're right, he's smart. Smart enough to cheat his wife. How much is he getting? I bet a lot more than $1,000 a month." Kitty tried to control her anger but fear overwhelmed her.

She was used to a personal allowance from her father's trust that had been well over six figures a year. She'd always had several credit cards with no limits, a closet full of designer clothes, and a new Jaguar convertible every two years.

"What about my car?"

"It's paid for. You'll have to take care of the maintenance, but there's no debt on it," Jim explained.

"You didn't tell me about Matt. How much is he getting?"

"Actually, there isn't any money for him. He'll live on his earnings."

"How much is that?" Kitty demanded.

"Kitty, you know he's broke. He's got to turn his business around. He's living in a friend's apartment, just like you are. If you two lived together, you'd have more money," he said, looking at her. He hesitated, and then said, "You two were crazy about each other. Can't you work this thing out?"

Kitty looked away. "Please, Jim, don't talk about us being crazy about each other. Matt has a hell of a way of showing all that love you talk about. So don't give me that nonsense."

Suddenly an awful thought ran through her mind. *How much does Jim's wife know?* Mortified, she asked, "Jim, does Marilyn know?"

He shook his head. "No, you're my clients. I never tell Marilyn anything about my clients. That's strictly confidential. As far as I know, no one knows."

She resisted the overwhelming urge to slap him. "This is the worst insult I've ever had. Do you hear me?" she insisted. "An insult!"

"Kitty, I'm sorry, truly sorry. This is the best we can do right now."

An inner voice cautioned her. *Control yourself. Take a deep, slow breath. Praise and thank God for this moment. He has a plan for you. There is peace in this moment.*

She hesitated and stared at Jim. Suddenly, she went limp; she was exhausted. She had to get out of there. She wanted to run and never stop. "I must go. I can't talk. It's too devastating."

Jim reached out to hug her but she turned away. "I'm here for you," he said. "I know Matt will work everything out. He's more concerned for you than you'll ever know. Believe me, Kit, when I tell you that."

Kitty called Chip's number the minute she got in the car. She looked at the phone. *My cell phone – who's going to pay for that? How will I pay for all these things with $1,000 a month?* She panicked. She was ready to hang up when she heard Chip's voice.

"Kit, honey, how's it going?"

She told him about her visit with the lawyer. They talked for about 20 minutes. Chip listened. He was always a good shoulder to cry on.

"Chip, what will I do? How will I live?" Kitty babbled hysterically.

"I understand why you're so upset. You know I'm here for you.

Don't worry." His reassuring voice helped Kitty. She listened intently to his words of encouragement. "You have more going for you than you realize. You'll get through this. You're a strong woman, Kit. The perfect job will come along. Don't worry. You know I'll help you."

Chip's soothing voice and wise counsel calmed her. "Let me say a prayer with you," he suggested.

Kitty seethed with anger at the thought of prayer. But she didn't want to offend him, so reluctantly she agreed. "Chip, I hope you and Caroline are right. I hope there's a God pouring His love and abundance on me. If there is, He has a strange way of showing it," she said. "Go ahead, say your prayer."

"Lord, your daughter is frightened," Chip began. "She's in the midst of a terrible storm. She needs to know you're with her. She needs to know you're holding her in the palm of your hand. She needs to know she has nothing to fear. Take her heart in your tender hands and soothe her, hold her, let her feel your powerful love for her this moment. Show her your light and wisdom and peace."

There was silence and then Kitty took a long breath. "Thank you, Chip, you're a sweetheart. I do feel better. God has already shown me His love by giving me you," she whispered. "Thanks. I better not use up any more minutes on my cell phone."

"I love you, Kit," Chip said as she was about to hang up.

"I love you, too, Chip."

**

After Kitty ended their call, Chip called Matt to see how he was doing. Matt, like many men, kept his problems to himself. He assured Chip he would be fine and thanked him for being there for Kitty. "You know I appreciate it," he told Chip. "It's just one of those damn things we have to work through. We'll make it. I know we will," Matt assured him. Right before they hung up, he asked, "Did Kit say anything to you about her visit with our lawyer?"

Chip hesitated. "She mentioned it."

Matt laughed. "Thanks, Chip, you're always the diplomat. You're a good friend."

Chapter 35

Trust

*"The Lord protects and defends me.
I trust in Him and He gives me help."*

(Psalm 28:6)

Matt went back to work as soon as he was released from the hospital, and Kitty continued her job search with greater urgency. She counted every penny and kept records of everything. Although she wasn't used to being frugal, she was surprised at how well she stretched her money.

At first, she kept playing over and over in her head how Matt had taken advantage of her ignorance and cheated her. The more she thought about it, the angrier she got. She couldn't even talk to him. She waffled over whether she should get her own lawyer or trust that it would all work out.

Except for Caroline, she hadn't told anyone what was going on. However, word got out, so she admitted to one of her close country club friends that it was true. She and Matt were having financial problems and were getting divorced. Her friend urged her to get her own lawyer.

"It's survival of the fittest," she told Kitty while writing down the telephone number of a competent female divorce lawyer. "It's him or you."

On the other hand, Caroline cautioned her that court cases and lawyers could perpetuate the problem. "You can't get blood from a stone. If you're meant to get your own lawyer," she said, "God will open the door for you at the right time. Be patient."

Kitty never mentioned getting a lawyer to the children. As angry as she was, she tried not to discuss her feelings about Matt with them.

On the morning of November 1, Kitty woke up in a cold sweat. She kept thinking over and over, *I've got to get a job. Any job.* She was jittery. She made coffee and sat down in her prayer corner, but she couldn't concentrate. She jumped up to get water, then sat down again to pray. But she couldn't focus. She jumped up to skim the help-wanted ads and decided, as she started reading, that she'd pray later.

Suddenly she stopped. *Get a hold of yourself. Keep your appointment with God. I'll come back to the ads afterward.* She finally forced herself to go back to her prayer place.

"Oh God, I want to praise you, but I'm having trouble. I'm scared. Are you home, God?" she pleaded. Then she remembered a psalm Caroline had written down for her, and scurried to find her handbag.

She searched through it, but the psalm wasn't there. Then she remembered putting it in the drawer of the nightstand. Caroline had written out Psalm 3 with her personal interpretations following each verse.

Kitty read verse 1:

"I have so many enemies, O Lord, so many who turn against me."

Caroline's interpretation:

"My greatest foes are my negative thoughts, my regrets about yesterday, my fears about tomorrow, my scarcity, thinking about all the things I don't have, my grudges. These are my real foes. My fears and inner turmoil are created by my own thoughts and doubts."

Kitty read the next verse:

"They talk about me and say God will not help her."

Caroline's interpretation:

"I am the one talking about me when I tell myself I don't have time to pray! I rationalize my lack of prayer with the typical cliché, "God helps those who help themselves," and I make excuses to myself. I tell myself I have too much to do to waste time praying. "I can pray later, not today!" Oh Lord, help me be faithful to you. Help me to find special time for you."

Verses 3 and 4:
"But you, Lord, are always my shield from danger. You give me victory and restore my courage. I cry to the Lord for help. And from His sacred hill, He answers me."

Kitty copied the psalm and Caroline's notes into her journal. She added, "Lord, I can't believe how perfect this psalm is for me. You do protect me. You do take care of everything. Thank you, thank you, thank you. I know you are taking care of me. I know you are preparing the perfect job for me." She rested her head against the chair and let her whole body go limp, slowly guiding her thoughts back to reality.

Putting her journal away, Kitty refocused on the jobs section. The very first ad that caught her eye was for an assistant to the development director of a small liberal arts college. At first she hesitated.

Then she repeated to herself, "Lord, you are always my shield from danger. You give me victory and restore my courage." *Why not go for it? They won't hire me. I have no experience. But I'll give it a whirl.*

She called the college and to her surprise they asked her to come in that afternoon. She interviewed with the head of human resources and the director of development.

The director told her, "We don't answer phone calls. We request resumes. But when you called today, we were interested in your experience. Raising money is an art. You have it or you don't. It doesn't matter if you've raised it for charity or for a profession. Once you have the skill, you can use it anywhere." She told her they would call her the next day.

Kitty's heart was beating so fast she was sure the director could hear it. As the woman walked her to the front door, Kitty was sure she hadn't gotten the job.

But the director called her that very same night. She wanted Kitty to start immediately. Kitty hesitated. She felt a twinge of excitement mixed with fear. Thanksgiving was only three weeks away and she wanted to have her family for dinner. She knew absolutely nothing about how colleges were run or how to raise money for them.

The words from Psalm 3 ran through her mind: *"You, O Lord, are* always my shield from danger. You give me victory. You restore my courage." She said to herself, "Okay, Lord, here goes." She didn't want to appear desperate, so she said she was available a week from Monday.

The director seemed pleased. "Meet me here at 8:00 a.m. Monday after next," she said. "I'll have our HR person go over your benefits and get all the paperwork taken care of so you can get started."

Kitty was so excited she almost dropped the phone. "Thank you, God, thank you!" As soon as she hung up, she called Chip.

He was enthusiastic. "Kit, you'll be great. That's one wise woman and one lucky school. Remember when you called me right after your meeting with your lawyer, and you were so upset?"

"I remember," Kitty assured him.

"I went out on my deck and prayed for you. I told God I thought He was being a little harsh on you," he laughed.

Kitty interrupted. "You're right; you're absolutely right. He is."

"But, Kit, Jeremiah 29:11 flashed across my mind. 'I have a plan to bring her prosperity, not disaster, plans to bring about the future she hopes for.' I knew then that everything would work out for you. You're going to have so much fun entering into a whole new adventure in life. Let's pray together."

Chip prayed and thanked God for Kitty and her job, Matt and the children, and for the new home God was preparing for her.

As soon as they hung up, Kitty called Caroline. She was about to call the children, but changed her mind. Susan and Doug were coming for dinner. *It'll be fun to surprise them.* So she called her husband instead.

Matt was delighted for her. She told him she was afraid; she didn't want him getting any ideas that her life was easy. She wanted him to know how hard this was for her.

"It may seem hard to you now, but once you begin the job, you'll be surprised at your success," Matt said enthusiastically. "That college is getting a jewel, don't you forget it. You're a crackerjack fundraiser. Don't underestimate yourself."

Although she was still angry with him, she appreciated his encouragement and invited him for Thanksgiving dinner. He thanked her about three times. The more she worked on her peace process, the better she felt about Matt.

By dinnertime, she was alive with excitement waiting for Doug and Susan to arrive. She set the table with her mother's cloth. Holding it close to her face, she thought about her mother, as she always did when she used it. *Mom, help me do well.*

She put a bottle of wine on ice. She was serving salmon filets with grilled asparagus and a leafy garden salad. She wanted the evening to be festive, so she turned on the music and lit candles. She took a last-minute look at herself in the mirror and adjusted her suit, pushed her black hair back, and smiled with approval.

She was trying to decide whether she should tell Doug and Susan about the peace process. Susan had asked her about it the last time they were together. *I think it could help them. But suppose they think it's silly?* Kitty was rolling this over in her mind when she heard Susan's key in the lock.

Kitty couldn't contain herself. The minute Susan and Doug walked in the door, she gave them both a big hug and kiss and burst out, "What do you think happened to me today?" She told them all about her interview and her new job.

"Mom, I'm so proud of you. You're the perfect person for that job," Doug said, laughing. "That school won't know what hit them when you take off," he said, rubbing his mother's shoulders.

"You know, Mom, as difficult as our family situation has been, do you realize how much you've grown in the past four months?" Susan asked.

Kitty poured the wine and they toasted her job. They toasted each other, and then they toasted Matt and Ken. They toasted Chip. Then Susan looked her mother in the eye and said, "Mom, about this process you and Aunt Caroline are doing. You're so secretive. Can't you tell us?"

Kitty flushed with embarrassment.

"Come on, Mom," Doug prodded, "Spill the beans."

Kitty bit her lip. "If I tell you, no wisecracks – deal?"

They agreed.

She told them about Caroline, and how she'd resisted hearing about Caroline's newfound peace. She explained the process and how she focused on a different principle each week. When Kitty saw how receptive they were, she decided to tell them about her daily exercise of praising, asking, and listening. The more she got into it, the more she told them. Both Doug and Susan were attentive.

Kitty was sure they wanted to make some sarcastic remark. For a minute, she was sorry she'd told them so much. Doug broke the silence. "Mom, that's awesome. Why did you think we would laugh? It's amazing the effect it's had on you. I'd like to try it. Wouldn't you, Susan?"

Susan looked across the table at him. "I've been asking Mom about it for a while, but she wouldn't tell me anything. Chuck's told me a little bit about it. He said both his mom and dad are following it, and it's made the biggest difference in their family."

"What do you mean, both parents are following it?" Kitty asked, thinking Susan didn't really know what she was talking about.

"He said his mom has changed a lot in the past year. She's more relaxed and fun to be with, and she seems to juggle all her activities without any struggle. She takes care of the family without stressing out over all the pressures."

"What did he say about his dad?" Kitty asked.

"I shouldn't have said anything," Susan confessed. "He told me his dad started reading his mom's book. His mom doesn't know it, but Chuck and his dad are both experimenting with it. The book apparently suggests you try the peace process for 30 days. Chuck and his dad are on their twelfth week. He said it's helped him gain clarity about things and feel better about himself."

Now Kitty was silent. *Nick's practicing the peace process?* She looked intently at Susan, listening to everything she said.

"Mom, I'd like to try it," said Doug. "Tell me what I have to do. You can teach Susan and me together."

"Maybe some other time," Susan said, "but not right now."

"Well, Mom," Doug said, "You and I should go to lunch. Let's set a date now."

They scheduled a lunch but Kitty felt a little disappointed. She had been about to tell them about her experience with the third psalm, but when Susan said she wasn't interested in practicing the peace process, she decided not to.

Chapter 36

Hope

"Be concerned above all else with the Kingdom of God and what He requires of you; and He will provide you with all these other things."

(Matthew 6:33)

Kitty didn't realize that taking the job at the college made her children eligible for free tuition. *I'd love Susan and Doug to come here. I'll wait before I mention it.*

Kitty fit right in with the other people in the office. All her worrying about her ability was for naught. The development office was a small, three-person department, and her boss was on the road most of the time.

Kitty did all her shopping for Thanksgiving the weekend before and set the table Monday evening. She got up early Thursday and started the turkey. This was the first Thanksgiving that Kitty had ever cooked without help. She even baked two pies.

Matt and Doug arrived on time to watch the game. Kitty ran in and out of the room serving them beers and snacks while she prepared dinner. At first it seemed strange. But as the day progressed, it seemed so right – Matt and Doug watching the game while she and Susan worked in the kitchen. Everything was perfect. Kitty was pleased with herself. They talked to Ken and Chip on the phone before they sat down for dinner. Everyone helped clean up.

On December 15, just three weeks before she had to move out of the Frenches' townhouse, Kitty found the perfect apartment. It was in Narberth, a small, close-knit, family community on the Main Line. She rented the first floor of an old Victorian house on a month-to-month basis. She adored it. And Narberth was closer to Fairmount, the area of the city where Doug and Susan lived.

Kitty excelled at her job. She arranged dinners, sent out press releases, contacted businesses, went to meetings, and solicited donations. She arranged art shows, theater parties, and sightseeing trips to raise money. She kept track of alumni. She was so immersed in her work she didn't have time to worry.

She also read several books on finances and money management. She approached money management like a game, in spite of her limited income. Kitty faithfully paid herself first by putting 10 percent of her income into a 401(k). She gave another 10 percent of each paycheck to charity, and she started reading the real estate section of the paper. She was determined to buy a house someday.

As the weeks went on, Kitty's focus changed from her pain and disappointments to Matt's and the children's pain and disappointments. She became less self-absorbed and more focused on her family's feelings. She loved her work and enjoyed interacting with the staff. She also enjoyed the students who worked in the development office. They told her about their dates and often asked her for advice on various issues.

As the year progressed, she kept returning to Chip's question, "Who is Kitty Murphy?" *He was right.* She actually laughed to herself when she thought about her obsession over the Bradshaw name.

At first Kitty talked to Chip several times a week. In one of their conversations, she told him he was right about her family, and that she was discovering who she was. She admitted she liked the new Kitty. "I realize my parents always wanted me to be me," she confessed to Chip. "I was the one worried about being a Bradshaw." But the busier she became, the fewer phone calls she made to her uncle.

Kitty had Matt and the children over for dinner every Sunday night. Occasionally, Caroline and Nick joined them. She was faithful to her daily praise meditations, scripture reading, and journal writing.

Chapter 37

Strengthens the Weary

"The sovereign Lord has taught me what to say,
so that I can strengthen the weary.
Every morning He makes me eager
to hear what He is going to teach me."

(Isaiah 50: 4-5)

Kitty was winding up the school year. Graduation was on May 11. She was juggling all of her responsibilities and doing it quite well when she received a phone call from one of Chip's friends, Buddy.

"Chip's very sick," he said. "He has pneumonia again. But this time, it looks like he may not pull through. I thought you'd want to know."

Kitty felt her own lungs restrict, like she couldn't get enough air. She remembered feeling this way the day her dad died. "Lord, please don't let Chip die," she begged.

Fortunately, Kitty's mantra, "Do it now," kept her ahead in her work. She was fairly well caught up at the office, and her director told her to go to California. "Don't worry about us," she said. "Go with peace of mind."

Kitty couldn't afford the ticket price quoted to her over the phone, but she was going, no matter what it cost. A student helped her find a cheaper fare over the Internet, and she paid for the ticket with her American Express card. She remembered the lawyer cautioning her about using it. *This is an emergency, and I'm glad I have it.* She had more than $1,000 in her savings account, so she'd be able to pay the bill at the end of the month. *Praise and thank you Lord, for my American Express card.*

Ken met Kitty at the airport and drove her right to the hospital to see Chip. She tried to hide her dismay when she saw him. He had weighed around 145 pounds when she was there last summer, but he now looked as if he carried barely 100 pounds on his fame. His ashen gray skin stretched across his skeletal bones; his eyes protruded from his head. The doctors were hopeful that Kitty could take him home in a day or so.

"Kit, I'm so glad you're here," Chip said, reaching for her hand. "I feel bad taking you away from your family. But I'm glad you're here."

She leaned down, kissed him, and stroked his forehead. "We're going to get you better," she promised. But in her heart she knew Chip would never get well.

He smiled weakly. "Of course we are," he agreed.

Kitty had two days to get Chip's apartment ready for his homecoming, and she rushed around preparing for his arrival. Large vases of fresh flowers brightened every room, while Puccini's melodies played in the background. When Kitty saw Chip walk through the door, she bit her lip to control her emotions. His shirt and pants hung over his frail, decaying body. "Welcome home, darling," she said, kissing him on the cheek.

The first week went by quickly. Betty, a lovely woman from the hospital, came every day. She taught Kitty how to help Chip with his oxygen, and she taught her little things that would help make him more comfortable.

Almost every day Kitty and Chip sat on the terrace for as long as he could take the sun, which wasn't long. He told her he was excited about his recent baptism and confirmation into the Catholic Church. His eyes sparkled in spite of all the medicine he was taking, and he shared with her the notes he'd written about his funeral.

At first, Kitty tried to resist such conversation.

"You're going to be fine," she said. "Let's not talk about it."

Chip didn't talk about his funeral again for several days. But he was growing weaker.

One day while Betty was there, he told Kit, "Kit, you're right. I'm going to be fine. I'm going to be gloriously fine, but it'll be in heaven with Grant and Fran. I don't have much time left. I want you and me to talk with the undertaker and the priest together. It will help both of us."

He reached out and gently took her hand.

"I'm sorry to put you through this, Kit. But it's important that we're honest and that we talk about all the things we need to talk about before it's too late." He leaned over and gave her a kiss. "You are my pride and joy, you know. I love you. You and Matt and the children are like my own children. I thank you for sharing them with me."

Then he was silent and soon dozed off in his chair. Betty helped Kitty understand why it was important that she discuss Chip's funeral arrangements with him.

The priest visited every day. Kitty was impressed with his humor and his gentle way of speaking. He spoke openly to Chip about death without being stern or gloomy. Two days later the undertaker and the priest came to discuss Chip's funeral arrangements. Chip insisted Kitty sit in on every meeting about his funeral. When the undertaker and priest left, he reviewed every detail with her.

Buddy and Ken took turns helping her. She was grateful they were there. When they came, she would go to the store and take a long walk. Chip had a slew of friends and neighbors parading in and out of his apartment. There was so much food that every day Ken took extra to the AIDS shelter where Chip had volunteered.

Kitty kept her family posted on Chip's progress. Some days he was better than others. She walked around in a fog. Her daily appointment with God helped her focus more on Chip than on what she was going to do when he was gone.

Before she knew it, she had been in California ten days and was focusing on the courage to appreciate all her blessings. She started out praising and thanking God for soaking Chip, his friends, the funeral parlor employees, and her family in His love. She asked God to help her be thankful for all the people in her life.

But she felt inadequate taking care of Chip, and was uncomfortable discussing his death with him. She wanted to be a comfort to him but she felt awkward and clumsy. Unsure what she should say, Kitty prayed, "I praise and thank You, Lord, for lighting my way and showing me what I should do or say today to help Chip." She flipped through her

Bible to find Psalms, and the page fell open to Isaiah 50. Verses 4 and 5 immediately caught her eye:

> "The sovereign Lord has taught me what to say,
>   so that I can strengthen the weary.
> Every morning He makes me eager
>   to hear what He is going to teach me.
> The Lord has given me understanding."

Kitty began crying. *Oh God, you do speak to me. I do trust you will speak through me to Chip, just as you have spoken through Chip to me.* She had many sorrows in her life but this was the first time she was aware of a profound sadness, as well as an overwhelming joy.

She ran into Chip's room to tell him what just happened but he was asleep. She hoped she would have an opportunity to share this experience with him before he died.

The next day, Buddy came in at about 11:00 a.m. "I called Ken and suggested he take you to lunch," he said gently. "You need to get out. Really, Kitty, you and Ken need to talk. He'll be here in half an hour."

Chapter 38

Healing and Forgiveness

"The fruit of the spirit is love, joy, peace, patience and kindness."

(Galatians 5: 22-23)

At first Kitty's conversation with Ken was strained. They talked about the bit part he had in a movie; they discussed Kitty's job, and they shared stories about Chip.

Finally Ken looked at his mother. "How are you doing, Mom? I know this is a tough one for you."

Kitty sighed. "It is for you, too. Chip's absence will leave a big hole in both our hearts." She plucked a purple grape from her fruit salad and ate it.

Ken nodded his head. "I'll miss him," he admitted.

"Kenny, you'll probably think I'm crazy, but I have these strange conflicting feelings."

"What do you mean?"

Kitty shook her head. "Oh, it's nothing. I guess I'm just upset."

Ken looked at his mother. "Mom, your whole life has been turned upside down. No wonder you have mixed emotions."

"It's weird. I've never experienced feelings like this before."

"What do you mean? What kind of feelings?"

"When I think of life without Chip, an overwhelming sadness comes over me; and yet, at the same time, I feel joy." She looked at her son. "Do you think it's possible to experience two conflicting emotions at the same time? I can't explain it."

"You feel sadness and joy all at once?"

"Yes, that's exactly what I'm feeling, sadness and joy together. Talk about mixed emotions." She laughed. "Maybe I'm losing it." She told him about her morning prayer and how she had suddenly been overwhelmed with joy as she read the scripture passage in Isaiah. She felt like dancing and singing. "And yet I don't want to lose Chip," she explained. "I already feel a void, an emptiness without him." She shook her head.

Ken raised his eyebrows. "Sadness and joy mixed together? I've never had that experience. It's different. Maybe the Holy Spirit is sending the gift of joy to console you."

Kitty appeared to be thinking. "That's an interesting thought. Where did you get your spiritual wisdom?"

His answer took her back. "I got it from you."

"From me?" Kitty questioned. "Thanks for the compliment, but I can never take credit for your spiritual formation."

"Didn't Chip tell you he gave me your book, *The Peace Way*?"

Kitty was surprised. "No, he didn't. I'm surprised he never said anything."

"Mom, he loves that book. We both do. It's helped both of us a lot these past few months."

Kitty smiled. "I never knew." She pulled a linen handkerchief from her bag and wiped tears from her eyes. "Are you practicing the peace principles?"

Ken smiled. "Yes, I spend 15 to 20 minutes every morning praising God and meditating on the peace principles for that week.

Kitty's face betrayed her shock.

Ken laughed. "You're so surprised. Chip started a prayer and praise night. We meet one night a week to praise and thank God together for the peace secrets for that week. Then we meditate on them and have dinner. We now have six guys practicing the peace process."

"I don't know what to say. Chip never told me this," Kitty said in a hurt tone.

"I think he wanted to surprise you," Ken explained. "He didn't think he was going to die. He was planning to come back east in July."

"I'm sorry that visit will never happen," Kitty muttered.

"We were coming together. I was looking forward to it," Ken confessed. He hesitated. "But Chip will be in a better place."

"I hope so."

Ken leaned over the table and looked into his mother's eyes. "I've learned a lot about God's love and the secrets to peace from him and from your book."

"So I noticed. You're much more relaxed; you seem more at ease," Kitty said, encouraging Ken.

"You know, Mom," he said thoughtfully, "I was always searching for something but I wasn't sure what it was." His brown eyes were intense. "I studied different religions, hoping I'd find peace.

"The truth is, I pushed you away with my self-righteousness," he admitted looking straight at her. "Since I've been focusing on the Peace Prayer of St. Francis and the peace principles, I realize how obnoxious I must have been. I was so self-righteous and critical of everyone. No wonder you ignored me."

"Yes, you were a little self-righteous, but I hardly think we ignored you!" Kitty laughed. "I guess we all get self-righteous when we think we've found the secret to inner peace."

"But that's just it. I didn't find the secret to inner peace. I was miserable. I was so into myself and my opinions."

She nodded. "I have to admit you were obnoxious when you tried to push religion down our throats."

He laughed. "I realize that now. The peace principles are helping me get a better understanding of myself and others. They're helping me see that peace is wrapped up in the little things we do: a smile, a kind word, or enjoying people for who they are, and not who I think they should be."

"You *have* changed," Kitty commented. "Ken, I get a kick out of you calling them *my* peace principles, but you know they aren't mine. I'm trying to live these principles but I've only scratched the surface. I have a long way to go."

Ken smiled. "You've come a long way. I know you didn't come up with these principles, but you introduced them to Chip, who introduced them to me. I like calling them my mother's peace principles."

Kitty laughed. "I'm sure Caroline will love that."

"Meditating every day helps me be less stressed out. I don't get as frustrated over the daily unexpected interruptions in my life like I used to. I have you to thank for that, Mom." He leaned over the table. "I pray every day for the grace to spread God's love."

Kitty looked straight at Ken. "Ken, I'm so happy for you."

Leaning an elbow on the table and looking into his mother's eyes, he said, "Mom, I want you to know I'm sorry about your trust fund. I feel like I'm the cause of all your financial problems. I kept pushing you to put your trust in high-risk stocks."

"Oh, Kenny, no. I did it myself. It wasn't your fault. I'm a big girl. Your dad and Uncle Chip begged me not to do it."

"Well, I realize now that I was afraid of failing; I didn't want to go into Dad's business. But once I did get into the business, I wanted to impress you."

Kitty laughed. "You did impress me, you really did, and you are quite a salesman."

"I think *pushy* is a better word," Ken said with a laugh. "You know, Mom, I was driven by fear. I never realized how many fears I had until I began meditating on peace. I always felt inferior to Susan and Doug." He looked down at his meal.

Kitty didn't say a word. She waited for him to continue.

"I wanted to win your approval. I was determined you would change your trust fund, then you would think I was as smart as Doug and Susan, and you would brag about me to your friends."

"Kenny, you didn't have to impress me. I always thought you were as smart as Susan and Doug."

"Did you really, Mom?"

"Of course I did!" Kitty protested.

"I'm not trying to put you down or make you feel bad, but I never felt you loved me as much as you loved Doug and Susan. You always treated them like grown-ups and me like a child."

Kitty didn't say anything. She took a sip of water. She looked over at Ken. "It's funny you should say that because Susan also thinks I treated her like a child."

"Susan feels the same way?"

Kitty pursed her lips. "She does."

Kenny didn't say anything. They continued eating in silence.

Kitty thought about what her oldest son had just said. *What he says is true. If I'm honest with myself, I never treated him with the same respect I gave Doug and Susan. Praise and thank you, Lord, for this moment, praise and thank you for Kenny, and thank you for the graces you are sending to us right now.*

Ken finally looked up. "That's all behind me now. I'm getting so many insights about myself and you and our family. I'm not trying to hurt you or put you on the spot."

Kitty reached across the table and touched his hand. "I guess as a family we've been very good at pretending." She sighed. "When we slow down and reflect on ourselves and the way we relate to God and others, we get a more honest picture of the good, the bad, and the beautiful." She smiled. "Don't be afraid of hurting me. Besides, maybe I need to hear it. I'm glad we're having this conversation. Okay?"

"Thanks, Mom. I've wanted to talk to you about this for a long time. But I didn't want to hurt you," he said again. "I already told you I always felt like an outcast in our family. I always felt different. I was very lonely."

"Ken, I'm so sorry if I made you feel that way." Kitty felt devastated.

"I'm not saying it was your fault. I just felt aloof, different. I didn't realize how very lonely I was," he hesitated, "until I began asking God to wash away my feelings of loss and loneliness. When I wrote my thoughts in my journal I realized I had this tremendous loneliness." He looked over at his mom. "I think that's why I was so angry. I tried to please you and everyone else, but I never could please you."

Kitty was listening. Her vision was blurring with tears but she was attentive to what he was saying. "I'm okay. Don't stop," she reassured him.

"I think I felt different because I'm not a Main Line Philadelphia type of guy. Doug and Susan were preppy dressers, good students, and good athletes. I liked baggy pants and sloppy shirts, and what did I excel in? Nothing! Doug was the man around campus. I was the do-nothing brother."

"You were the best photographer in the school."

"Mom, you don't have to defend me. I appreciate it but I'm really getting a handle on who I am and what my purpose is. I realize I don't have to be considered the best at anything. I just have to be the person God wants me to be."

"I'm sorry, Ken. I'm sorry I wasn't there for you."

"That's okay, Mom. You had your own frustrations."

"I think I had unrealistic expectations of myself and everyone else," Kitty confessed.

Her son laughed. "I'll agree with that."

Kitty tried to explain. "That was the way I was raised. You didn't worry about what your children thought or how they felt. You told them how they were to behave and that was it. You expected them to do what they were told. Of course, you didn't do what we told you, and that's where the conflict came in."

"That's probably why I had so many fears," Ken said. "Mom, a lot of times I was angry with you and Dad because I was afraid I wasn't as good as Doug or Susan. I was afraid I wasn't living up to the Bradshaw name. I knew I just couldn't be all that I was supposed to be as Douglas Bradshaw's grandson."

"Kenny, I'm sorry. I'm so sorry."

"It's okay, Mom. I think that's why I made such a big thing about religion. I knew something you guys didn't know and that made me feel important." He looked at his mother. "Does that surprise you?"

Kitty shrugged her shoulders. "Nothing surprises me anymore."

"I realize now I was searching for a God to make me look better than anyone else. I was sure you loved Doug and Susan more than me. I wanted to show you how smart and intelligent I was. I wanted to do something great that would make you love me."

Kitty's eyes filled up again. "Ken, Dad and I never loved you any less than Doug or Susan. The three of you are all so different and unique. What can I do to help you see that you are very special and that we love you for being you?"

Ken smiled. "Mom, you've already helped me with your peace meditations. I know God loves me and has a special mission just for me. I know He puts people in my life who help me. I don't have to force my views on others. All I have to do is practice the peace meditations and surrender my loneliness, fears, frustrations, doubts, despair, pride, and desires to control others to God, and He will light my way." He laughed. "Do you realize, Mom, that you gave us this?"

Kitty sighed. "I'm glad I gave you something. Kenny, I love you. I want you to know that. You've given me so much since I've been here; I never would have gotten through these days without you."

"It works both ways. I love having you out here."

Kitty looked at her watch. "We've been here two hours. As much as I hate to go, we better get moving. But before we go, is there anything else you want to talk about?"

"No, I think I've covered everything."

They stood and embraced.

Kitty smiled, put her arm in Ken's, and they walked out of the restaurant.

Chapter 39

Peace, One Heart at a Time

*"May the God of peace provide you with every good
thing you need in order to do His will."*

(Hebrews 13:21)

Kitty returned to the apartment, refreshed and exhilarated. Other than talking about his funeral, she hadn't chatted much with Chip since he got home from the hospital. But tonight Chip seemed more alert and eager to talk.

She prepared a light dinner, as she did every night. Tonight, he relished it. She was thrilled watching him enjoy every morsel. He looked at her with a big grin. "That was delicious, Kit. Thanks. How are you coming along with your peace process?"

"It's growing on me," she said, laughing.

"What are you working on this week?"

"Appreciation." She laughed nervously. "Ken tells me you have a weekly prayer praise night."

He looked at her. "I wanted to surprise you. Ken and I were planning to come east this summer. We thought we'd invite you to pray with us and then share with you all the things we've learned."

"Were you going to teach me how to juggle my daily life with grace and ease?" Kitty asked gleefully.

Chip laughed. "I don't think you need us to teach you how to juggle. You do a pretty good juggling job every day." He got more serious. "I'm sorry, Kit; I didn't get a chance to tell you before Ken did. I want you to know how much your peace principles have helped me."

"That's okay," she said, giving him a kiss on his forehead. "I'm actually deeply moved that you started a men's group practicing the peace meditations and spreading God's love."

"I saw the difference in you when you were here last summer. I had to try it. It's obviously working for you," Chip said, smiling. "I've prayed, reflected, and thought a lot about these principles. They are powerful, life-altering principles. Although each one is a little different, they interrelate."

Kitty nodded. "Caroline and I have talked about this. I'm just beginning to see that enjoying the moment and being grateful go hand in hand."

Chip added, "And we can't enjoy the moment and appreciate our gifts unless we forgive. And we can't encourage others unless we're happy with what we have right now. Each principle is an integral part of the others. Don't you agree?"

"You're right. They definitely do interrelate, but I think it's going to take me a lifetime to put it all together," she confessed.

Chip didn't comment. He seemed to be staring into space. Then he repositioned himself in his chair. He was so thin that he had to sit on three pillows. Kitty jumped up to help him adjust the cushions but he put his hand up to stop her.

"I'm okay. I'm enjoying this," he said. "I began reading *The Peace Way* last summer. When I meditate on the peace virtues, I visualize God soaking me in His love and washing away, with a big soft sponge, my loneliness. I shared my visualization with Ken and Bud.

"In our weekly meetings, we would praise and thank God for soaking us in his peace. We'd pause and silently visualize it. Then we shared what we visualized." He laughed. "We usually had very different pictures about God soaking us in his love, but we all agreed that visualizing helped make God's presence in our lives more real." He looked at Kitty. "Kitty, I learned that when you start your day with the peace meditations, you have a deeper desire for the presence of God within you. It's a springboard to other prayers." He closed his eyes and stopped talking.

"Chip, are you too tired to talk?" Kitty asked.

He slowly opened his eyes and spoke softly. " I'm fine. I'm trying to find the words to tell you what I learned from meditating on the peace principles and practicing them. Remember the song *Little Things Mean a Lot?*"

"Sure," Kitty answered.

"The peace prayers helped me realize that every little interaction we have with someone can create peace or conflict." Chip's voice grew stronger as he shared his thoughts. "When you think about spreading peace one heart at a time, as you put it, it means being conscious of everyone we meet, smiling at the people we pass on the street, saying thank you to the checkout woman at the supermarket, or saying a prayer for all the other people stuck in the same traffic jam we're stuck in. It means when we feel put out or annoyed with the person we're living or working with, we have to stop and remind ourselves we want to spread peace in this moment, to this one person."

"Wow, Chip, the way you said it makes it sound kind of cool."

Chip laughed. "I see you're picking up some college lingo."

"I guess I am. Tell me more about what you're doing."

Chip was more energized, like his former self. "At night, before I go to bed, I ask our Lord to show me the areas where I could have spread peace and didn't. That's when I began realizing the hundreds of little opportunities I have every day to spread God's love. I never really thought these little things were important. Now I try to ask myself, 'What's important to that person right now?' The most crucial thing I can do for a person right now is validate them and help them appreciate who they are."

Kitty nodded her head in agreement. "I'm also realizing more and more how critical the little everyday encounters are. But I never thought about validating the woman at the supermarket or people I meet throughout the day," she confessed. "Do you think we need to validate people we don't even know?"

"I think spreading God's love, wherever we go, whatever we do, means spreading God's love in all the tiny, seemingly insignificant activities of our day."

Kitty sat up straighter. "I'm a little confused about something. I think you said you think about what's important to the other person and you try to validate that. When you do that, aren't you becoming a people pleaser? Like you told me I was trying to be a Bradshaw rather than be myself?"

"Ah, that's a very good point. We want to be God pleasers, not people pleasers."

"What's the difference?"

"There is a big difference. When we let God's love radiate through us, we genuinely care about our dignity as human beings and the dignity of others as human beings. We are equal. We are both God's children. We love others as we love ourselves. When I show appreciation to the cashier at the grocery store, I am treating her as I want to be treated. On the other hand, if I do something that compromises my dignity to please another person, I am treating myself as a nonperson and the other person as a deity. This behavior hurts both parties."

Kitty frowned. "In other words, people-pleasers perceive themselves as inferior to the person they want to please. They see the person they want to please as superior; therefore they compromise themselves to please the other."

"Precisely. That's what creates conflict and injustice in the world. One group of people thinks they are considered subservient to another group of people, and they act accordingly. But this behavior creates repressed anger."

"That's an interesting way to look at it," Kitty said. "I never really thought about that."

"Another cause of conflict and injustice comes when a person or group of people think they are entitled to exclusive rights or privileges to which others are not entitled. They feel that their money, position, power, or intelligence makes them superior. These subtle feelings are obstacles to finding God's love in our hearts, because we make things, power, and position our God."

Kitty stared at Chip. "I think I felt that way all my life. I never thought about it until just now. I always felt entitled. That's why I had such a hard time when we lost our money. It wasn't the loss of money as much as the loss of position." Kitty leaped up from her chair. "Until you just said that, I never realized what a snob I am."

Chip looked up at her. "I wasn't pointing the finger at you, Kit."

"I know that. But do you realize that you were talking about me?

That's how I was. I didn't realize it until just now. But I definitely thought I was entitled to privileges because of my position, money, and intelligence."

"Kit, don't be so hard on yourself."

"I'm not. I'm just seeing aspects of myself I never saw before. Chip, I never appreciated how truly blessed I was. I thought the money and position were my birthright." She put her hand up to her mouth. "Oh, I'm ashamed to admit what I just realized: I thought I was better than Caroline because I came from a more educated, wealthier family. We were close friends but I thought I was entitled to more privileges and recognition than she was."

Chip gazed at her with warm and compassionate eyes. "Those are big insights."

"I'm realizing what a control freak I was. I always tried to mold people to be the people I thought they should be. I thought I knew what was best for everyone."

Chip laughed. "I think trying to mold people to who we want them to be is a human trait we all have to battle."

"I guess you're right. But I never realized until tonight what a spoiled brat I've been. Thank you, Chip. You have a way of helping me see myself as I really am." She faltered. "What will I do when you're gone? Who is going to help me see what I need to see?"

"I'm not worried about you, Kit," he said gently. "You're on the right road. You'll be fine. Just keep praising and thanking God, and all will be well."

"One thing I'm learning," Kitty interjected, "is that if I truly love a person, I'll encourage them to be who they were meant to be, not who I think they should be."

Chip smiled. "When we praise and thank God for his love, we slowly realize we're frail brothers and sisters in his human family. We need to be soaked in His love so we can love and appreciate ourselves and each other. When we do that, it's easier to encourage people to be who they are meant to be."

Kitty smiled. "*The Peace Way* really is a how-to guide for peace in the heart, the home, and the world, isn't it?"

"I think so," Chip agreed. "We are all one in God's love, and He needs us to be his peace instruments. When we find God's love in our hearts and spread it, we are planting peace seeds everywhere we go. I believe that's our purpose in life: to spread peace seeds throughout our world." He stopped, took a breath, and laughed. "I don't need to preach to you, Kit, you radiate God's love."

"You're sweet for saying that, Chip. I wish it were true. I'm just beginning to see how self-centered and selfish I've been."

Chip shook his head. "You can't see yourself as I see you. I don't see you as selfish; however, if you think you're selfish, praise and thank God for realizing it." He smiled and gave her a wink. "Remember, we praise God for everything and let Him work out the wrinkles."

"When we get upset with ourselves," Chip continued, "we become impatient and intolerant of others. I think God wants us to acknowledge our weaknesses and place them in His care so we can focus on Him rather than ourselves. Praising Him in all things helps us do just that; it helps us focus on Him rather than ourselves."

"Chip, you're amazing. It is true. When I get upset with myself, I become tense and impatient with everyone around me. The next time I feel upset with myself, I'll try praising God and asking Him to continue showing me ways to overcome my weaknesses." She giggled. "I'll be doing a lot of praising and thanking." She laughed a deep, belly laugh.

Chip looked intensely at Kitty. "This is off the subject," he said, "but I've wondered why you never asked me to help you financially. How have you managed to live?"

Kitty smiled and shrugged her shoulders. "I watch every penny. I realized other people manage to live on less than what I'm making. I am determined to be a good money manager. Believe it or not, I've even saved a little money. I'm very proud of that."

"Being a good money manager helps you be more peaceful," Chip told her.

"I do feel more confident about taking care of myself. Managing my finances wisely has helped me enjoy more peace."

"If you think you can manage without any help from me I'd like to leave everything to the AIDS shelter, in Fran's and Grant's names. Would you have a problem with that?"

Kitty was touched. "Chip, you're a dear to even ask me how I feel about how you leave your money. It's your money and you should do with it what you want."

"Yes, but if you need it to live, I should leave it to you."

Kitty thought for a moment. "Well that would certainly make life easy. But I think God is teaching me how to trust Him to show me the way to be financially responsible. We're going to be okay. Besides, I think you should leave everything to the shelter. It will help keep the memory of your family alive."

"I have one more thought about spreading peace." He squirmed in his chair, trying to get comfortable. "Imagine this," he said. "What if everyone planted peace seeds all day long, wherever they went, and in everything they did? Peace seeds would bloom everywhere."

Kitty listened intently. She was so excited to see Chip energized.

"You're saying that if we introduce the peace principles to more people, they would start doing what you're doing?"

"Yes, that's my point. Think about this, Kit," he continued. "I've seen more than one life change from these principles. It's meant to be one heart at a time. But suppose you could introduce it to 20 or 30 people at one time? If you could do that it would spread faster and to more people."

Kitty stared at Chip. "But how do you do that?"

"You've already introduced it to six guys. Now I think it's time for you to take it to a bigger audience. You're the next link in the chain. Kit, *you* must spread peace now."

Kitty was taken aback. "But, Chip, I don't think I'm the one to do it. I took to heart all the things you told me about myself. I can't believe how selfish I am. I was living in a bubble and I'm just now beginning to realize I'm not superior to others. I'm grateful to you for pointing it out to me, but I'm the last person to teach others how to spread peace."

"But that's exactly why you're the perfect person to share your story and experiences with others. These principles change people's hearts. They can change the world if enough people live by them."

"How could I possibly do that?"

"God will lead you. Just stay open."

Kitty wasn't convinced. "I only know Caroline and a few others in Pennsylvania who are practicing the peace principles. I'm not the one to spread it to a wider audience."

"One way to begin is through church groups," Chip advised.

"I don't know any church groups."

"I'm praying you'll find the church community that is right for you. God made us a community of people. We need to surround ourselves with people who believe in God and want to spread His love."

"Why do you think I need to go to church?"

"You'll go through periods when you doubt God's love. You'll doubt the peace principles, and during those periods you'll get strength from your church community. We need each other. We can't go it alone."

"I don't know, Chip." Kitty hunched her shoulders slightly. "I'm doing just fine without a church. I've already had my doubts but I'm still practicing the peace principles because they make sense."

Chip smiled, and in his usual gentle way he said, "Kit, God will lead you. And one day you'll go into a church and you'll know that's the church for you. You'll know you're home."

"When that happens, I'll think of you," Kit promised.

"When you do, be sure and say a prayer for me," Chip requested. He squirmed in his chair and closed his eyes.

"Let me get you a cup of tea," Kitty suggested.

"No, thanks." He adjusted his pillow. "Kit, promise me you'll continue praising God and living the peace principles, and promise that you'll share them every chance you get." His voice was growing weaker. He was perspiring, and the little bit of color he had in his face faded.

"Chip, how about some tea?" Kitty said again, trying to control the panic in her voice.

"I'm tired. Sorry, Kit. Kindly help me to bed."

She managed to help him into bed, and his head fell back on the pillows.

"Don't go," he pleaded, reaching for her hand. His voice was so weak she could hardly hear him. "Stay with me."

Kitty sat beside him as he dozed off. She was afraid to leave him. He started making a strange gurgling noise. *Do I dare leave him to call the doctor?* He continued gurgling and she tried to free her hand to go call for help, but he grasped it tighter.

He opened his eyes for a brief minute, smiled, and breathed a deep sigh. His head fell to one side and his grasp weakened. He stopped breathing.

"Chip, don't leave me. Oh my God, what will I do?" Kitty cried. She threw her arms around him and held him close.

Ken came in some time after. He gently pulled his mother away from her uncle. "He's gone home to Fran and Grant," he said softly. "Now he knows real peace, Mom. Let's say a prayer for him." Together they kneeled by Chip's bed, arm and arm, and through their tears prayed that the angels would be there to welcome their beloved Chip.

Chapter 40

Farewell for Now

"There are many rooms in my Father's house,
And I am going to prepare a place for you."

(John 14:2)

The next day Ken and Buddy stayed with Kitty while she reviewed funeral arrangements with the priest and the undertaker. They did everything exactly as Chip wanted. He wanted a viewing with a closed casket in the church the night before his funeral Mass.

On the afternoon of the viewing, Kitty and Ken went to the funeral parlor to bid farewell to Chip before the funeral director closed the casket and moved his body to the church. Engulfed in loneliness, Kitty stood by the casket, praying, and whispering to Chip.

"Thank you, my dear Chip, for loving me," she said as she touched his hand. "I do praise and thank God for you. Thank you for all you taught me. Thank you for your patience with me." She stroked his shoulder. "I'm glad you're not in any more pain but I'm going to miss you so." Tears rolled down her cheeks.

"Thank you for being in my life." She leaned down and whispered, "You knew you were leaving me. You tried to teach me that a full life is a roller coaster of sorrow and joy, night and day, life and death, winter and spring. Thanks for teaching me that."

She stared at him for a while, stroking his hand. "May you be enraptured in joy, light, life, and spring forever. Go now to Fran and Grant, your mom and dad, my mom and dad, and to God." She wiped her eyes, leaned over, and kissed him. She put a *Peace Way* pin on his lapel.

She whispered in his ear, "You're the most courageous person I ever knew." Kitty whispered good-bye, and was ready to nod to the undertaker to close the casket, when a hand gripped her shoulder.

"Kit, are you okay?"

She felt that old tingling feeling she always felt when she heard Matt's voice. Turning, she saw Matt, Susan, and Doug standing next to Ken.

"You need your family," Matt said, as he reached out to hug her. "We're here for you."

She fell into his arms and sobbed.

"It's going to be okay, Kit," Matt assured her, stroking her hair. "It's time to go."

The next morning, Matt squeezed Kitty's hand as they walked hand and hand behind Chip's casket while it was wheeled into the church. Throughout the funeral, Kitty felt the same peace she experienced the first time she went to Mass with Chip. *God, You are so great. Thank you for Matt and Kenny and Doug and Susan and Caroline and all the people I work with. Thank you for Chip.* She also thanked God for giving Matt and her another chance.

Right at that moment, Ken leaned over and whispered, "Uncle Chip had such a great influence in helping me find peace in my life, Mom." Through his tearful eyes he asked, "Next time you come to California will you go to Mass with me?"

Kitty smiled through her tears, nodded, and squeezed his hand.

She gazed at Matt sitting next to her. He'd gained weight and looked healthier than he had in a long time. He turned toward her and their eyes met. He smiled and grasped her hand. Bright sunlight filtered through the stained-glass window.

She stared at the windows. It was like she was in a dream. She heard the music but it was far away. She watched the service but she didn't see it. She was too tired to think anymore. *There is peace in this moment. I praise and thank you, Lord, for bringing us together and soaking us in your peace.*

Acknowledgments

I am grateful to all my clients, friends, and colleagues who have urged me to write a book on the joy and freedom that comes from living the peace principles. You know who you are. I hope you are not disappointed that what was intended to be a nonfiction, how-to book turned into a novel. I think you will enjoy the way the story introduces the five secrets to inner peace.

I was in the process of writing a self-help book when Kitty Murphy was born, and the novel, *Juggle Without Struggle,* wrote itself. Although Kitty Murphy is fictitious, several people who read the manuscript asked me if they were Kitty. Kitty was born in my head and her life is based on no one in particular, but I think we all have a little bit of Kitty in us when we are confronted with some of life's more challenging experiences.

Writing the first draft was easy. The difficulty was in the editing, research, and rewriting. Five years and lots of challenging moments later, *Juggle Without Struggle* is finished, thanks to many wonderful people. I am deeply grateful to Elizabeth Kennedy and the fellow members of her book club. Your feedback was an enormous help. I wish to thank Megan Rohr, Molly Baker, Gina Foley, Bridget Devine, Clara Meyers, and Bridget Rahr.

A special thanks to Jacqueline DeBianca's friends, Cheryl Baldwin, and Dr. Jonathan Cohen, for your professional insights and valuable advice.

Barbara Costner, you are a great copy editor. Bill Greenleaf, every lonely author needs an editor who encourages and builds him or her up like you do. Jacquie Murphy, I appreciate you taking the time from your summer vacation to read my book. You'll notice I followed your suggestions. Thank you also to Sherrie O'Neill and Mary DeCarlo. You encouraged me to keep going when I grew doubtful.

M.Q. and Ted Reimel, your suggestions made *Juggle Without Strug-*

gle a more interesting story. Euse, Harry, Vince, and Guy, you constantly inspire me with your faith and your love for your work. When I felt like quitting, I thought about you and all the challenges you've overcome.

Marcy and Carol Wolfington and Kassie O'Neill, you are good sports to take the time to read and give me honest, helpful feedback. Martie, your constant encouragement and marketing expertise are invaluable. Alex and Patricia, I cherish the open and honest conversations we've had sharing our experiences with the Peace Meditations.

I appreciate Euse and Frank Mita, and John Finegan's enthusiastic feedback from the male perspective. I want to thank Steve Mountain for his advice about the media. He was so right. Thank you also to Tim Flanagan for embracing the PAL principle and sharing it with so many people. I'm looking forward to coauthoring with you *Juggle Without Struggle for Men*. John Toland, Trudy Kelly, Helen Hobson, Kerri and Matt Manion, thank you for your enthusiasm for *Juggle Without Struggle*. Also, a special thanks to my longtime friend Betsy Bracken. You heard so much about the story, you didn't have to read it. You're a true friend and a wonderful listener.

Lisa Corcoran, Mimi Heany, Marta Kyle, Mary Q. Dwyer, and Andrea Downs, I thank you for being so open and honest about what you liked and didn't like. I took your advice to heart. I also want to thank Martie Bernicker for your constant encouragement. You are the best.

I praise and thank God for my team – Mary Pat Palmer, Mary DeCarlo, Denise Kane, and Michelle Garwood for dropping everything they were doing to read the latest draft. Your humor, enthusiasm, and hard work made a big difference in the completed manuscript. Every day you help me juggle my daily work with greater ease and a lot less struggle. I don't know what I'd do without you.

I was blessed to have assistance from four dedicated and talented graphic artists, Frank Barone and Harry Hatzistavrakis, Rip Muhlenhaupt and Tom Roskelly. Harry designed the original cover. Rip and Tom used their creative surgical skills for helping along the way. God does have a plan, and I thank Him for sending the Advantage Media team in to help me cross the finish line. Thank you for your patience.

A special thanks to Yanni Romaro, Louis and Adele Correa, you're the best.

To four special people in Brian's office who graciously took so much of the struggle out of my daily juggling, Nancy Ladd, Desiree Foulds, George Fitzpatrick, and Bobbie Dougert, thank you, you are truly angels. Pam Wright, thank you for never saying no.

I am deeply grateful to Msgr. Cunningham, Jeanne Baker, and the staff at St. Isaac Jogues Parish for keeping the Adoration Chapel open 24 hours a day. You gave me the opportunity to withdraw from the busyness of life and just be in the presence of Our Lord. It was in these quiet moments I learned the secret to finding inner peace and spreading it one moment and one heart at a time. Thank you.

To five special and very unique women, Miriam, Jeannie, Ione, Alice O'Neill, and Michele Aragno, I thank you for your interest and encouragement. You always lifted my spirits when the going got tough. I appreciate your direct and honest questions and feedback from a young mother's point of view. Your thoughts are a very important part of this book. Thank you. I am blessed to have the five of you in my family. I love you more today than yesterday.

God blessed my husband, Frank, and me with six wonderful sons. I am deeply grateful to Frank Jr., Brian, Joe, Mike, Bill, and Vince for encouraging and helping me in everything I do. Thank you from the bottom of my heart for caring so much. I love you more than you'll ever know.

Last but certainly not least, I want to thank my husband, Frank, for his patience with me through the time-consuming process of writing this book. Thank you for making me laugh when I wanted to cry and for making me take time off when I needed to, but didn't want to. I love you.

My appreciation goes to the many people who influenced my life and encouraged me to live the Peace Principles. You are each an important part of this book. Thank you, dear readers, for embracing the Five Simple Peace Principles and spreading them wherever you go, whatever you do, one moment, one heart at a time. God Bless.

Testimony by Brian J. Gail, Bestselling Catholic Author
American Tragedy in Trilogy

I first heard of the iconic Peg O'Neill forty years ago. My own dear mother (who died in 2002) was one of her early volunteers at *Birthright* – an organization Peg founded to help poor and very often frightened pregnant teenagers.

It was said Peg founded *Birthright* because she didn't think the Philadelphia Pro-Life community was doing enough at the time for the mother of the child. Not surprisingly this belief, and apostolic response, was somewhat controversial at the time. As word of the organization quickly spread, girls began arriving at *Birthright's* front door from all over the city. Often she and her volunteers learned about the pregnancy before the girls' own parents did. One night that almost got Peg killed. As the story goes, Peg asked one scared teenager if her parents knew of her pregnancy and as it happened they did not. Peg offered to accompany the girl to her home in the northeastern section of the city to share the news. Within minutes the father excused himself and left the room. Moments later he returned—with a shotgun aimed directly at Peg.

About ten years later, while traveling on business for a company she started with her brother, Peg was shocked to discover that there were a number of parishes throughout the country that were unable to offer daily Mass because of a shortage of priests. She was deeply troubled by this and immediately launched a second apostolate which she called *Prayer Power*. Its mission: to pray for vocations to the priesthood. Within five years, *Prayer Power* had over 5,000 women praying for over 1,000 priests.

Peg O'Neill raised six mythically independent sons while working side by side with her husband on a number of entrepreneurial ventures.

Suddenly, having arrived at a cruising speed in mid-life that set land records for women 30 years younger, Peg O'Neill was told she had cancer. When first advised of her condition, she reportedly shrugged and said, "Just one more thing for God's 'to do' list." Over the next 20 years the disease spread. She would endure six painful operations, a long litany of difficult treatments, and a whole counter full of mostly ineffective medications.

Did it slow her down? You be the judge. She helped one of her sons start and build a highly successful business, became as she liked to say a "hands-on" grandmother for 16 grandchildren, and oh, by the way, wrote a book.

You are now holding that book in your hands. It is in its essence a survivor's manual for women who have taken on the greatest and most difficult challenges in life: divorce and single parenthood, isolation and poverty, the sickness and death of a child, and the kind of deep and immobilizing depression that puts hope to flight and flight to prayer. *Juggle Without Struggle* reveals an astonishing familiarity with pain and purpose yet a singular remedy that is as transcendent as it is practical. The book has a voice that we recognize. It is the voice of saints past sharing the eternal secrets of the mystical life with those who would climb the twin peaks of tribulation and consolation.

Juggle Without Struggle does one other thing. It answers an inter-generational question for thousands of Philadelphians who wondered aloud how this extraordinary woman accomplished all that she did in one lifetime. "It's a secret … well actually there are five secrets," she might have said with a wink.

They are secrets no longer.

Brian J. Gail
Bestselling Catholic author
American Tragedy in Trilogy

Endorsements

Author Peggie O'Neill has created a unique and compelling story that imparts the deepest spiritual principles for understanding life's challenges and finding inner peace. It's a modern parable, a story that turns on the real crisis of Kitty Murphy and how even her reluctance to connect with God opens a door to an epiphany that transforms not only her life, but those around her. You'll want to collect the five secrets and apply their power immediately.

Pat Ciarrocchi
TV News Anchor
Philadelphia

Peggie O'Neill's *Juggle Without Struggle* addresses the central dilemma of the human experience: how to be in this world but not of it. Drawing on a lifetime of experience as a wife, mother, friend and benefactress, Mrs. O'Neill presents these lessons in a book that is part novel, part self-help manual. Written around characters who are uncomfortably recognizable in their faults and foibles, her narrative brings these characters to the very limits of their endurance, and then leaves them to muddle toward their only way out, surrender to God's great love. Daily meditation on her five Peace Principles gradually transforms heroine Kitty Murphy and an expanding circle of her friends and family. The trials of these imagined figures bring home the point that the soul's yearning for God is a universal constant, irrespective of age, class, station or even self-awareness. The reader cannot help but wish for such peace in the lives of her own loved ones.

Emily Rice
Writer
Philadelphia Bulletin

The stories of these women and their journeys whispered to my soul. They are every woman! At the end of the day we are all looking for approval, strength, balance, wisdom, peace, and love. I related to so many of the situations they were dealing with and as the secrets were revealed I found myself applying them in my own life. This book changed me!

Sometimes life gets so busy and we get so caught up in the chaos of it all that we forget how simple things, like the 5 Peace Secrets revealed in *Juggle Without Struggle,* can completely change our perspective. Practicing the 5 secrets can immediately wash us over with peace. In spending that one- on-one time with God every day my relationship with Him became stronger, I felt safe, I trusted that He would take away my anxiety and fears, and because of that I am finally feeling that sense of peace I was so craving. This book has definitely been a blessing in my life. It showed me how to "let go, and let God" again.

Ali Landry
Actress, *Bella*
Mompreneur

Juggle Without Struggle reaches out to women of all faiths and backgrounds and calls them all back to two universal messages: "Trust God" and "Love one another as I have loved you" (John 13:34-35). The author clearly has listened to many wounded souls in her lifetime, and inside this book has left for us some golden nuggets of truth so profoundly contained in the "Prayer of St. Francis." This book is both a spiritual gift and self-help guide intended to show us the path to finding inner peace through daily time in prayer with God. Mission accomplished!

Liz McEwen
Wife of former Congressman, Bob McEwen
Hospitality Chairman of the Republican Congressional Spouses,
President of the Former Members of Congress Auxiliary (bipartisan)

Juggle Without Struggle comes alive with colorful and real characters, any of whom could easily be my next door neighbors. This book is a reminder that we all have our own problems and crosses in life. It also leads us to crave how wonderful our life can be if we take the time we need every day to follow the 5 secrets to inner peace. My favorite character is ‹Uncle Chip›, a true hero, who took a great tragedy in his life and turned it into an inspiration and a glory to God. I encourage people to read this book so that a seed can be planted in their own hearts to glorify God in all things and live every day to the fullest regardless of the sadness or suffering that is in their lives. To the author I would like to say, «Thank you and ‹well done my good and faithful servant.›»

Cindy Hertzel
Widow and mother of three
The Robert T. Hertzel Foundation

What is the Courage of One Project?

Courage of One (C.O.O.) for Peace is an idea that resulted from the culmination of Peggie O'Neill's life work in communication, leadership development, personal strength, and prayer.

Courage of One explores the inner strength that women have in the role of spouse, parent, friend, business leader, and member of the community. It is no accident that the initials "C.O.O." also stand for "Chief Operating Officer." As an executive herself, Peg always believed that every person was the "Chief Operating Officer" in her own life and that it was up to the individual to take charge, grow in it, and 'own it'. To that end, Peg developed the Courage of One tools as a guide. These are available in the format of books, meditations, and videos. These precious resources allow each person to experience for themselves the way to inner peace and trust in God's plan.

Juggle Without Struggle is the novel in the Courage of One products which shares a mother's source for inner peace.

What is the Peace Way?

The Peace Way is an invitation to live life to the fullest. It asks each reader to explore exactly why God has put them here on this earth. Achieving peace leads to clarity, inner strength, and the courage to peel back the layers of life and find the strength and wisdom to live life joyfully. It is a challenge to find the courage to break the cycle of fear and busyness in order to focus internally and to allow God's plan to be revealed *for* you in your life. It is only after you find peace that you are able to freely give it away to others.

This book and other Courage of One products are being handled by Peg's niece Mary DeCarlo, and daughter-in-law Alice O'Neill. This system has helped these two amazing, busy moms more than words can say. They consider it a great honor to share it with the world.

A portion of the proceeds from Juggle Without Struggle will be contributed to The University of Pennsylvania's bladder cancer research.

For more information or to contact them go to: info@courageofone.com

About the Author

Peggie (Wolfington) O'Neill was a native Philadelphian. The daughter of Eustace and Mary Margaret (Hayden) Wolfington, Peg was raised in Overbrook, Pennsylvania with six brothers and two sisters. Growing up in a household full of love, laughter and affirmation made her the dynamic woman who, throughout her life, touched so many. She and Frank O'Neill were married 54 years, raised six sons, and were blessed with 16 grandchildren. Peg considered her greatest gift and role to be that of wife, mother, and grandmother. Additionally, Peg worked in corporate America, founding her own consulting company. Over the years she inspired many to follow their passions. Peg authored communication-training programs for corporations such as Ford Motor Company and Carey International. Peg's passion for life and desire to help others led her to serve on numerous Boards and during her life of service she received multiple awards of recognition from business groups, charities, and the Catholic Church. Peggie O'Neill was always connecting people to one another. She did this in many ways. She was a humble instrument in answering God's call when asked to host her own TV show, "Passionate Leaders, Powerful People." She later began a holy hour to pray for priestly vocations which grew to over 5000 prayer warriors praying at the same hour every week. All of this and more resulted from a pivotal moment in Peg's own prayer life. It all began in 1965 when she followed the advice of a dear friend to make time for herself to pray every morning. That led to a daily routine Peg called the 'Peace Way' that she practiced for 46 years until she died of bladder cancer in September 2011. *Juggle Without Struggle* is Peg's gift to the world. It is her passionate legacy that she was determined to leave behind for her family, friends, and those she spent

hours with in chemotherapy and radiation treatment. Peggie O'Neill labored in her last days to capture the grace-filled wisdom that God blessed her with by writing this book as a significant part of her "Courage of One" outreach. It was her greatest desire to help others to connect (or re-connect) with God through the 'Peace Way' to discover their own inner strength and peace, so that they, too, could live life to the fullest every single day.